FOR EVER SERIES BOOK 2

FALLING *for* EVER

C. M. WYLLIE

Dub Press

www.cmwyllie.com

ISBN: 978-1-959583-09-7 (print)

ISBN: 978-1-959583-10-3 (e-book)

Content Warning

This book is meant for mature audiences and may contain content that could be triggering for some readers—including sex, alcohol, drugs, profanity, violence, bullying, verbal and physical abuse, domestic and dating violence, and suicide.

If you or someone you know is contemplating suicide, please call or text the National Suicide Prevention Lifeline at 988 or go online to www.988lifeline.org.

If you're the victim of domestic or dating violence, please reach out to the National Domestic Violence Hotline at 1-800 799-SAFE (7233) or go online to www.thehotline.org.

Playlist

- Chasing Cars, Nate Smith

- Mercy, Shawn Mendes

- Knowing You, Kenny Chesney

- I Shall Believe, Sheryl Crow

- Lies, Lies, Lies, Morgan Wallen

- the other girl, Kelsea Ballerini (with Halsey)

- Say Don't Go, Taylor Swift (Taylor's Version)

- Chains, Nick Jonas

- Boyfriend, Justin Bieber

- 10,000 Hours, Dan + Shay & Justin Bieber

- Steal My Love, Dan + Shay

FALLING FOR EVER

- All To Myself, Dan + Shay

- Perfect, Ed Sheeran

- Crazy Girl, Eli Young Band

- You Give Love A Bad Name, Bon Jovi

- You Shook Me All Night Long, AD/DC

- Body Like A Back Road, Sam Hunt

- Devil Don't Know, Morgan Wallen

- Save Yourself, Sense Field

- I'm With You, Avril Lavigne

- Dark Horse, Katy Perry (feat. Juicy J)

- Sugar, Maroon 5

- God & Guns N' Roses, Tyler Braden

- WAIT!, Kelsea Ballerini

- Runaway, Bon Jovi

Contents

For the ones who let their hearts lead, even when their heads begged
them not to.

I have no notion of loving people by halves, it is not in my nature.

~Jane Austen

Falling For Ever

Chapter 1

EVERLY

I leave the warmth of his body to tiptoe across the cool hardwood floor and ease the sliding door closed to shut out the frigid air, then I scoop the thick comforter off the foot of the bed and pull it over the sheet as I snuggle back in. He reaches for me in his sleep like he always does. Pulling my back to his chest, I hear his faint inhale as he nuzzles my neck just behind my ear. And like I always do, every cell in my body exhales at the ritual.

The chilled nights of the past week warn us summer is ending. My heart thuds with the knowledge. I don't like change. I like to know what's coming. And this fall is bringing changes in spades. I prefer the bubble we lived in all summer. Me and Julian and Blue Lake. All of them—Lilly and Noah, too. Pete and Shelley. Even the littles: Noah and Lilly's sisters. We function like a well-oiled machine and run the camping season like clockwork.

Why do things have to change? And how have I only been here less than six months? I almost can't remember myself before Blue Lake. Or maybe I just don't want to. To distract myself from my spiraling thoughts, I turn in his arms and wrap my fingers around the nape of his neck, curling them into the soft, spiky fade of hair there.

In the dull moonlight, his eyes flicker open and his lips part.

"Hi, Julie."

"Hi, Ever."

I lean in and press my lips to his. He knows what I want, and he doesn't make me wait.

Deepening the kiss, his hand finds my thigh just below my hip and lifts my leg to wrap around him, pulling me in close. Already aroused, he grinds into my pelvis delicately at first. Pushing up his oversized cotton shirt I sleep in, he fills his palm with my breast, squeezing just enough to make me gasp. He dips his head and takes my nipple in his mouth, sucking, swirling his tongue, making me squirm.

I press into him eagerly.

Quickly his lips are back on mine. His tongue delving in, stroking mine until I'm panting, arching my back into him. Breaking the contact only long enough to whip the shirt over my head, he leans in and whispers, "I know."

The building tension makes me quiver in anticipation. His words ignite a fire in me as much as his touch does. Without warning, he plunges his finger into me, eliciting a sharp cry. My hips lift off the bed to meet the force. His kisses are everywhere all at once—my neck, my ear, my breasts—while his hand drives me crazy. When his mouth joins his hands, it's too intense. I grip the sheet under me. My head twists from side to side. The noises I make from deep in my throat are half cry, half moan. I feel the pressure behind my eyes before the first tear leaks. It's almost always like this with him. This intense. So all-consuming that my body erupts.

"Easy, Ever. I got you, babe."

His words combined with his breath on the bundle of nerves at my center push me to the peak. He places his thumb on the sensitive bud as his finger crooks and meets his thumb from the inside, and I explode over the edge. While my body is still convulsing, he pulls his fingers out, and I whimper a little at the loss. It's only seconds before he fills me, guiding himself into me so swiftly I cry out. He laces our fingers and drags our hands above my head as he pushes into me over and over, kissing my cheeks, my lips, my neck. He's everywhere, consuming me. His thrusts are steady, deep, and give me no time to come down before I'm shaking with the building pressure again.

"Julie," I cry. "I . . . fuck me. I can't. Ung . . . uh . . ."

"Yes, Ever. You can. You will. So good. You. Feel. So. Fucking. Good." His words come between thrusts. "Come for me." He pants. "With me."

"I'm . . . yesss . . . Julie . . . ughhh." I come so hard, I sob. I feel him follow me, pulsing inside me, and I can't control my trembling. My body erupts, and I can't stop it.

As Julian's orgasm subsides, he rolls onto his back, taking me with him.

Curved into his side, half on top of him, my leg draped low over his body, I fight to control the waves of emotion rocking me. My sobs come out on shaky breaths, tears wetting his chest.

"Shhh, sweet girl. I got you." He takes the emotion overload in his stride.

It doesn't happen every time, but it happens a lot. I don't understand it enough (or at all) to explain it. And he never asks me about it afterwards. He just holds me and whispers sweet things until it subsides or I can rein it back in. The only rationale I can find is that it's all so intense that my body temporarily short-circuits. I have wondered if anyone else ever experiences this intensity during sex. I have no frame of reference except *him. Julian.* My very own walking thirst trap. Fuck, he's beautiful. And miraculously mine. Every time with him is intense. Old wives' tales surge through my mind, like going blind and other absurdities, but I get where they may have stemmed from. Right before an orgasm, sometimes a blinding white light flashes behind my lids. I'd open my eyes afterwards and see Julian watching me, eyes a dark stormy blue, pupils huge. My heart would swell and the pressure behind my eyes would build. The emotions would flood my system, and I'd want to crawl inside this man's arms and stay there forever.

All the love stories in my books don't lie about this. It's so consuming and beautiful it hurts. It hurts because the thought of it ending is unbearable. I have new respect for the strength it took my mom to move on with her life after my dad died. I still don't know how she did it, but I understand why she works all the time and why she chose her profession. A VIP flight attendant for the rich and famous keeps her literally jet-setting from one fantastic place to another. Seeing the world and being at the beck and call of the elite leaves little time to wallow in sadness. I never begrudged her absence growing up. And now that I have Julian, I commend her ability to reinvent herself after losing the love of her life. I don't know if I could do it.

Calmer now, I swipe my fist down my cheek and look up under my lashes, still resting the other cheek on his chest. His hand cradles the top of my head. When I meet his deep blue gaze, he sweeps his thumb back and forth across my forehead a couple times.

"Hi, pretty girl." The baritone of his voice vibrates my cheek.

"Hi, beautiful boy." He always calls me pretty girl, sweet girl or Ever.

Growing up, everyone called me Evvie, or Everly if they were mad. He's the only one who calls me Ever. I love that only he calls me that. And he rarely does it in front of anyone else, unless by accident. Then he usually adds the "ly" as an afterthought. I call him lots of things, usually something funny. My favorite is Julie, sarcasm being my second language. I originally called him that to get under his skin, but it quickly grew into a regular term of endearment. I mostly reply to his pet names with whatever the moment calls for. And right now, the beauty of this man before me is taking center stage.

Physically he's a specimen. But underneath the flawless physique, he possesses a heart of pure gold. He takes care of me the way he takes care of his body. I finally understand what all my beloved romance books have been spouting about. Part of me is sad that those books have lost some of their magic. When the real-life boyfriend is giving perfect book boyfriend energy, can you blame me? I can only hope it will always be this way.

Chapter 2

JULIAN

My girl is perfect. I don't know what I did to deserve her. Sometimes, I hold my breath waiting for it all to vaporize. The first time she broke down during sex, I panicked. I thought I'd hurt her or somehow traumatized her, but she assured me that wasn't the case but couldn't explain it beyond that. The best I can figure is that she's flooded with the intensity and it's her way of unconsciously letting it all out. Whatever the reason, it guts me every time. I hold her as tightly as I can and just breathe, waiting for her to come back to me.

Trauma isn't new to her—to either of us. And sometimes we can't avoid the triggers. Sometimes it's hard to recognize a trigger for what it is until you're in it. Maybe it's a response to overwhelm. All I know is that it makes me want to fiercely protect her from every shitty thing this life could possibly throw at her. Except me. I gave up trying to save her from me. I instead decided to try to be everything she could possibly need. I just hope I can be good enough to deserve her. This beautiful, sweet creature lets me see all of her when it's just us, skin to skin. In the light of day, she plays tough. She *is* tough. Compartmentalizes like a first responder. I guess that's what losing your military dad at twelve years old will do to you.

She'd stopped shaking in my arms and her tears had dried. Her body, relaxed now, drapes silently across me. I feel goosebumps rise on her skin, and I reach for the comforter that slid off us during sex and drape it over us without moving her. She snuggles into the crook of my arm as I tuck it around her. Skimming my finger down her cheek, I ask, "Sleepy?"

"Mmm," is the only response I get. Her breathing slows, turns rhythmic and tells me she's drifted off.

I lay there a while longer, staring at the dim ceiling. By the muted tone, it's still the middle of the night, but I don't want to reach for my phone to check and risk disturbing her.

My brain strays to the days and weeks ahead and how our quiet summer life is about to change. Change is good—great in this case. But upsetting the sweet balance we've found creates a low-level anxiety in my gut. I know she feels it too. She'll be starting college and I'll be learning to become an influencer, apparently. Or I already am—accidentally. Luke Ashley is going to show me how to capitalize on it.

Influencing and social media are the furthest things from a career choice I could have imagined for myself. But as Ashley pointed out, I can't unring the bell of the viral videos, so I might as well take advantage of it. And he is more than thrilled to show me how. He'd already convinced Allie. If there's one person I trust most in this world, it's her. If Ashley had won Allie over, I could give it a chance and see where it leads. Besides, having a lucrative business and income means I can offer Ever more than some nobody kid from South Point. And I did want to offer her nice things—things I'd never even dared dream of. Not only did I want to offer them to her, I also wanted them for myself. It takes a lot to admit that—even now.

After all the therapy, this train of thought still trips my heart rate. The guilt settles on my chest like an anvil. Snippets from therapy sessions I'd gone to right after Taya died—Allie's suggestion—flood my mind. And it did work—the therapy. Mostly. But old default settings run deep. I tap my chest in rhythmic succession until the weight begins to lift.

Dr. Claire Carver's face swims into my mind's eye. *You don't need to learn how to deal with your trauma. Your trauma is like a second skin. You need to learn how to accept love and happiness. How to accept that you deserve good things to happen to you and for you.* I nod my head like she's here talking to me through the screen, like all our online sessions. Logically I know I deserve love and happiness and good things, but sometimes when things feel too good, too perfect, I want to crawl out of my skin. The urge to look over my shoulder makes me want to shrink, hide. Like someone is watching me, and, if I act too happy, too comfortable, they'll come and take it all away. I have to remind myself that that feeling is the lie—not the happiness, not the contentment.

The pressure behind my eyes adds to my guilt and shame—and annoyance. I squeeze them shut and continue tapping my chest. *I deserve love. I am worthy of love. I am allowed to feel love.* A sob catches in my throat, piercing the silence, causing my body to jerk. I freeze, waiting to see if the sound and movement disturbs Ever, but she is still curled into the crook of my other arm, her breathing steady and cadent. I gently roll her away from me and spoon into her backside. Inhaling deeply, I bury my face in the space behind her ear.

In sleep, she reaches for my hand and pulls it to her chest, wrapping her arm around mine.

My Ever. Her sunshine scent reminds me of sunrise, which I can see creeping around the edges of the window shades. I've always been an early riser and marveled at the sunrise—even as a little kid in the trailer park. I'd awake to the sound of a distant rooster and leap up hoping to catch the sun peeking over the foothills that framed the little league field next door. I could see it from my bedroom window if I stood on the mattress pushed up against the wall—my bed. A new beginning, a fresh start.

Nothing bad had happened yet. The day brand new, the house still and quiet. I'd dress silently, sneak out the front door, walk through the dusty trailer park, squeeze under the curled-up chain-link fence and onto the outfield grass next door. I'd race the sun to the wooden bleachers and sit on the highest one, listen to the roosters on the neighboring farm calling out their morning greeting and wait for the first rays to kiss my face. Rain or shine, cold or heat, I showed up. Even the days the sky was fat with clouds, I'd wait patiently for one to move so the sun could peek through and send a ray my way.

Living in the foothills of Northern California means we miss most of the dim, foggy days. Even when a layer of gray can be seen blanketing the central valley below us, Mother Nature drew a line just before the elevation began to climb and the ground began to roll in soft hills below the Sierra Mountains. I love the area, if not the house I grew up in. The beauty of my surroundings outside the walls of the trailer kept me happy—at least happy as I knew it.

Back then I'd worked out the timing almost perfectly. I'd wait until the sun was at a certain place in the sky before I made my way back through the outfield, back under the fence and down the dusty road back to my house. When I did time it right, Hal Durham, the Little League field groundskeeper who lived in the trailer park on the parcel that backed up to the field, would just be coming out onto his porch to drink his morning coffee. He'd invite me up onto the porch and pour me a cup too, mostly cream and sugar, and let me join him. I'd sit quietly so he didn't make me leave and sip the warm, brown liquid that tasted better than anything I'd ever known. I couldn't help how loud my stomach growled though, and he'd make a *hmpf* sound before setting his cup down, going inside and coming back out with a PB&J sandwich and hand it to me. They were always the best tasting PB&Js I'd ever eaten. And combined with the coffee, it was my favorite meal. It may have had more to do with the calm, cozy setting than the actual food, but I was too young to know that. I just knew it was the best part of most days growing up.

My alarm vibrating my phone on the nightstand drags me out of the memory. I reach behind me, feeling for my phone, and tap the screen to stop the buzzing. As gently and silently as possible I slide my arm out from the soft grip of hers and roll away and off the bed in one fluid motion. Ever doesn't stir. I've perfected silence but squash the memories of how and why. Instead, I move into a downward dog pose, stretching my legs and lower back. Then I stand, straighten my spine and reach for the ceiling. I do this a few times along with deep, slow breaths before I complete my usual set of morning push-ups. I'm anxious about today. I don't want to leave her. *Change can be a good thing*, I chant as I go through the motions of brushing my teeth, washing my face and making coffee.

Dr. Carver would be proud. I smirk at myself. I know she'd have a field day with how much my calm comfort zone depends on the beauty sleeping upstairs. And I can't quite bring myself to care if it's somewhat codependent or unhealthy. If I deserve good things, why can't those good things start with her? Having her near me does calm me—like a giant exhale. I'm pretty sure it's the same for her. And what was the thing Dr. Carver said once when I first jumped headfirst into fitness? *It's human nature to be somewhat addictive. But you can choose to be addicted to things that help you or harm you. So I think you're on the right track with fitness. There are worse things to be addicted to. In fact, I'd venture to say this is a good thing—a great thing even. I'm proud of you, Julian.*

I don't want to believe I'm addicted to Ever. That makes what we have sound ugly and tainted. And it's anything but that. She is a thing of exquisite beauty—and not just in looks, although she could and does stop traffic. She's just so good, and she makes me feel like I'm good when I'm with her. As if my thoughts summon her, the creaking floor upstairs tells me she's awake. My heart thuds a little quicker, a little louder. *God, I love her.* So what if the main way we show it is physical. Fuck, we're so good at it. I smirk again and turn toward the stairs. *We deserve to be happy. We deserve to feel good.*

Why snippets of my therapy sessions keep popping up lately I'm not sure. The closer Everly and I get, the more I'm reminded of the only other person I think I loved. Maybe that's why. The parallels. I've only ever had two love relationships in my life. I can't say I ever loved my parents, at least not since I was old enough to name an emotion. Maybe I loved Hal, or even my grandpa McKay, but not in a way I acknowledged with actions or words. Just Taya and now Ever. I guess that's why Claire and all her sound bites are flooding my brain. They're good sound bites that are worth the recall, but I'd be lying if I didn't sometimes wish for a shutoff valve.

Therapy is a lot of work—if you do it right. Enter Claire Carver again: *You use this tool rather well—and rapidly, I might add.*

"I'd prefer to get all the digging around in old wounds and rebreaking done as quickly as possible so I can be on the other side already and move on."

"That's fair. But please know healing isn't linear. You don't just get over it once for it never to resurface again. Sometimes the things that trigger you may come out of nowhere, with no rhyme or reason. It will be up to you to dig a little deeper, figure out where it's coming from and get on the other side of it. And I'm always here to help."

"Thanks, Doc. Let's stick to the current meltdown and I'll let you know if I ever need you in the future."

"You're doing great, Julian. Really. I wish all my patients used therapy as thoroughly as you do."

Chapter 3

Everly

I'm alone. The way the light streams through the wall of glass tells me it's morning but still early. Julian's side isn't warm, but I leave my hand slightly under his pillow for a few seconds before I stir. I smile at how he always wakes before I do. Then I frown because today he flies down south to meet Ashley for the new business venture. Right after, I remind myself this is a good thing. The best thing! Julian deserves this recognition. I'm just not sure I'm ready for the whole world to fall in love with his body the way I have. I mean, unbeknown to us, millions already have. But now it'll be official, and he'll collect the paychecks to go with it. As he should. Knowing the story of how he grew up dirt poor makes me want this for him. Dreams weren't an option or even on the radar for him growing up. It was purely survival. That he can dream now and realize dreams he may not have even had for himself brings me joy. Makes me so proud of him. So why do I feel this sense of dread? Is it just the past trauma talking? Or do I sense trouble coming?

After getting up to use the bathroom and brushing my teeth, I still can't shake the feeling. I make my way back to the edge of the bed and give myself points for not crawling back under the covers. I'm staring down at my bare feet, toes nuzzling the fuzzy white rug beneath them, when his shadow fills the doorway. He's leaning on the doorframe, arms crossed over his chest when I meet his eyes.

"Hi, pretty girl."

"Hi, Julie."

"What's going on in there?" He tosses his head toward me but doesn't move other than that.

I know he means my head. He always asks that when I get quiet. He can read me well. I don't speak. I just shrug, hoping it looks casual and not sulky.

He's walking toward me now, and I lower my gaze to the floor again, but he kneels in front of me, his soft jogger-clad knees cushioning into the fuzzy rug either side of my bare feet. He rubs his palms up and down my thighs. Then he reaches up and hooks the dangling locks of my hair behind both ears and cradles my face, his palms now on my cheeks and jaw. I raise my gaze to meet his, so blue in the morning light that I blink against the radiance.

"I'm going to miss you." He says what I'm thinking.

"I already miss you. How long before you leave?"

"We've got time. I was also wondering if you would drive me to the airport. We could take the Jeep, and you could use it while I'm gone."

"Yeah, okay." I force a smile, make it reach my eyes and hope he doesn't see through it.

"Can I kiss you?" The flicker of mischief gives me pause because he doesn't ever ask to kiss me.

I nod though and lean my lips toward his.

He shakes his head slowly and says, "Stand up."

I stand, and he hooks his fingers into the waistband of my panties and pulls them down all the way to my ankles and nudges me back onto the bed. He kisses my inner thigh just above my knee. My sharp intake of breath brings his eyes up to mine. Watching me, he places another kiss a little higher on my thigh. My eyes roll back, and my lids fall. I arch my back and let my neck drop as his kisses get closer and closer to the vee between my thighs. His lips place featherlight kisses there first, seeking. Within moments my body responds, the bud of nerves hardens, my thigh muscles contract. I want to squeeze them closed, but he's there between them, so I press them to the sides of his face. I can't help it. I try not to squeeze, and the effort brings a moan from deep in my throat. The baritone of his voice, part chuckle, part moan, tells me he likes what he's doing to me. My hands fly to his hair, the soft prickly fade teasing my fingertips. My palms splay against the back of his head and hold him firmly to me when he begins to suck. As the pressure builds, I fight to keep my knees from clamping down on him. They begin to tremble with the effort. I feel his fingers slide into me, and I fall back onto the mattress. I raise my feet to the edge of the bed and use them to propel me down into his thrusts. I want more. I think I say it out loud because he stops kissing me down there to answer me.

"Tell me, Ever. What do you want?"

I'm so disturbed by the loss of his mouth I blurt out exactly what I want, crudely. "Fuck me, Julie. Please."

Then he's gone. His mouth, his fingers. I open my hazed eyes and see him stepping out of his joggers before he pulls his shirt over his head. Then he's climbing up my body and scooting me back onto the bed. He braces himself above me with one arm next to my head. With his other hand he guides himself to my center. I feel the tip of him, hard and ready, a second before he plunges into me with a force that's new. I'm wet and ready, so he sinks in easily, but the force rips a deep cry from my lips. It sounds like *yes* to my ears. So I say it again.

"Yes, Julie. More."

"I got you, Ever. Come for me."

He's driving into me with each word, hard and fast. And I'm not seeing, just feeling. My eyes are shut tightly and I'm digging my nails into his hips, inviting him to go harder. It's almost painful but in a good way. And it's taking me up and over. "I'm there, Julian. I'm going to. Ughhh . . ." I'm convulsing around him.

He slows his thrusts. He knows everything is sensitive now, heightened by my orgasm. He's patient. When my body stops convulsing, he wraps his arms around me and rolls us without breaking our connection so that I'm on top. Straddling him, I sit up and rock back and forth. His face goes slack, lips pouty when it feels good, but he doesn't close his eyes like I do. He watches me. I want to close my eyes, but I make myself stare back at him. He reaches out and caresses both my breasts. His big hands envelop my modest chest.

"So beautiful, Ever." He squeezes them before he drops his hands to my hips and lifts me off his length and drops me back down as he rocks into me. Then he does it again and again until the frenzy builds, never once unlocking his gaze from mine.

I want to close my eyes and just feel, but I can't look away from what I'm seeing in his. I feel the pressure behind mine before the well blurs my vision. I feel him tense, I feel him swell inside me.

As the first tear slips down my cheek, he convulses with his orgasm, holding me down tight to him while he empties himself deep inside me. He reaches up to caress the tear off my cheek with his thumb while his fingers wrap around the back of my neck and pull my face down to his. He kisses me so tenderly it makes my heart ache. Our bodies are still joined intimately when he wraps his arms around me, hugging me so tightly I feel his heartbeat against my own.

"I'm going to miss you, Ever."

"You already said that." His rumbling chuckle makes me smile against his chest. I love making him laugh. I love the deep sound. And when I make him laugh, I'm usually rewarded with a hug. Like now, he squeezes me tighter, then rubs his hands up and down my back, dancing his fingers along my spine.

"I don't want to leave you."

I don't respond, because I don't want to sound needy—even to my own ears. I'm aware that my world begins and ends with him. I'm aware that I don't really have a life that is mine. *It is mine.* I gaslight myself. He's mine. But what else? What am I really doing with my life?

"Come with me."

I raise my head to look at him. He's looking up at the ceiling, so I fold my hands on his chest, rest my chin on my hands and wait. I can see the wheels turning, and I know mine are, but I need him to say more before I let my thoughts run away.

"How fast can you be ready?"

"To be gone for four days? What about Fit? Brew?"

"I know. I'm being selfish. I don't want to sleep without you."

"To be fair, we don't sleep much." I'm rewarded with his laugh and a playful pinch on my ass. My stomach turns to butterflies.

"Shower. Pack. Let me work this out. We leave in thirty." Then he presses a soft kiss near my ear and whispers, "Say yes."

"Yes." I hop off the bed and rush into the bathroom, closing the door behind me. *It is mine.*

***

He worked everything out perfectly. I shouldn't get used to him handling the details of my life for me, but I like it. And it calms me in a way I'd never felt before. *Depending on people just sets you up to crash harder if they ever stop.* I push that thought from my mind and reach for his hand across the center console of the Jeep. I showered, got ready and packed in twenty-seven minutes. The only reason I think it worked is because Luke Ashley already planned to send his private jet to fly Julian to Southern California for their planning meetings. Money really does make everything easier. Julian would have two full days of meetings, then the last two would be spent filming content, providing they reach a fair agreement.

"You can spend the meeting days exploring and the content days filming with me. If you want . . ."

I'm not so sure about being in the content videos, but I can't wait to explore LA. I'm also insatiably curious about Luke Ashley. He's seemingly captivated the two people closest to me, and I need to see why.

What I know so far is that Ashley created ASH (Ashley Strength & Health) and took it to household status, especially in Southern California. With a string of fitness centers, a merch line and a viral YouTube channel of his own, he knows exactly what it takes to be successful in that arena. Allie met him when she attended his three-week training in the spring, and they'd been inseparable ever since. He's the one who told her the Fit promo videos went viral. He offered to help Allie and Julian capitalize on it. That none of us knew they gained that kind of attention is another story. Sylvie ran the Fit website. She offered to because that had been her profession before getting divorced negated her need to work, so she offered to oversee Fit's website for a discounted membership, which Allie happily agreed to. Neither she nor Julian liked navigating social media but knew it helped to have it. Sylvie had to know the videos blew up, had to be the one getting paid. Granted, I don't understand the nuances of social media, influencing and virality, but I know someone gets paid when content gains that level of hype. Hopefully Ashley will show Julian and Allie how to take back control, especially Julian. It's his image in the videos.

Julian hasn't confronted Sylvie about the videos yet, if he even plans to. Ashley and Allie advised him to wait until after their discovery and planning meetings. At the very least, going forward she would have to credit him in them. Without a social media presence, there was no one to tag originally. If all went well, after this week there would be. I say well, but the idea of social media constricts my throat and gnaws at my chest. Without realizing it, I take a deep breath, hold it while I count to four and exhale. Julian clasps my hand in his and brings the back of it to his lips. We're now seated in Ashley's private jet, cleared for takeoff. I think he assumes I'm nervous about the flight, and I don't clarify. I don't want to think about my past experience with social media. The present gives me enough to dwell on.

Sometimes I wish my life began the day I met him. Realistically I wouldn't give back any of the shitty times because there is good that I wouldn't trade. Like my sister, Via. Even my mom and dad. They weren't around like some other parents were, but we never doubted they loved us. And we didn't know the difference. But the town I grew up in my whole life held no sentiment for me anymore. Not my house, not my schools or my *friends*. Just Via. My dad died while deployed. My mom almost never came home anymore due to her VIP flight attendant job and preferred it that way. Except for Via, who still lived in our old house with her fiancé, I could erase Oak Valley from my memory and never look back or miss it. Looking back makes my breathing shallow, my skin tingle and my vision go dark around the edges.

Chapter 4

Everly

Seven Months Ago

*D*O *THE PLANET A FAVOR AND LEAVE IT. WE'VE GOT ENOUGH SLUTS, FAKE FRIENDS AND HOMEWRECKERS ALREADY. BYYEEE @its.everly.davi s And if you're just joining us, beware: this bitch will try to steal your man!*

The post included my yearbook picture with devil horns added to it, demon eyes in place of mine and flames in the background. It hadn't gone viral by internet standards, but everyone in my school, town and pretty much everyone I'd ever met had seen it. I slam my laptop closed and shove it into my backpack. I swallow the lump in my throat and blink back the tears. Fuck them and fuck this place. I stand up from the tree I found to sit under at lunch—alone because that's my new MO. I dust off my jean shorts and head to the parking lot. I don't care if I get cooked for cutting class. I'm not going back in there today.

As soon as my car comes into view in the student lot, I notice the dangling side mirror first. The flat tires next. The two I can see are completely deflated. Walking closer, I can't stop the tears or the heaving breaths when I see the word slut carved into the hood and the deep scratches in the sides that stretch from bumper to bumper. I decide right then that I'm leaving. The school for sure. The town, probably. The planet? Not even a little bit, Fuck these small-town bullies. My mind is brave, but I'm just tired. I turn around and aim straight for my locker. I'm taking all my shit and never coming back.

Hopefully the damage to my car is repairable. I call for the roadside assistance my mom insisted both Via and I have in case we get stranded and request a tow to my house, which would also get me a ride there. I take it as a sign of good karma that I'm not, in fact, the devil the bullies claim I am when the tow truck driver shows up within twenty minutes and I can get the fuck out of there before classes let out. Besides my brief encounter with Dr. Franklin, he's the only other person I've run into. Thankfully. It's just me and him in the parking lot while he hooks up my car and hauls us both home. I can tell he wants to ask me about the vandalism, but I do my best impression of the doctored yearbook photo and give just enough super bitch energy that he doesn't.

When he pulls up to my house, I ask him to back my car into an area on the side of the garage designed for RV parking and hidden behind a wooden gate. I sign the receipt, and he leaves. I stand in the front yard staring at the closed gate that hides my car and the evidence of the nightmare I've been living since the night of Kendall and Chase's party. Or more accurately, the morning after.

As I look up the slant of the driveway at the house I grew up in, the only home I've ever known, I'm resolved. It doesn't feel like my home anymore. If I let myself dwell on it too much, it will break me. I don't have a home. I'm barely eighteen years old and I don't have a home. I give myself a minute, then square my shoulders and take a deep breath and tuck the sorrow and anger away the way I saw my dad do when I was young. Military training taught him how to compartmentalize, although I didn't know that's what it was called back then. But I observed the restraint it took for him to exist in civilian life. I assumed it's why he preferred to be deployed, off fighting for some cause to being here with *a bunch of privileged people who don't recognize the price of their freedom.*

My back pocket buzzed with a text from Via.

Saw the post. Checked your location. OMW.

Her text has pressure building behind my eyes again. This time I let the tears fall unchecked and walk up the front path into the house. Ten minutes later, Via finds me face down on my bed, no longer crying, but the evidence is unmistakable. I feel her weight dip the edge of my mattress.

"I called Allie."

I roll over and sit up, dragging my fists down my cheeks. "What'd she say?" I don't ask her why. I know why. We're out of options. If she hadn't done it, I would've.

"She's excited to see you," Via says, sans emotion. We both learned it from our dad. My mom's MO is the opposite. She overhypes every-thing. Different execution of the same tactic. Squash it. Tuck it. Ignore it.

"I'm fucking up my plan. Senior year. College. Everything."

"This is bullshit, Evvie. I know you didn't do what they're saying. Ryan knows it too. He even argued with Chase about it, but he won't give me any details. He just said he didn't realize what a pussy his best friend is." She turns her head to look me in the eyes, and I see hers shimmering with unshed tears. Her knuckles turn white as she clenches the edge of the mattress. She's pissed, not sad.

That creates a warm glow in my chest. My eyes well up too.

Knowing Via is on my side, believes me, and Ryan too, is all I care about. Not really, but they are the most important. I don't want to care that basically the whole town thinks I'm a slut. But I do. The bigger part is that all this has derailed years of planning. I have no idea what I'll do with my future now. Not that I've decided on a college or a major yet. I just knew I was going and I couldn't wait to get there. Now, I don't even know what the rest of senior year looks like, much less college. "It is what it is. I'm not going to stay here and take it anymore. I can't."

"I know. I'm so sorry, Evvie."

I nod once, rub my palms down my thighs, take a deep breath and stand to begin packing up my life. "Me too."

Chapter 5
Everly

Present Day

We fly into Van Nuys Airport, where a car and driver wait to drive us the twenty miles to Ashley's home office in Malibu, CA. Thirty minutes after we land, the driver turns off Malibu Canyon Road onto a private gated road leading to Canyon Crest, Ashley's estate. The sprawling grounds of his estate are nestled into the hills above Pepperdine University and boast ocean and canyon views.

Allie and Ashley greet us at the door, while paid staff whisk our luggage away to our rooms. Yes, rooms, plural. Allie knows Julian and I are together, living as a couple in her house back on Blue Lake, but maybe she just needed to give me my own room to feel like she's being a responsible guardian. I'm technically an adult now, so I don't see the need. But I'm not prepared to have that conversation in the foyer of Luke Ashley's jaw-dropping home two minutes after arriving.

After shaking hands and small talk greetings, I can sense Ashley is anxious to get down to business. But formality prevents him from saying it straight out. Instead, he asks, "Would you guys like to take some time to rest, get settled?"

"Uh . . ." Julian looks at me before answering. I just smile at him, then at Luke and Allie. "The flight was pretty restful. No airport hassle. Quick. Smooth," he says to our host.

I nod in agreement.

"Yeah, thanks for that," I chime in. "I thought about exploring the Pepperdine campus and maybe the beach if you guys don't need me for the meetings."

"Of course. It's a perfect day for it. Sean can take you wherever you'd like to go," Ashley says, referring to the driver who picked us up and brought us here. He introduced himself as Sean and disappeared as soon as he opened our doors and set our luggage inside.

A woman, who Ashley introduced as Clara and one of the people who took our luggage, appears and offers to show me to my room to change and grab anything I might need for my exploits.

As I turn to follow her, Julian snakes his hand out and clasps mine, lacing our fingers. He pulls me to him and kisses me sweetly on the cheek. "Have fun today. Text me if you need anything." He speaks quietly but not like he doesn't want anyone to hear. Then he bookends it with another kiss just in front of my ear.

The little puff of breath sends shivers down my arms and heat to my lower region. I can feel my face go crimson. I squeeze his hand quickly as I turn and release it to follow Clara up the stairs. "You guys have fun too. Don't work too hard." I add a wink to all three of them over my shoulder, which earns polite chuckles all around.

***

Pepperdine's Malibu campus takes my breath away. The location alone would be enough, but from one of the libraries you can hear the waves crashing in the distance. I could live here. Okay, maybe not here exactly. As far as the curriculum went, it wouldn't be my first choice, but the daily exposure to salty negative ions would make up for that. While I could've explored the campus all day, the beach calls to me. I've only been to the beach a handful of times in my life, and they were all before I turned twelve, when my dad was still alive.

Sean dropped me off at the guard shack at the entrance to Pepperdine, where I collected a map and learned I could walk to the beach. The walk back to campus up the steep hill is another thing. After thoroughly wandering the campus, I'd text Sean when I was ready to leave, his idea, and ask him to pick me up at the beach instead. I don't know when Julian, Allie and Ashley will be done with their meetings, and they didn't suggest a time for me to return. The campus security guard told me the mile walk to the beach would take fifteen to twenty minutes and warned me to use caution crossing the Pacific Coast Highway. I jog part of the way there and love the burn in my legs and lungs and the salt in the air. I miss running outside.

Once I cross PCH, I nab a spicy fruit cup and a bottle of water from the vendor parked strategically next to the crosswalk. Taking my snack, I find a quiet stretch of shoreline and plop down in the warm sand. I dig my toes in while I eat the tangy, chili-seasoned fruit and watch the surf crash into the shore. The sun kisses my face as it begins its slow descent into the ocean. The salty air teases my hair, the moist breeze waving the locks. I don't know how long I sit there watching the powerful ebb and flow when I hear the familiar bass of his voice.

"Hi, pretty girl."

I turn my head and squint up into his beaming face, shielding my eyes from the glare of the sun. "Hi, Julie." I can't stop the smile from spreading into my cheeks and crinkling the corners of my eyes. He's so beautiful. And he calls me "pretty girl."

My heart flutters when he dips down next to me and leans over to press a kiss to my cheek. He looks so sexy in his thin athletic shorts and sleeveless tee. His tan, rippled torso, exposed by the gaping armholes, makes my mouth go dry. I unconsciously wet my bottom lip with my tongue, drawing his gaze down. His blue eyes, so bright in the sinking sunlight, darken. He reaches out and tucks a strand of hair behind my ear and dips his head to claim my lips, softly at first. But it never stays soft, not with us.

I part my lips, and he does too. I meet his tongue. He tastes sweet and I wonder if he can taste the Tajín on mine. If he does, it must not offend him because he sucks mine a little before he ends the kiss.

"I missed you." We say it together, then laugh at our timing.

Julian adds, "Hey, so, it's Taco Tuesday."

I arch one eyebrow in question, grinning.

Taco Tuesday is apparently a regular thing for Ashley, and now Allie. Julian asked Sean to take him to me when he finished his meetings. With my location in his phone, he found me at the beach to tell me Ashley wanted to make us dinner tonight—his Tuesday tradition apparently.

We spend a few minutes watching the waves crash and pound the sand. I share my fruit with him, feeding him bites off my fork and kissing him between bites. I'm low-key intrigued to see Ashley in a casual setting like dinner. And I'm completely hyped to observe him with Allie. I know they're together. They aren't trying to hide it. I've just never seen Allie in a relationship, and I want to see for myself if he is good enough for her. Billionaire, fitness celebrity aside, I want to know if he is a good person. Yes, he is unselfishly teaching Julian everything he knows.

"How's Ashley?"

"What do you mean?"

"Like, is he nice? Does he seem like someone you can trust?" I pop another bite of fruit into his mouth and giggle while he chews it enough to answer me.

"He does. Very genuine guy. Generous with his knowledge. Seems completely smitten with Allie."

"Whoa. Smitten, even. Must be serious. You used the word smitten."

Before I can react, he scoops his hands under my ass, squeezing hard as he does, and lifts me up and over his lap. Then twists with me in his arms and has me on my back in the sand underneath him in a blink. "So sassy. Always so sassy." He plants a smacking kiss on my lips and touches his nose to mine.

"You love it," I say and give him a bratty *duck lips* face.

"I do." His eyes turn darker blue, like the ocean behind us, his expression serious. "And I love you."

I think my heart actually stops for a second, then triple thuds against my ribcage. I part my lips on a sharp intake of breath. My exhale sounds unsteady, even to my ears. I'm not sure I'll ever get used to him telling me. "You sure?" I try to sound cheeky to camouflage the butterflies twirling in my stomach.

One corner of his mouth goes up in a smirk. He sees right through me. He sits up on his knees between my legs and pulls me up so I'm sitting now with my legs bent on either side of him, never taking his eyes off mine. "Yeah, Ever, I am." He kisses me so deeply it takes us both a second to catch our breath. "I wasn't sure I could love anyone—*would* love anyone again. But the whole time Ashley was talking and walking me through his game plan, I couldn't stop thinking about you. About us. That I could give you a life. A good life. And I realized that's all I want. A life with you. A good one. Would you . . . want that? With me?"

I stop smiling as the gravity of his words settle on me. I nod my head slowly at first and then quicker.

His smile spreads, showing his teeth, and deepens his dimples. Then he pulls me up by the hands, stands and throws his arms around me, lifting me off the ground.

Instinctively, I wrap my legs around him, hug him with my whole body, tuck my face into his neck and I breathe in his scent. God, I love the way he smells. I kiss his neck just below his ear and rasp, "I love you too, Julie."

Gone are the melancholy visions of college campuses, impressive libraries and what might've been. All I can see is Julian and me together. It consumes me. And my heart feels full. It's okay to love my life, even if it's not the one I thought I'd have. Maybe this one is better.

"Let's go eat some tacos in a mansion, with a billionaire, and suss out this guy and see if he's good enough for Allie."

I find I'm giddy now at the thought of the next few days here. He kisses me again, soundly on the lips, and sets my feet on the sand. I gather my flip-flops and bag and reach for his hand as we make our way to the car and a patiently waiting Sean to take us back to our temporary home.

***

"Really, I'll do all the heavy lifting—or rather my team will. The only thing that changes for you is flying down here once or twice a month to film content." Ashley says this to Julian as we all dine casually around the kitchen island bar on homemade tacos, which are incidentally the best tacos I've ever eaten. And beyond healthy, according to our host. Over the surprisingly casual family-style dinner, Ashley (he's known and called by his last name, except by Allie, who calls him Luke or Ash) shares the ins and outs of this new business venture. He'll be the investor in Julian's new company, The McKay Method. For a percentage, Ashley would essentially fund and spearhead making Julian the next big thing in the fitness world—as a branch of the Ashley conglomerate, but its own entity.

From the little I know and understand about basic business, it sounds legit, if a little too good to be true. But watching Allie with him might've given me the reason for his generosity. They are clearly, as Julian said earlier, smitten. It's frankly beautiful to see. He is this specimen of virility, wealth and savviness who seems genuinely excited to share it.

Julian is quiet through dinner—not awkwardly quiet but reserved. He seems hopeful, asking insightful questions and trading ideas with both Ashley and Allie. I mostly say nothing except when I can offer encouraging sentiments like "That sounds promising," or "Ooh, that would be fun," and "Amazing."

At least, I hope I sound encouraging. I mean every word, but it's hard to take our relationship out of the bubble we've formed it in. I'm protective of it, of him. Is protective the right word? Maybe I'm being possessive. I don't like the thought of that, but I've never had anyone like Julian in my life before—not a boyfriend or committed relationship before him—and I'm a little out of my element, to put it mildly. When we finish the meal, I gladly offer to clean up as a thank you for the hospitality and let them continue their business planning. It's a great excuse to listen and not feel required to chime in with inane declarations. I feel pulled in two. I want every good thing for this sweet, beautiful man, but I don't want it to take him away from me.

So lost in my thoughts, I don't notice the lull in conversation or my guy walking up behind me at the sink until he's sliding his arms around my waist. He places a quick kiss on my neck. I tilt from habit to give him better access.

Ashley speaks up from behind us like we were in the middle of a conversation, telling me I'd zoned out on the group discussion and missed part of it. "Yeah, Ev, thank you for clearing the plates, but leave it. Let's go for a walk and a soak after."

Playing it off, I dry my hands and smile, nodding. The four of us, each couple holding hands, head out the back door off the kitchen/dining area and down the stairs of his deck to his private beach access. No wonder Allie doesn't want to come home.

As if I'd summoned her to me with that thought, she snakes her arm through mine as we walk along the beach. "You were quiet throughout the business talk. What do you think?" She talks low enough that we won't be heard over the sound of the waves.

Julian raced Ashley down the beach anyway and they're now walking and laughing their way back toward us. It reminded me of how my mom always teased my dad about men never growing up. It's cute watching them act like boys and drives home how much he and I live in our isolated bubble of Blue Lake. A bubble of our own making, but a bubble, nonetheless.

"It sounds like an incredible opportunity. One he shouldn't pass up—especially if you trust Ashley the way you do."

"He is probably the most generous person I've ever met."

"Forgive me if I'm out of line here, but I think love looks good on you."

Allie squeezes my arm with hers and giggles. "I do think I love him. And I think he loves me."

It's dusk, so I can't see if she's blushing, but her words sound like she probably is. "You think? Or you know?" I ask like we're besties, which is how she's made me feel since I moved to Blue Lake—like an equal.

"I know. He wants to marry me." This she says quietly, leaning into my ear.

"Oh my God, Allie, that's . . . wonderful." I all but squeal it, prompting the men to look up from their animated conversation and focus on us. We both giggle nervously and turn toward the ocean to watch the waves.

"Will you move down here then?" People have teased me before about flashing forward twenty years in any given situation. I think it just makes sense to prepare for every possible outcome. Less likelihood for unexpected drama, chaos or hurt.

"That would depend . . ."

"On . . .?"

"Julian. You. Your plans for the future. Julian already owns half of Fit and Brew. If I do decide to move down here full time, I might want to divest my interests."

"You mean like sell your half to Julian?"

"Or you? What are your plans, Evvie? Do you want to go away to college? Get your degree online?" She trails off, giving me a chance to respond.

"I've thought about that a lot lately. Especially since coming here. Seeing Pepperdine. And that library. So beautiful. It's always been my dream to go away to school. But dreams have a way of changing. And I think mine has."

"Yeah, they do." Allie's face takes on a wistful expression as she says it. "Maybe you'll travel for something else now. With someone."

"Did you know Julian and I would become a thing?" I ask her bluntly.

"What? Nooo. I mean, it may have crossed my mind that there would be an attraction. But I saw you as two kindred spirits, I guess. It just seemed like you two would get each other. Beyond that, I didn't give it any deep consideration. I'm glad that you have each other though. To see Julian open up to someone, care about someone the way he cares about you, makes me so happy."

"He says the same thing about you." My reply has a sad smile creeping over Allie's face. I want to ask her about it, but I don't, because I know what it's like to not want people to ask me about my sad smiles.

So I change the subject instead. "The thing is, I can study and earn a degree anywhere. So, I think you're right. I can swap 'going away to school' for traveling for fun instead. I like that. Even if it's just coming down here with Julian for now. I mean, this place is a vacation all by itself." I spread my hands to encompass our surroundings.

Giggling, Allie agrees, "It really is."

Chapter 6

EVERLY

Watching Julian film content is beyond hot. Joining him is even hotter. Ashley runs a tight ship. He planned the trip so that all content films in one day, but it's a long, thorough day. The morning content is four kickboxing combos and three talking pieces that takes about three hours. The afternoon takes another three hours and includes short reels, motivational clips and a few behind-the-scenes/lifestyle shots. That it all takes place on Ashley's property is a bonus.

Julian can use any of the models Ashley has on staff, but he insists I be the model when they need one for his videos. I'm flattered but so nervous. Turns out, because we work well together and know each other so well and have done these routines together countless times, it only takes one video for me to forget we're filming and just enjoy working out. I mean, the director would yell "cut" and have the assistant fix things like hair, sweat and angles. Besides those interruptions, it's easy to fall into our routine. What isn't easy is pretending I'm not thirsting to get this sweaty, ripped man alone and naked after a full day of proximity with said sweaty, ripped man.

Now that we're done for the day, we have the evening off. Tomorrow, we'll be on the ASH private jet first thing in the morning headed back to Blue Lake via the Oak Valley airport—a day earlier than planned. We're in the green room off Ashley's home studio and alone for the first time in hours.

"Thanks for doing the videos with me. Made it so much easier. We have a groove." Julian is wiping his arms down with a damp towel and looking at me in the mirror.

"I agree. I wasn't sure I would like it, but it was kinda fun. Except the assistant who liked to monitor your glisten factor. I think she likes her job a little too much." I frown at his knowing smirk.

"Hmm, I don't think I've ever seen you jealous before. I think I like it." He lifts his eyebrows and tweaks his lips to the side.

"Am I giving jealousy? I thought I was just annoyed. I mean, if Callie is there to make sure we don't look sweaty on camera, why is yours the only sweat she inspects?" I roll my eyes.

"Fair point." He turns from the mirror, snakes his arm around my waist and pulls me in to plant a hard quick kiss on my lips. "Maybe you're just not as sweaty as me."

I don't let him off with that quick kiss so easily. I wind my arms around his neck and keep my lips pressed to his. I tilt my head just enough to invite him to deepen the kiss. He obliges. It feels like forever since he's kissed me. We don't make a habit of kissing at work back in Blue Lake either, but today just felt . . . long. If I'm being honest, maybe I low-key want to mark my territory. I don't love acknowledging that might be part of it, but I've had enough therapy to be self-aware.

Self-awareness be damned.

Working out with Julian always gets me a little keyed up. We've been simulating workouts for almost eight hours now, so my keyed-up has escalated to full-blown hot and bothered. I clench the sides of his shirt in my hands and pull him tighter to me. His musky scent, part sweaty man and part pure Julian fills my nostrils. I push the damp fabric up his body, flat palms sliding up his chiseled abs.

He lifts his arms, allowing me to swipe it over his head. As soon as I do, he snakes his hands inside my workout shorts, gliding the shorts over my hips with his hands.

I whip my sports bra over my head.

Hunger emanates from his midnight-blue eyes as he lifts me and places me on the dressing table, my back to the mirror. Within moments, we're panting. His low, baritone chuckle tells me he knows exactly what he's doing to me, and he likes it. Capturing my lips in a searing kiss, he picks me up off the dressing table and carries me to the sofa. We're not talking and this isn't sweet. It's hot and fast and wild. As we both come, he holds my body down tight to his and pants through his orgasm and our kiss—our lips against each other but not actually kissing anymore.

I forget where we are or to care to be quiet until he shushes me. "Fuck, Julie, ugh."

"Shhh," he breathes heavily into my ear, which only increases the shudders and the intensity of my orgasm.

My man thinks of everything. I'm not sure I could've found a coherent thought in this moment with GPS and a tour guide. But afterwards, he picks me up and carries me to the connected bathroom before we make a mess on the nice couch. He stands me in the shower and joins me.

The icy jolt of spray shocks me out of my sex-drunk haze. We shower quickly. After the long day and the hot sex, I could've curled up with my beautiful man and passed out for the next eight hours. Technically we could do just that with our night off, but I'm guessing we'll be joining Allie and Ashley for dinner at least before we turn in for the night. I'm pretty sure we've already been in the green room longer than necessary. The pre-embarrassment of facing anyone when we walk out of here flames my cheeks. I look up to see if Julian is tracking my reaction. He is. Always.

"Hi, sweet girl." He drags his index finger down my nose and taps my bottom lip as he says it.

"Hi, hot boyfriend." I attempt to squash my unease with the sass I know he likes.

He winks and gives me a sweet, soft kiss. "There she is. What's going on in there?" He taps my forehead.

"I think we might have just announced that we had sex in here." I turn around and give him my back when he twirls his finger at me to do so. I think he's going to scrub my back. Instead, he starts washing my hair. His fingers massaging my scalp make my eyes roll back in my head.

"I don't give a shit who knows. I'll make love to you again right now." His words send a tingle through my lower body.

He dips my head toward the spray, letting water and suds sluice down my body, then presses a kiss to my shoulder and turns me around. Pressing his hands to my cheeks, he pulls my lips to his and kisses me deeply. He pulls back and pins me with his azure eyes, his lashes spiky and wet. "You're my girlfriend. We live together. I think people know we do it."

He plants a kiss on the tip of my nose, and I can't help but giggle, embarrassment forgotten. This is one of the many reasons I love this man. I want to tell him that, but I don't. I don't want things to get serious right now. I like when he can pull me out of my head and everything feels light and happy and playful. I can breathe when it's like this—when we're like this. It feels like nothing else matters and I could keep floating on this plane of existence forever. I can't wait to be back in our Blue Lake bubble.

As we're putting on fresh clothes, a knock on the door and Callie's singsong, muffled voice penetrates my bubble. "Julian? Just wanted to run over some final edits with you when you get a sec."

I turn to the mirror and start brushing out my wet hair, hoping to hide any reaction my face might give away.

"Be right there, Callie. Thanks," he calls loud enough to be heard through the door. He comes to the dressing table and stands behind me, placing his hands on my shoulders.

I mess with my hair a couple seconds longer until I can no longer avoid his eyes without giving myself away.

He squeezes my shoulders and winks at my reflection.

"So, Callie's an editor now?" I arch one eyebrow at him in the mirror.

He gives me his adorable half smile and runs his hands up and down my arms. "I guess I'm about to find out. Wanna go with? Wait here?" He asks the last question with an unspoken *or*... at the end.

"I think I'll head out to the beach and catch the last sunset." I look down and busy my hands needlessly straightening up items on the dressing table.

Kissing the side of my head and gently squeezing my biceps, he says, "I'll meet you down there as soon as possible. Tell the sun to wait for me." He winks when I make eye contact again and play along by nodding my head with a half smile at his silly request.

When he closes the door behind him, I throw down the make-up brush. Not for the first time, I wonder what the hell I'm doing with such a beautiful man. Everywhere we go, women want to throw themselves at him and do. I mean, that's why a few random workout videos of him went viral to begin with. Granted, we didn't get out much to have to deal with it on a daily basis, but I see the writing on the wall. I'm not sure I'm prepared or cut out to deal with everyone wanting my man. I want to throw a toddler-level tantrum, but I settle for shoving my shit into my bag, hastily straightening up the green room and slamming the door on my way out to the beach. I cringe at the sheer brattish behavior—very unlike me, but I can't deny the satisfaction of the door rattling in its jamb. Yeah, I'm supposed to talk about my feelings, but I'm better at pretending everything is fine. It's what good military brats do. I mentally salute myself as I stalk out of the building.

***

Sunsets in Malibu rival those I love at Blue Lake and today is no exception. As the fiery orb makes its final descent into the sea, a breeze sweeps over my skin, swirling strands of hair across my face. I shiver. With the increasing darkness, the temperature drops. I didn't think to bring a sweater. When I feel the first chill, I tell myself I'll be warm as soon as Julian shows up. He doesn't show. I stand and dust the sand off my shorts, ready to trek back up the stairs to Ashley's. Whatever editing Callie needed him for, it's taking longer than he said it would. I don't want to admit it to myself, but I'm sulking. The whole thing is magnifying how much I don't know what I'm doing with my life—except living his.

Granted, I've been learning and loving all things fitness and thinking about where it might lead me. I can see myself making a satisfying career out of it on some level. Maybe not doing exactly what Allie, Julian and Ashley are doing, but I know I could add my own qualities to the mix. I've even had the small hint of an idea forming lately about what I might contribute. I'm just not ready to voice it yet, and considering my simmering annoyance, I can't even summon those kinds of future thoughts. I'm pissed, and I admit, I don't want to calm down.

My irrational anger and I stomp up the steps in near complete darkness. As I approach the back slider, I can see all three of them, Allie, Ashley and Julian, talking in the kitchen, and my anger ignites into full-blown fury. The small, sensible voice telling me to calm down is extinguished by the neon-green resentment and jealousy. I feel like the supporting character in someone else's life. And haven't I always been? Staying out of the way. Doing what was expected. Never making waves.

Tasting what it felt like to be the star of the show only spotlighted my feelings. This doesn't feel like my life. It feels like Julian's, and I'm along for the ride. I want to sneak past them and hide in my room, but my evil twin slams the slider and stalks past them without a word instead. Their conversation halts and I can see the smiles and greetings freeze on their faces in my periphery as I storm through the open hallway to the stairs.

In the bedroom we share, I pace, wishing I could throw something or break it. The adrenaline rush doesn't leave any room for rationale. I just pace and heave. I don't recognize this hothead I glimpse in the mirror with each pass by the dresser. The click of the door halts my forge. I place my hands on the wooden surface, not looking at my reflection. I don't want to see that girl. I don't know her. I don't look over at him either or acknowledge him in any way. I know it's him though. Just like I knew he'd come. And I feel like a brat—ashamed even. Maybe I acted like that just to get him to follow me. That pisses me off more. I don't want to be this girl. I'm *not* this girl. Except that right now I am. And now I can't get away from myself and how I just acted. Now I have to face him. My nails curl on the wood surface with a faint scratching sound.

He comes up behind me, placing his fists beside my hands on the dresser top, his arms bookending mine. He dips his head down and rests his chin on my shoulder.

I can't avoid him forever. I look up into his eyes reflected in the mirror—a soft, calm blue. Piercing mine, I see patience and sweetness looking back at me. Pressure immediately builds behind mine. My emotions are at war. My heart races in my chest like a thousand hooves. Shame is quickly snuffing out the flames of my anger.

"Hi, pretty girl." He tilts his head when he says it, so his nose tickles my temple, and his words push soft puffs of breath into my ear.

It sends a flood straight to my belly and lower. I close my eyes and lean my cheek into his, but my stubbornness digs in its heels. "Don't, Julie." My voice hitches, and I clench my stomach muscles to force a steadiness I don't feel.

"Talk to me, Ever. What's going on in there?"

"I don't know, okay? I'm pissed. And I'm pissed that I'm pissed. And I don't wanna talk about it—especially with you."

His eyebrows disappear into the hair spilling onto his forehead on my last words. He lifts his head off my shoulder like I smacked him. "Okay." He steps back but doesn't stop watching me in the mirror. Lifting his hands off the dresser, holding them out low at his sides, he asks, "What can I do?"

"I don't know, Julian. Okay?" I blow a breath through my puffed cheeks and add, "Fire Callie?"

His smirk at my Callie remark sends a grudging smile to my own lips.

"There she is," he says, his smirk going full-blown, closed-lipped smile, crinkling the outer corners of his eyes.

He turns me from the mirror and wraps his arms around me so tight I work to inhale a full breath. My arms hang at my sides at first, but his heavy sigh has me hanging them loosely around his hips. I never want to hurt this man. Ever. The tug of war inside me has my head spinning so I can't form coherent thoughts. Then a traitorous tear slips from my eye. I brush my cheek on his shirt to hide it, but another one takes its place. I sniff to keep my nose from running, which I know alerts him to the tears—if he didn't already know.

"Ever . . ." He drags out the end of my name on a sigh like it hurts him to say it.

I know he doesn't like to see me upset. And therein lies my struggle. I want to stamp down my emotions so he's okay. *When do I get to feel my feelings?* I ignore myself. "I'm fine. I just wanna go home." As soon as the words come out, my old room flashes through my mind. Not Blue Lake. My childhood bedroom in Oak Valley. I don't really want to go back there. *Do I?* I love my life in Blue Lake. With Julian. But right now, it doesn't feel like my life. It feels like his life. In Blue Lake, I feel like his equal. His partner. Here, I feel like some tagalong with no life of her own. But is my life in Blue Lake even mine or ours? Or is it his with just more lines for me as a supporting character? It began as a fresh start, a way to escape, get away from all the bullshit in Oak Valley, but meeting Julian and working at Fit changed that. Now I want it to be my life. I want to be a contributing part of the life I have *with* him. And that means it's on me to decide what that looks like. At some point I have to be able to say what it is I want, what I envision. I also have to know what that is before I can say it.

Quiet, agreeable Everly is going to have to speak up for the life I hope to have. And while that isn't my MO, I am coming around to it—speaking my mind more. The reason for that, I know, has everything to do with the breathtakingly beautiful blue-eyed man before me and the way he makes me feel seen and understood. That my outer self is slowly reflecting my inner self is a testament to that. A small part of me worries that's proof it's all about him, but he's never made me feel that way. The opposite in fact.

"About that . . ." The timber of his voice rumbling against my ear wants to soothe me, but his words trip my heartbeat.

Chapter 7

Julian

My arms tighten around her as I say it, even when she tries to pull back to look at me. I hold on a few seconds more before I loosen my arms enough for her to tilt her head back and pin me with her storm-cloud eyes. That she waits for me to continue reminds me yet again how good this young woman is at compartmentalizing. And why her losing her shit resonates deeper. She doesn't throw fits and welcome the drama like most young women her age. That she did lose her shit tells me her nervous system is overloaded with a bunch of shit she's not saying. I want to do nothing more than whisk her back to Blue Lake where her smile meets her eyes, her laugh is infectious, and her body is fluid. Not rigid like it is now. What I have to say isn't going to help that. And being the fucking reason for that is making the tattooed spot on my chest ache.

"Ashley wants some personal content for the brand. He's . . . sending Callie and Auz home with us for a couple days."

After a short beat, she nods against my chest. She releases her loose hold on my waist to drag a fist down her cheek, and I know she's tucking it all away. *Fuck!* I hate myself a little right now. Like this is my fault somehow. I want to tell her that I'm doing all of this for us. Instinctively she knows this. I'm pretty sure she knows this.

"Okay, I'm . . . gonna grab a drink . . . some water from the kitchen and then finish packing. Want something?" She says all this without looking at me as she turns toward the door.

"No, thanks. I'm good." When she opens the door, I add, "Ever?" She stops midway through the opening but doesn't turn around. "It's only a couple days. Okay?"

"Yep, I know. We'll show them Blue Lake. It'll be great for the brand." She continues toward the stairs on the last part, not waiting for a reply.

Rubbing my chest, I tell myself that her feeling comfortable enough to throw a fit is probably a good thing. But when it came to facing me and owning it, she backed down. Became agreeable and retreated into herself. I want to be her safe place. I want her to show me all her sides and know that I'm not going anywhere. The timing of this content trip is not ideal. And Callie could dial down the focused attention. I mean, I know it's her job and the brand is essentially me, but if someone—anyone—were showing that kind of attention to Ever, putting their hands on her all day long, I'd probably want to rip their head off. No, not probably. I know I would. And maybe it really is her job and she's not trying to be flirty. It certainly didn't feel like the same kind of obvious attention that Sylvie and her Fit flock give me.

By the time I packed my clothes and flopped down onto the bed, Ever still hadn't returned from getting herself a drink. The anxious thud in my chest hadn't quite diminished, so I started counting my breaths. Deep inhale for a count of four. Hold for a count of four. Exhale for a count of four. I visualize my happiest place with each breath. It lulls me.

We're at the cliffs. It's Ever and me. Noah and Lilly. The midday sun is toasty and we're about to jump. The water is sure to stop the sizzle on our skin. The rush of the leap. The splash breaking the glass surface. The plunge of the silky coolness enveloping me. Popping up into the light, I reach for her. She floats just out of my reach. I swim toward her and stretch my arm out to catch her, but she dips under the surface again, so I wait for her to reemerge. When she doesn't, I turn in circles searching . . . looking for bubbles, ripples. Nothing. I slip under, looking for her in the murky water. Nothing. My chest aches with my held breath. When I can no longer hold it, I propel myself to the surface again, heaving air into my lungs.

My eyes bolt open. I'm clutching my chest, sucking air into my lungs. The room is dark. The hand clutching my chest flies to the side and finds her, and my brain rushes out of the dream and into reality. I'm here in bed, and Ever is next to me, sound asleep. I regulate my breathing quietly, hoping I don't wake her. The last thing I remember is doing a relaxation technique, waiting for Ever to return. I guess it worked because I must've fallen asleep. The day was exhausting and long. It's no surprise I crashed so hard. I gently rise from the bed to get water and see a full glass on my nightstand. I take quiet gulps and settle back onto the mattress. I don't want to wake her, but the pit in my stomach won't go away, so I roll onto my side and pull her into my chest. I inhale deeply with my nose pressed to the nape of her neck. Always warm sunshine.

Her hand reaches for mine and pulls it to her chest. She doesn't stir beyond that.

I count my inhales and exhales until her scent pulls me under again.

***

Ever is the epitome of a composed, gracious guest as we say our goodbyes to Ashley and Allie. She's mostly herself, if not quieter and more reserved. I don't push and instead mirror her energy. It's a default setting of mine—a survival instinct, my therapist told me once.

Ever doesn't know much about where I come from or how I grew up, except that I used to live in Southy, where her closest friend, Lilly, grew up. Lilly is three years younger than me and the oldest of her siblings. That she doesn't know me is not a stretch, despite the size of that shitty little town, and frankly, a relief. Besides, Julian McKay didn't grow up in South Point. Jayce Keller did—mostly unseen. Like most everyone else in the mobile park. Unless they warranted a visit from the sheriff's deputies, which my parents did on more than a few occasions. But that was my parents. No one paid attention to the quiet kid stuck in a shitty situation. And as I got older, I stayed gone as much as possible—a proven technique for staying off their radar and out of their codependent dysfunction-disguised-as-love shit show.

When I crashed into Allie, literally, over three years ago, and she asked my name, I wanted to disappear so completely that I choked giving her my real one. I spit out my middle name instead, along with my mother's maiden name, McKay. My grandfather, my mom's dad, is one of the few bright things I remember about my childhood. He came around a few times before he and my grandmother moved to

Florida. I was ten the last time I remember seeing him. He always asked if I was okay, happy. And I always said yes because I knew that's what my mom wanted me to say. It's twisted to me that little kids just want to make their parents happy—even shitty parents. Kids who want to please their parents above all learn to mask their trauma and perhaps set themselves up for the kind of meltdowns my girl encounters when faced with a storm of emotions. Anyhow, I couldn't say for sure why, but Jayce Keller disappeared that day. Aided by the loss of Taya and threats from Russell Bennick, her father. I didn't want to exist without her anyway. She gave me something in my miserable life to look forward to. Without her, I didn't care to be Jayce anymore. I didn't want to be anyone anymore. Allie changed that.

She's one of less than a handful of adults to ever show me kindness. Teachers didn't notice me, and I liked it that way. I much preferred they looked through me, like I wasn't even there, to their sad sorry looks. Or worse, the concern that could warrant a visit from Child Protective Services, which would just get my ass kicked once they left. I could tell from a young age when they did see me, they looked at me differently than the other kids, pitying, although I didn't know it at the time. I just knew I didn't like it.

Besides Allie and my grandpa McKay, there was only Hal, the groundskeeper for the Little League fields next to the trailer park. I snuck over and watched games during baseball season. When there weren't games, Hal mowed the grass or dragged the infield on his quad. He let me ride on it with him when I was really young. Once I got big enough to reach the pedals, he let me drive the mower while he dragged the field. Eventually, he paid me for my time. It wasn't much, and the older I got, the more I realized he probably couldn't afford to do it. So I quit showing up. That's how I wound up working for Russell "Rusty" Bennick on his property, mucking stalls, weed eating, whatever he told me to do. He needed a ranch hand, and I needed the job. That was how I met Taya.

Chapter 8

JULIAN

Seven Years Ago

"Hey, pretty girl. Yeah, you love ear scratches, don't you?"

"That's Sugar. She's a flirt, especially with guys."

My hand freezes, and I turn at the sound of her voice. The girl it belongs to walks through the barn doors as she speaks, backlit by the sun, and all I can think is *she looks like sugar*. Warm, sunbaked sugar. Her golden hair looks like it's been set on fire. Her frame is slight but tall for a girl. Her jeans scrunch at the bottom, pooling around her boots that kick up dust as she walks.

"I'm Taya. You must be the new hand my dad hired."

"Yeah, Jayce." I hold my hand out to shake hers.

She looks down at it, brow arched and swats the back of it like a backwards high five and giggles. "Okay, Jayce. Don't let Sugar sweet-talk you into more oats, because she'll try. She can be very persuasive." She strolls past me as she adds, "And she usually gets what she wants."

My head spins a little as I watch her breeze past me and out into the corral. *Is she talking about the horse?* I'm barely fifteen and don't know much—or anything—about girls, but it seems like her words mean more than what she's saying. My father was like that. His words wouldn't match his meaning, but it usually meant I was about to get my ass kicked. I learned to read people early to avoid things like that. I can't get a read on her though.

She treks through the stable corridor, and as the sun moves down her body, her hair changes from glowing to sandy blonde, swaying against her belt loops with her strides. Once outside the barn and in the corral, she calls to the other horse with kissing and clucking noises. "Cookie!"

Sugar and Cookie. That's what she reminds me of, a sugar cookie. Golden skin, sparkling sun-kissed hair. My mouth waters and my jeans feel tighter. Embarrassed by my reaction, I adjust myself discreetly and turn my back on the corral to focus on Sugar. She's nuzzling the hand I left dangling on the stall gate. The one Taya slapped but didn't shake. I give Sugar a few more scratches, then grab the rake to muck out the rest of the stalls. As animal crap goes, horse is the least offensive. I don't mind the work. It feels good to use my muscles and work outdoors.

Working for Mr. Bennick will make me stronger. My arms, back and legs ache already, but in a good way. And his property is close enough that I can ride my bike to and from work. The curvy highway between the trailer park and his ranch isn't the safest road for a bike, but South Point doesn't have sidewalks or bike lanes. Most roads barely have shoulders, but I'd make it work. When I told him

I couldn't ask my parents, Bennick offered to pay me in cash so I didn't need my parents' permission or a work permit. If I could save up enough, I could buy something better than a bicycle—maybe a motorcycle—when I turned sixteen. I don't know how to ride one, but I know they're cheaper than cars.

The sooner I have my own transportation the better.

Whinnying has me lifting my head from the stall I'm mucking in time to watch Taya fly through the center of the barn riding Cookie.

Dust and hay dance in her wake, her hair flying behind her like glowing ribbons of gold. Sugar tosses her head, snorts and dances in her stall as Cookie gallops past her.

I clamp my hand onto the top of my head to anchor my ball cap in place and duck my head against the gust of dirt and debris whipping through the barn. I turn my back to it and face Sugar as Taya and Cookie streak down the dirt road and up into the rolling foothills of the pasture. "Shhh, pretty girl. I got you. I know. They left you behind."

She bumps her muzzle against my hand and ducks her head over the gate.

I rub my hand absently up and down the white streak on her nose and watch the image of horse and girl grow smaller with distance. I flip my ball cap backwards and touch my forehead to her soft muzzle. I've never been around horses before, but I like this one. And I like the smell of the barn too. I don't understand the tightness gripping my chest. I feel the same way when my parents start screaming at each other and breaking stuff, trapped in the compact spare bedroom of our trailer, hoping their drama didn't find its way down the hall. Knowing I couldn't make it through the front door, the only door, without drawing attention to myself, I stay as quiet as possible and wait for the chaos to stop.

Watching Taya and Cookie fly across the ground and disappear within minutes looked freeing. I think I want to know that feeling—the wind slapping against my face while the thunder of hooves carries me away far and fast from the reminders of my shitty life. I decide to busy myself on the property until she comes back. Then I'd ask her to teach me to ride. I'm not sure if I'm allowed to do that, but something tells me she'll let me know if not. It doesn't hurt to ask. And she doesn't come off like she'd be afraid to tell some hired hand no.

An old wooden picnic table I discovered just outside the barn has seen better days, so I'll sand it down, make it look nice and possibly give it new life. It will be perfect for eating lunch or taking breaks. And fixing it up means I'll avoid the splinters it would surely give me otherwise. I find some sandpaper in the toolbox inside the tack room. It's not on my to-do list or even a priority, but since my regular chores are done and I want to wait for Taya to return, it's a good way to pass the time and look busy while I wait. Plus, I can sit down while I do it. My legs and back ache from all the bending and scooping. I hope the small pieces of sandpaper I found hold out until she shows. I'll buy more tomorrow to finish the project. Some stain too.

The sun has just begun to dip low behind the foothills when I hear the clomp of horse hooves. Then Sugar whinnies from her stall, greeting her friend. I look up, watch Taya rock and sway in the saddle as Cookie plods into the barn. Just as I convinced myself she either didn't see me just to the side of the structure or she was ignoring me, she stops before entering the barn and pins me with her sage-green gaze.

"You trying to make something out of that heap of kindling?"

"Maybe. I like it." I look down at my handiwork as I answer.

"Suit yourself, but if you decide it's not worth it, it'll make a great bonfire starter."

I stand on ever-stiffening legs and follow her into the barn. As I come around the corner and through the sliding doors, she rolls out of her saddle like it's part of her. She starts to unhook the saddle, and I rush to help.

"I can manage, thanks." She sounds almost annoyed.

"I don't mind helping. I was . . . I wanted to ask . . ."

"Spit it out." Yep. Clearly annoyed. Now I'm sweating.

"Could I go riding with you sometime? Maybe on Sugar?"

"Gotta little crush?"

My face flames at her question.

Before I can stammer a response, she adds, "I told you Sugar is a flirt."

Ohhh, she meant the horse. I force a chuckle, relieved. "I just . . . It looks . . . cool. I wish I knew how to ride like that."

"Well, Sugar would love it." She considers it for a second. "Sure, we can do that. But you can't tell my dad. He'll go ballistic. Worse than a prison guard. But he's gone a lot this time of day for one thing or another. We can ride then. Just get your shit done before so you don't get in trouble. Or fired."

"Noted. Thanks. I . . . don't know . . . anything—"

"It's cool. I got you. Nothing to it once you know the basics. You'll love it. And Sugar will love you more than she already does."

My cheeks go crimson again.

Why does the mention of a horse's affection embarrass me? Maybe it's just a reference to anyone or anything loving me that does it. My stomach heats up like my cheeks and flutters too. "Can we start . . . go . . . ride tomorrow?"

Her giggle fills the barn and echoes off the empty stalls. "Yeah. Tomorrow's perfect. He plays poker. He'll be gone all night."

"What about your mom?"

"What about her?" she snaps and kicks a pebble with the toe of her boot. "She lets me do what I want." She shrugs as she says it, but the crease between her brows contradicts her words.

"Okay. I can get all my stuff done pretty quick. I'll wait here for you."

She's taken the saddle, blanket and cinch off and set them on the ground beside Cookie as we talked. I scoop them off the ground and grunt a little with the effort and stiffness.

"I told you I got it." She doesn't say it with venom but leaves no room to argue. I ignore her and take it into the tack room. I return with a brush and begin brushing the horse down. She goes to the tack room and returns with a hoof pick and cleans Cookie's hooves while I brush.

I have no idea if I'm doing it right, just mimicking what I've seen on TV or in movies.

When she finishes the hooves, she holds her hand out to me, asking for the brush without words. I place it in her hand and lead Cookie into her stall. Taya returns with a couple carrots. I wonder where they came from. She keeps two for Cookie and hands me one and tosses her head toward Sugar. "Here, take it to your new girlfriend."

I dip my head as I chuckle to hide the flush coloring my cheeks again. I turn toward Sugar's stall as she whinnies, eyeing the carrot in my hand.

Before I finish giving it to her, I hear Taya say, "Nice meeting you, Jay. Remember to stay off my dad's radar so you can stick around. Get your work done."

"Noted. And it's Jayce."

"I know. I kinda like Jay. See you tomorrow."

Chapter 9

JULIAN

Six Years Ago

"Taya?" I hear her voice the moment I step inside the barn. Not words though. My heart drops at the sound of her sobs, then slams into my ribs and hammers like it wants out of my chest.

"Go away, Jay. I just wanna be alone."

"Not gonna happen." I find her sunk into the corner of Sugar's stall, legs pulled up to her chest, cradled by her arms with her forehead pressed to her knees. Unlatching the gate brings her head up, and her waterlogged sea-glass eyes break my heart. Dropping to my knees in front of her, I clasp her face in my hands and raise it to mine. "Talk to me, Tay. Tell me what it is."

"She did it. She finally did it. She got out. She's gone."

"Who, Taya? What happened? Your mom?"

She barely nods her head within the confines of my hands as fresh tears spill down her cheeks.

"Where'd she go?" Her broken sobs give me my answer, as much as I hoped it wasn't so.

Mandy Bennick struggled with depression since before Taya was born and never bounced back from postpartum psychosis unless aided by drugs that left her comatose or manically happy. Either way, she checked out of her life long before Taya was old enough to know any different. Her dad, Rusty, pulled out all the stops to keep her happy or at least able to portray happiness to the town he unofficially ran. Today, her mix of pills and cocktails turned fatal. And while Taya always proclaimed she liked the freedom of a checked-out mom, I know she wished their relationship were different. We shared that sentiment.

Taya rises up onto her knees and scoots onto my lap, straddling me.

I drop my hands from her face, resting my soft fists on the hay floor.

She grips the sides of my neck and jaw, curling her long fingers into my hair, and pulls my face to hers. She kisses me frantically, and I let her for a moment.

I rub my hands up her body, neck, stopping when I get to her cheeks. I softly pull away from her lips, locking gazes with her.

Eyes glazed, she leans in, trying to resume her kisses.

"Tay." I try to reach through the haze of her grief.

"Stop, Jay. I don't want to talk. Just kiss me."

I hold her face in my hands and stare into her liquid green eyes. What I see there tells me I won't penetrate her pain with words. I sigh and pull her lips to mine. I deepen the kiss, mimicking her urgency—an urgency I don't feel but sense she needs.

She peels my shirt up over my torso, and I lift my arms, letting her drive the fabric over my head. I reach behind my neck and yank it up and off. She crosses her arms over her stomach and yanks the hem of her Guns N' Roses T-shirt over her head in one motion. Then she's kissing me again, skin to skin except for the thin fabric of her bra.

Within minutes I'm not thinking about talking or stopping. I don't care that the hay pricks my skin when I pick her up and lay her back, covering her body with mine. It's soft enough, and the sweet smell reminds me of her. Her scent always smells faintly of horses and hay and green grass. Underneath, her shampoo or soap or maybe lotion teases a hint of coconut but never overpowers the essence of the outdoors.

She's pulling at my hips now. Pressing hers up into mine. We've made out before. Lots of times. But we always stop before we go too far. Before clothes come off. This time is different. She won't stop.

Somewhere inside my brain, a faint voice tells me I should stop. But she's kissing my neck. Her warm breath and soft raspy voice fill my ear, raising the hair on my arms and neck. Goosebumps follow.

"I want you, Jay. Please, just make me forget." The reminder of her mom brings me back to earth.

"We shouldn't. Not now. Not like this."

She braces her hands on my shoulders and shoves with everything she's got.

I roll off her onto my side as she sits up, resting her forearms on her raised knees.

She lifts her hands and drags them through her hair at her temples. Without looking at me, she says, "Go away."

"C'mon, Taya, don't be like that."

"Don't fucking tell me how to be. She's dead, Jay. She's not in the other room ignoring me like usual. She's fucking gone forever. Okay? I just wanted to numb the pain. Even if it was just for a little while. You don't wanna help me do that, then leave."

I stare at her profile, racking my brain for the right words. A tear slides down her cheek, and I reach for her. I rest my fingers lightly on her shoulder and place a soft kiss there. She turns her face until her cheek rests on the back of my hand. Looking into the broken green pools, I know I won't deny her anything. "Okay, Taya, it's okay. I'm right here. I got you."

She throws herself into my arms, the force knocking me back onto our hay *bed*. Straddling my thighs, she begins unfastening my jeans. I watch through hooded lids as she slides them down my hips, lifting to give her access. She stands quickly, pulling her sports bra over her head as I push my jeans off each calf with my feet. She shimmies out of her jeans, kicks them to the side, then repositions herself on my thighs. I reach up to timidly hide her breasts, covering them in each palm, but my touch has her arching into my grasp, her nipples hardening at the contact. My hands squeeze instinctually. Her body rubs against me, and moisture glazes the growing stiffness between my legs. My hips rise to meet the pressure of hers. The friction isn't new, but our complete nakedness makes the sensations new, more intense, and somehow more real. We're floundering in our inexperience but eager and urgent.

My hands clamp hard onto her hips and drive the grinding motion, causing our breaths to hitch and our hearts to hammer. I slide them up her torso, circle her nipples and pinch them between my thumb and finger, hard. I sit up, take one in my mouth and suck. My pulse throbs in my crotch.

She's moving her hips back and forth along my length, and it gets more slippery with each thrust. With my free hand I reach down to touch the wetness of her center. When my thumb finds the bundle of nerves, she throws her head back in a deep moan. I'm mesmerized by her long blonde hair falling over us, her soft tan skin against mine, moving and responding on pure instinct.

On my own instinct, I dip my finger into her heat. She rocks into the invasion in a clear invitation of more, and I oblige by adding another. Her rocking turns to grinding as I plunge in and out, but I can tell what I'm doing isn't enough. I slide my fingers out of her, clasp her hips and lift her. I turn and lay her beneath me, kissing her softly.

She doesn't want to be soft. She sucks my bottom lip into her mouth and nips it almost painfully.

Before I kiss her, I pull back and look down into her eyes, dark emerald now. "Are you sure, Taya?"

"I want you, Jay. Now. More than I've ever wanted anything. Please."

I kiss her deeply, quickly. "Okay. Okay, Taya." I'm scared to cross this line, but I'm more scared not to. I want to be here for her, give her what she wants, even though I know it's just a crutch. My choices sucked. Leave her alone in her grief or give her this crutch. I won't refuse her.

Taking myself in my hand, I guide it into position between her legs and into the slippery heat. I meet resistance and ease up.

But Taya is single-minded in her resolve. She locks her hands onto my hips and, with surprising force, pulls me into her. Her wetness helps, but I feel the pierce. The short cry that rips from her throat tells me it hurts.

I freeze. She lets me. I rest my forehead on hers, panting, fighting for control over my urge to keep driving.

"It's okay, Jay. Keep going." I know without knowing she welcomes this physical pain, hoping it drowns the emotional pain.

"Shh, Taya, give it a second, okay?" I rain little kisses on her face—temples, forehead, cheeks, lips. She lies still under me, eyes closed, while I kiss her. When I stop, she opens them, and we stare at each other. I slowly move inside her.

She reaches her palms to my cheeks, rubs tenderly, encouragingly. She tries to hide the wince of pain. But I also feel when it stops hurting because I slide in and out more easily. Her eyes glaze over just before they roll up and her lids shutter down. Her lips part on a long exhale—part moan, part breath, as her hips rise to meet each thrust. I don't know how much longer I can hold back, or if I'm supposed to.

Instinctively, I know there is more I could do to give her what she wants. My inexperience has my carnal impulses taking over. I want to slow down for her, but she won't have it. So I drive in and out, over and over, until the buildup becomes too much. Her nails dig into my hips, leaving divots. I relish the pain as a fair turn for the pain I caused her. I groan into her neck as my orgasm rips through me and pulses into her.

As my brain returns to earth, the first thought that slams into my mind is that we didn't use a condom. *Fuck!* We are the typical stupid, irresponsible teenagers. *Fuck!* I can't change it now. I'd been carrying one around in my wallet for a while. I just didn't think to get it. *Stupid!* But I can give her a release I know she didn't get with mine. I don't know how exactly, but I've never wanted anything more. I need her to feel good, great, loved. I think I do love her. We've never said it, but I think it must feel like this. I'd do anything for this girl. I'd take her place right now, trade my mom for hers.

I push that chilling knowledge from my mind.

Instead, I focus on kissing her neck. She arches, giving me better access, and holds my head to her, encouraging my attention. Pulling out, I trail kisses down her body until I'm between her legs. I place featherlight kisses to her center.

Her body responds, a hardening bead. I suck it gently into my mouth, flicking my tongue over it. Her body arches off the ground as my name floats out of her mouth, her voice low and husky. Pushing my hands under her, I lift her to meet my lips more fully. I don't use my fingers for fear she's too sore, but I make up for that with my mouth.

Her legs lock tight around me.

I increase my intensity and pressure, causing my body to reawaken. I ignore the urge to plunge into her, but I do test a finger, slowly penetrating her soft heat.

A gasp rips from her lips, followed by a long, "Yesssss."

I nip the bud with my teeth and add a finger. Her legs lock like a vise as she pulses around my fingers. I slow my motions, mouth and hand. Her fingers in my hair pull slightly while holding my head in place against her as she pants through her orgasm. When her arms and legs go limp, I rest my cheek on her lower abdomen and she pets my hair idly. I scoot up until I'm lying even with her. As reality sinks in, I cringe inwardly that our first time was on a stable floor. But I don't have long to dwell on it.

Taya interrupts my thought spiral with, "C'mon, let's go to the drugstore and get Plan B. And some condoms." She rustles the hair on my head playfully. Gone are the torment and pain of losing her mother. I know what Plan B is, but I've never known anyone to need it before. I wonder if we should go to a nearby town where no one knows us—knows her. No one knows me already. But everyone knows her.

We sit up, side by side, not looking at each other now.

"What about Rus—your dad?"

"He'll be busy with . . . the formalities."

I turn my face to hers. Even in profile I see hers fall, eyes filling with fresh tears. "I'll drive, okay?" I grab her hand and stand her up, then hug her naked body to mine, threading my fingers through her hair.

"Okay." Her chest rises and falls with her deep breath. And just like that she tucks her pain back in. "Thanks, Jay. I . . . I love you."

"I love you back. I mean it, Taya. Always. Okay?" I vow naively. Completely believing every word I say.

She nods against my chest, takes another deep breath, then steps away and begins collecting her clothes.

Chapter 10

EVERLY

The plane is now at cruising altitude, so I unbuckle to get a drink. I'm still floored by this level of wealth and wonder if this is my mom's daily reality as a VIP flight attendant. Still, I walk toward the bar like I've done it a million times.

The flight attendant meets me there. "Can I get you something? Mimosa? Coffee?" She smiles and waits for my reply.

I planned to just get some water, but as Callie's tinkling laugh hits my ears, I change my mind. "Ooh, a mimosa sounds great. Do you have pineapple juice?"

"Of course. Would you like both pineapple and orange juice?"

"Yes, please."

"I'll bring it right over."

Callie has taken my spot next to Julian and is in an animated conversation—about content, I hope. I take the seat on the other side of the plane directly across from them. As I settle in, I look up at the click I hear. Austin "Auz" is snapping shots of our flight. He aims his lens at me, and I smile self-consciously. He doesn't click until I start to look away.

"Going for natural, unposed stuff," he explains.

I smile again and nod as the flight attendant, Trina, hands me a tall bubbling glass.

The first sip tickles my nose and puckers my lips. It's delicious. I open the Kindle in my hand. It's been a while since I lost myself in a book. I always have a book loaded and ready to read—several actually—but I haven't found time to unplug into a fictional world lately. And since I don't have any new releases cued up, I open my comfort book and begin to read. I could've journaled, but the drink in my hand is giving vacation vibes, so I indulge. I really do need to update my go-to comfort book. This one is over thirty years old. I turn to chapter three right away to begin on my favorite *first* chapter. *If I'd written it, I would've started here.*

This book really is outdated now, but maybe that's what I like about it: The simplicity of the characters not having social media and cell phones and text conversations. Content and branding and highlight reel lifestyles. I feel it first. Before I even look up from my Kindle to find Julian piercing me with eyes that rival the blue of the sky. Callie has vacated my spot and is now scrolling through the images on the back of the camera Auz used to capture the flight—their heads bend toward each other while he points out and captions the ones he likes best.

Swinging my eyes back to Julian, I catch his little half smile as he places his hand on the seat next to him, silently asking me to join him. My stomach does the little flip it always does when this man shows me what I mean to him. I lower my eyes and smile, then dart silently across the aisle into the seat beside him.

As soon as my ass hits the chair, he buries his nose behind my ear and inhales deeply. His slow, warm exhale tickles my ear and sends heat coiling in my lap.

I pinch my knees together and lean into him.

"Your drink smells yummy," he says, bringing his nose to the corner of my lip.

"Want a sip?"

"M-hm." He kisses the corner of my lip as he hums his answer.

I turn my body toward him, intending to extend my glass, when he captures my lips fully and kisses me, sucking my bottom lip softly. "Mmm."

Giggling quietly, I pull back. My bottom lip popping out of his mouth makes an unintentional pout. The heat swirling in my lap is turning to pressure and the pressure is making me squirm. I try to hide it by shifting my position, but his darkening eyes tell me he sees the effect he's having on me, and now the pressure escalates to throbbing.

"Try some." I press the flute into his hand. I close my free hand into a loose fist and press it into my lap.

He takes the drink and sips it slow, never breaking eye contact.

I do though when I watch his throat as he swallows. I swallow too. "I . . . I'm going to use the restroom." I stand up quickly and turn toward the back of the plane and the lavatory. His low baritone chuckle follows me as I scurry from our seats. Closing myself into the tiny bathroom, I lean back on the door and wonder if I will ever get used to my body's immediate and complete response to this man. I also wonder for the millionth time if we are special or if everyone in love feels like this?

In these moments, shit like Callie fades into oblivion. It feels foolish now to think I'd ever have to worry about anyone coming between us. He never fails to make me feel like his world begins and ends with me. And I know mine does with him. Even images of attending Pepperdine can't sway me now. Whatever life I could dream of would be nothing without him. I don't even hate that I'm giving wife-of-the-fifties energy. Maybe love can be the priority and everything builds around it.

Like in your books? I hear my sister's voice in my head.

When I return to my seat, Julian is on his laptop flipping through what looks like footage from the last couple days of content.

The shots of us catch my attention. We look hot. I know we're glammed up and it's heavily produced, but I'm impressed. Trina appears and lets us know we're landing soon and to stow our belongings. I can't wait to be home. It seems like we've been gone forever. I sigh just picturing Blue Lake.

Julian reaches for my hand and, linking our fingers together, brings the back to his lips for a soft kiss and settles it in his lap. He holds it until we're on the ground, then stands to retrieve our bags and deplane.

Chapter 11

EVERLY

"You're welcome to stay at our place, but if you want more privacy, there is my old apartment over the café. It's small but has everything you need," Julian offers to Callie and Austin sitting in the middle row of seats in front of us.

"If we're not intruding, we'd love to stay with you. Might give us more opportunity for the personal content Ashley's looking for," Callie answers over her shoulder for both of them.

Auz nods, agreeing with her, munching on a protein bar.

Julian squeezes my hand.

We're in the back of the black Escalade Ashley had waiting at the airport in Oak Valley to take us to Blue Lake. Just being this close to home calms my system. And because I'm calmer, I find I don't mind Callie and Austin staying with us. I'm even a little excited to show off the place I love so much. I'm proud of this life we're building.

But at the mention of Julian's apartment and its vacancy, I'm reminded that Lilly and Noah are gone now. Away at school, starting their freshman year. The twinge of jealousy pulls the corners of my mouth down. I quickly force them back up into a smile. I'm happy for my friends. I don't mind getting my degree online. I can continue to build a life in Blue Lake while I do it. With Julian. I meet his eyes and give him a wink to let him know I'm on board.

We're a team, I remind myself.

***

Once Callie and Auz are settled into the two spare rooms, we venture on foot to Brew to show them the resort. It's all but shut down now, with a few local stragglers visiting and soaking up the last of the warm days. Julian and I jog there, but it's a choreographed event with Auz capturing stints of running and Callie *cutting* to fix shadows and misplaced hairs. The five-minute jaunt takes thirty minutes. The more we stage our *real life*, the more grateful I am that I deleted my social media. Of course, Ashley (and company) is trying to convince me to reactivate my accounts. Or better yet, start new ones. I'm entertaining the latter—challenging Julian that I will if he does.

By the time we get to Brew I'm wishing we'd brought suits to jump in the lake. Callie wants to get some yoga/stretching shots on the beach. I'm thrilled to take off my socks and shoes and bury my toes in the sand. I whip my T-shirt over my head and plan to do the poses in my sports bra—if nothing else to avoid the sweat stains on my shirt.

"Ooh, I love that, Ev. Julian, can you take your shirt off too?" Callie notes his arched eyebrows at her request. "Oh, c'mon. Sex sells and you've got sex appeal in spades. Besides, you two together will make every married couple in the world want to join a gym."

Julian rolls his eyes, wiggles his brows at me on the last remark, shrugs his shoulders and whips his shirt over his head. We save the floor moves for the end, so we don't have sand clinging to us in the other shots. By the time we're done, the sun is much lower in the sky, but it's still a slightly cooler oven outside. When Callie finally says, "That's a wrap," Julian picks me up and tosses me over his shoulder like a sack and runs into the lake, dunking us both. As I'm coming up for air, I see Auz whip his shirt off, balance on one foot to pull off his Converse and plunge in after us. Callie's tinkling laugh follows. She picks up his camera and begins snapping, not bothering to check the quality.

"We're done for the day, Callie, get in here," Auz shouts, tossing his head sideways to swing his soggy hair out of his face. It's met with more tinkling laughter. "Get in or I'll come up there and carry you in."

"Fine. God, you're a pain in my ass." She kicks off her shoes and tosses her tank top on the sand. "These denim shorts are going to weigh twenty pounds when they're wet."

"So go in your underwear," Auz calls back.

"You wish," she counters.

"I kinda do," he says under his breath.

Julian's arms snake around me from behind, so I turn and wrap my legs around him. With a soft kiss, he says, "Let's go get us all some towels." He carries me out of the water as Callie is heading in. Setting my feet on the sand, he calls out, "Grabbing some towels, guys. We'll be right back." To me, he says, "Race ya," and takes off up the beach.

I take off after him, knowing I'll never catch him.

"Hey, stop doing cool shit when I don't have a camera," Auz yells from the water.

Seeing Austin's attention to Callie makes me hate her less. Combined with Julian's undeniable affection for me, I'm feeling like myself again. Content, calm and happy. I even enjoyed making content. Our beach session was kinda hot and sexy. Maybe that's why Julian wanted to race me to the towels—alleviate the tension. But we don't need much to wind us up. Our sexual tension seems to always lie just under the surface.

I catch him at the bottom of the stairs leading up to his old apartment, but only because he stopped and waited for me.

"Hi, pretty girl."

"Hi, boyfriend," I say, trying not to sound out of breath. My beautiful man isn't winded in the least. He's so frickin' hot and still dripping lake water. Since he doesn't have a shirt on, I grab the waistband of his shorts, pull him to me and plant a smacking kiss on his lips.

I take a step back, and he slinks his arms around me, grabs a handful of my ass with one and presses my lower half to him with the other. My hands glide over his soft and warm skin, past his abs, pecs and neck till my fingers wrap around the back of his head, where the spiky fade of hair is almost dry. I pull his face to mine and take the kiss deep from the instant our lips touch. The hand on my ass moves to my hip and lifts my leg to drape over his hip as he grinds into me.

The sound he makes deep in his throat rumbles against my chest.

I pull back, panting, and remind myself where we are. I put my hand on his chest and lean my top half back from him, leg still curled around him. As I lower my leg, he plants tiny kisses on my lips, cheek, ear. His breath is warm and tickles my ear.

"You get the towels. I'll grab four waters from the fridge," he says low and sexy, like it's dirty talk.

I smirk and turn to climb the stairs. His exaggerated sigh tells me he's watching me walk away. The smirk turns to a grin that hurts my cheeks. "Julie?" I pivot on the stairs.

"Yeah?" His hands brace on the deck rails as he looks up, squinting.

"Thanks for being such a great boyfriend."

His dimples dent his cheeks with a smile that creases the corners of his eyes.

"I mean it," I continue. "Even when women clearly want you, you're just . . ."

"Just?" He's playing coy and cocky, but he sobers and says, "There is no one else for me, Ever. Just you."

My stomach somersaults and my cheeks ache with the force of my smile. "Me too." I turn and jog up the stairs to get the towels.

Chapter 12

JULIAN

Thank God today is a slow day at Fit. Callie insists that having the gym open to patrons and conducting business as usual is perfect for content, but once Sylvie saw what was happening, she inserted herself into everything. And rallied her posse to join in too. On one hand, I could be grateful to Sylvie for the viral videos in the first place, but everything from this point on would not be about her, and I'm not sure she gets that.

Callie and Austin handle it expertly though and prove why Ashley trusts them to travel all the way to Blue Lake just the two of them and capture the footage they need for the McKay Method launch. They're masters at redirecting Sylvie's . . . energy. Not only that, but they also make her feel important. I'm impressed by the professionalism and even more confident about Ashley's vision for my future. But by the end of the day, I'm also exhausted. That was a lot of female energy inside Fit all day long. But Callie and Auz are confident they got plenty of footage and will be headed back to Malibu first thing tomorrow morning.

Ever had online classes today, so she stayed home where it would be quiet. She said to call if we needed her and she'd pop over. But they opted for live classes content today, which Sylvie happily orchestrated. I missed my Ever girl though. We're such a team now and work together like a well-oiled machine. And with the long day today, it feels like forever since I've seen her. I've enjoyed the last couple days making content for our new business—okay, enjoyed is a strong word. I don't mind it because I'm excited for what it will mean if it blows up the way Ashley thinks it will. If we do it right, I'll never have to worry about finances again. I don't even know what that's like. I've never known. But seeing how Luke Ashley lives gave me a glimpse. I want that for me and my life with Ever. I'm starting to feel like someone she deserves. As exhausted as I feel, I want to celebrate. I pull out my phone to text her.

Me: Hey. Wanna do pizza for dinner tonight?

Ever: Totally. Want me to order?

Me: Yes please

Ever: I got you. Eta?

Me: 15-20

Ever: On it

I send a kiss emoji in response, which she hearts. I'm not sure I recognize myself anymore, and I'm perfectly okay with that. I envision things with this girl that never entered my radar before. Things like a family—a real family, with love, loyalty and kindness. A nice house. With nice things. And nice vacations.

"Hey, bro. You ready?" Auz drops his hand on my shoulder, snapping me out of my reverie. "We're all packed up."

"Yeah. Yeah. I'm all set. Hungry? How's pizza sound for dinner?" I clap my hand on his shoulder as we head for the door. I see Callie already at the Jeep through the glass entrance.

"Hell, yeah. I'm starved."

***

I can't wait to get through dinner and shut my brain off for the night. Today drained me, but in the best way. Everyone seems to be on the same page. As soon as we finish our pizza, we all retreat to our rooms to shower and relax. Alone in our room with Ever, the weight of the day slips off me like a loaded-down backpack.

"You look exhausted. What about a salt bath?" Ever steps behind me and wraps her arms around me, hands splayed on my chest. She places a soft, wet kiss on my shoulder as she meets my gaze in the dresser mirror.

"Will you be joining me in that bath?" I place my hands over hers, lacing our fingers, and wrap them around me tightly. It's late and I'm sure she's as tired as I am.

She ducks under my arm, spinning around to face me. "I think that might defeat the purpose of the relaxing bath."

"Oh, I disagree. I think it sounds like the exact thing that would relax me the most."

"Well, we aim to please." She plants a sweet kiss on my lips and turns toward the bathroom.

"We? Is there someone I should know about?" I call out as she disappears into the adjoined bath.

"Funny." I hear her muffled reply along with the rush of the tub faucet.

I strip off my clothes and wander into the bathroom as she's sprinkling sea salts into the water. When she stands, I reach for her waist, rushing my hands under her top and up her ribcage, lifting it up and over her head. I peel the thin strap of her bra off her shoulder and place a kiss where the strap used to be. I slide my hand around her and fill it with the breast that spills from the cup, dragging the other strap down and filling that hand too. My thumb and finger tease each nipple, causing them to harden.

She arches and tips her head back on my shoulder, tilting her face toward mine. Her lips are slightly ajar, her eyes closed.

I pull a little, prompting a half sigh, half moan from her. The exhale that hits my face is sweet and warm, like her. "Turn off the water." I drag my hands from her breasts to her back and nudge her shoulder blades toward the faucet.

She opens her eyes, a little dazed. "No bath?"

"Uh-uh. I've got a better idea."

She nods and reaches for the knob, shutting the flow off as if in a trance. She turns to me and reaches her arms around my neck.

I scoop her up, and her long legs curl around me as I walk the ten steps back to the bedroom. At the edge of the bed, I set her on her feet and slip my hands into the waistband of her athletic shorts and drag them easily down her body.

We face each other, naked now. I tuck a lock of hair behind her ear and curl my fingers behind her neck, pulling her lips to mine. She kisses me so sweetly and urgently. God, she's so perfectly mine—ready and eager. I rarely see glimpses of my shy girl anymore. She's bolder now, comfortable, and I'm here for it. I let her set the pace and follow her lead, utterly hypnotized. And she does, perfectly.

Rolling onto my side afterwards, I take her with me. We're lying sideways on the bed, so there are no pillows. I cradle her head and mine on my arm and place a kiss on her temple. I taste the salt of what I imagine are tears, though she's not crying now that I can tell. It doesn't happen as often as it used to. I like to believe it's because she's healing—that we both are. I know I feel more whole with her. I hope—think she feels the same with me. I lean my head back to look at her.

She swipes her cheek against my skin before she looks up at me.

More tears? "Hi, pretty girl." My eyes bounce back and forth between hers, assessing her state of mind.

"Hi, pretty boy."

I squeeze her in response, relieved. "You think I'm pretty?" I tease back.

"The prettiest." She tucks her head again, rubbing her hand in lazy circles on my stomach.

I chuckle and kiss her forehead. "Sleepy?"

She shrugs in answer. "Are you?" She sits up as she asks.

I sit up with her and scoot toward the headboard, leaning against it. I reach for her hand and pull her to me.

She curls into my side, draping her leg over mine, and resumes her lazy circles on my stomach. Her finger finds the trail of dark hair below my navel, and her nail traces it up and down.

"I think if you keep doing that, it won't matter in a few minutes if I am or not."

She looks up at me under her lashes as her hand dips below my junk and lightly grazes back up to my navel. On her way back down, she stops to draw circles around the head of my dick, which twitches in response.

My girl is keyed up like I've not seen yet, and I'm here for it. I roll her onto her back and can't wait to give her what she wants. And I do until she's breathless and quivering and crying my name.

Once the shudders subside, she drapes against me, spent. I'm not sure if anything has ever felt better. I thank God and the universe for the gift of this vision in my arms, in my life, as I cradle her and scoot us both under the covers. I don't elaborate in my prayer of thanks, afraid to draw too much attention in case the powers that be realize they made a mistake and take it away. As if in answer, she places a sweet kiss on my chest.

Rubbing my thumb up and down her shoulder, I whisper, "Hi, sweet girl."

"Hi, sweet Julie." Her words are thick and breathy. "Your turn?"

I can't help the smile that etches my face. Even spent, this gift, my gift, is thinking about me. "Shh, let's go to sleep. Wanna go to sleep?" Nothing compares to knowing my girl is sated and happy—that I made her feel that way. I love her so much it hurts. I only want her to be happy, and please God let that happy be with me. I think it is. I believe it is.

"M'kay." Her breathing is deep and rhythmic within minutes. I stroke her back to the rhythm. Just when I think she's asleep, she murmurs, "Julie?"

"Yeah, Ever."

"Thank you for being the perfect boyfriend."

I stamp down the rush of panic the label puts in my chest, inhaling and exhaling slowly and deeply, once, twice, a third time until my nervous system settles. *I can be perfect for her. I am perfect for her. Just like she is for me.* My arm grows heavy tracing the line of her back. The rise and fall of her body against mine lulls me soon after.

Chapter 13

Everly

I slept like the dead, and I now understand that expression. If I've ever had a better night's sleep in my life, I can't recall. With Julian's body still spooned around mine, I hesitate to move. I want to get out of bed and brush my teeth before he wakes up, then sneak back into bed and finish what we started last night. I feel bad for falling asleep on him, but I'd also never had an orgasm like the one I had last night. Granted, I only have my experience with Julian to base it on, but I might've left this plane of existence momentarily—like an out-of-body experience. *Does everyone have sex like us? God, I hope so.* If I were a cat, I'd purr.

As soon as I start to shift, he tightens his grip. In seconds I know he's no longer asleep. He nuzzles my neck and places a kiss behind my ear.

"I'm just going to brush my teeth. Wanna come?" Realizing my choice of words, I amend, "Want to join me?"

His endearing little chuckle hits my ears before he says, "I'll take option A. And I have an idea how to avoid morning breath."

As ideas go, it might be my new favorite. The most intense for sure.

Afterwards, we slide right back into our spoon position, spent, his arms snug around me, both catching our breaths. I want to overthink how much we do *it*, but I squash the train. I'm too busy catching my breath and marveling at how fucking delicious it all feels. *Surely there is no such thing as too much sex. Right?* I make a mental note to ask Lilly her opinion next time we talk. For a couple of minutes neither of us speaks or moves, except to regulate our breathing. I'm drawing lazy circles on his forearm with my fingernail when my phone dings with Via's ringtone.

"Shit." I snag my phone off the charger. "Hey, Via. I'll call you right back. Okay, two minutes." I feel his kiss on my shoulder before he pulls his arms back from my midsection as I disconnect the call and set the phone down on the edge of the nightstand.

"Your sister, the cockblocker." His deep voice rumbles against my back before his lips return to my skin.

"Her timing is improving. Don't you think?"

"If we're grading on a curve, sure. But I wasn't quite ready to let you go." To prove his point, he nuzzles his cheek across my shoulder. His spiky facial hair raises goosebumps on my arms.

Sitting up, I turn and brush a lock of hair off his forehead and get lost in his penetrating blue eyes. "Hi, boyfriend."

"Hi, lover." His eyes are half-mast and a little sleepy, his voice deeper with the morning hour.

My stomach flips on the new endearment. God, I love this man. And I want to kiss him so badly. "I'm brushing my teeth, then coming back to kiss you."

"Before or after you call Via?"

"Via can wait."

"In that case, I'll brush mine too." He swats my ass as I roll off the bed and stretch on my way to the bathroom.

***

Walking down the stairs ten minutes later, I pull the phone away from my ear as Via squeals.

"He proposed," she screeches.

"Wait. What? You're already engaged. I was there. We had a party."

"No. I know. But he wanted to give me—I'm getting ahead of myself."

I snicker. "Okay. Start from the beginning. Tell me everything."

"He took me to Half Moon Bay. Just a quick overnighter. But after dinner, we went for a walk on Maverick Beach. It was low tide, so we made it all the way to the end where the big rock wall is. He pointed to the sunset, and when I turned to look, he said, 'It's beautiful, isn't it?' And when I turned back to answer him, he was kneeling in the sand with a ring. *The* ring. His grandma's ring. He'd been waiting for her to get back from her trip to get it."

"Oh my God. Did you cry?"

"Duh. Thank God for waterproof mascara." We both giggle. Via sobers and adds, "We want to get married right away. I mean, we already live together. And . . . we wanna do it at Blue Lake. Like at Brew. On the beach. Would you . . . could we . . . Would it be impossible to pull off?"

"Noooo." *Yes.* "Definitely not impossible. Let me talk to Julian. I think we can make it happen." And I realize how badly I want to make it happen for her. The idea of pulling it off with Julian excites me. Working together, planning the event as a team, doing something for someone who's part of my life—my old life. And maybe that's why. Some part of me wants to show off my life and my relationship to the haters in Oak Valley. Guess I'm not as evolved as I like to think. I want Julian to agree to this more than I've wanted anything in a long time—except him. I always want him more than anything else.

***

"They're getting married." I set the phone face down on the bar and reach for my coffee.

Julian leans against the counter across from me and sips from his mug, eyeing me over the rim. "Well, they're engaged, so that's a reasonable next step," he responds, lowering his mug.

"It's just so fast. I mean, I guess they're already living together, so what's the difference?"

Julian's eyebrow arches at my logic.

"For them," I add.

He lowers it and smirks.

"They wanna do it here. At the beach on Blue Lake. Before the weather gets too cold."

"So . . . right away . . ." Julian's eyes look beyond the kitchen, and I can see the wheels turning before he says another word. "This could be fun."

"Really?" My eyebrows lift as I wait for him to elaborate. Sipping my coffee, I watch him begin to nod, his gaze unfocused like he's deep in thought.

"Yeah. Pete and Shelley could help. It could be sweet."

"Ah, what a little romantic you are." I hide my smile behind another sip of caffeine.

Julian rolls his eyes and drains his cup. "I got your romance. Want me to show you upstairs in the—" Julian cuts off what he was about to say, clearing his throat, as Auz walks into the kitchen scratching his chest and yawning. He's dressed and looking ready to go except for the sleepy stretch. "Hey. Morning. Want some coffee?" Julian turns to grab a mug out of the cabinet behind his head on Auz's nod.

"Hey, Auz," I call as Callie appears right behind him. "Morning, Callie. How'd you guys sleep?" I ask and feel the blush hit my face, wondering if we'd made too much noise last night or this morning.

"Good." Callie smiles her answer. "It's so quiet here."

I catch Julian's glance, and his half smile is gone before anyone else notices except me. It makes my tummy flip. I clear my throat. "Good, great. Yeah, it, uh, took me a minute to get used to the quiet at first. Almost too quiet." I smile in agreement. "So, what time do you guys head out?"

"Ashley's car service will be here in about thirty. We got some great footage. He'll be pleased." Callie takes the cup full of coffee Auz hands her and smiles sweetly at him.

"Yeah, we stayed up late going over it all last night. Good stuff," Auz adds, smiling back at Callie.

I watch them for a couple seconds like a tennis match and realize I never had anything to worry about with Callie. She and Auz clearly have something between them—whether they're ready to admit it or not. "Awesome. Love to hear it. I'm gonna grab a quick shower before you guys head out. If you need anything . . ."

"I got you," Julian finishes for me, nodding at them, walks over and places a sweet kiss on my temple. His hand slides down my back to rest on my ass like it belongs there, sending a rush of heat to my lower region.

I so love this man. My body does too. I step away and move to the stairs before I abandon my manners and shamelessly drag him with me. *Maybe we do have too much sex.* I quickly shake my head at the thought. *Nope. That's not a thing. It can't be. It's too . . . Calm your tits, Everly.* I climb the stairs with a ridiculous grin on my face.

***

"**Y**ou're really okay with this? A last-minute wedding? At Brew Beach?" I'm packing lunch and snacks for our day at Fit, addressing him across the kitchen.

"Yeah. I even texted Pete already. And yeah, we've gotta work out the logistics, but it sounds like Via wants something simple, intimate. I think it could be special."

"You know Chase will be the best man. Which means Kendall will come too."

"I thought about that. If you're okay with it, I'm okay with it," he says. "I mean, they played nice at the engagement party, right?" He's watching me closely as he asks.

I shrug my shoulders in agreement. I am excited for Via. Blue Lake is an incredible backdrop for a sweet little ceremony. I can already see it: clear string lights, lanterns, maybe even a fire in the pit, and if Mother Nature cooperates, a majestic sunset like only Blue Lake can deliver. Without Oak Valley and its bullshit not currently here in my face, I have all the confidence in the world. Julian's excitement only adds to my bravery.

We decide to FaceTime them at Brew later and set some basic plans in motion—include Pete and Shelley so we're all on the same page. I'm weirdly hyped to plan this for Via. It feels a little like coming home. I'm not even nervous to see Chase and Kendall. My life feels good, safe. I'm happy, confident and love where I'm at.

Julian steps into my line of vision, interrupting my seven-mile stare and my thoughts.

I focus in on him and smile.

"Hi, pretty girl."

"Hi, boyfriend."

"What's going on in there?" He ducks his head down and to the side, his intense blue eyes blinking at me through a frame of thick dark lashes.

"I'm just . . . I don't know . . . so happy. I'm excited to do this for Via. And maybe a little more than excited to show off my new life." I smile with the heat taking over my face, embarrassed to admit it.

"I'm happy I'm part of the life you want to show off." He taps my nose and uses that finger to drape a lock of hair behind my ear, making tears prick my eyes.

I lower them so he won't see, but he knows me too well now.

I can tell he wants to ask me about it but doesn't want to push me. Instead, he jumps on my tucking-it-away bandwagon, which makes me love him more. He meets me where I'm at. Always.

"C'mon, sweet girl. Let's go start another day in the life we love, huh?" He pulls me to him with both hands on my ass for a quick kiss and grabs my hand as he pulls me toward the door, snagging the lunch bag I packed off the counter as he does.

Chapter 14

JULIAN

Will she ever get to a point where she doesn't tuck away her thoughts from me? The anxiety, the pain? I want to push, make her talk to me, but I don't. She does talk to me, open up to me, more and more, tucks it away less and less, but I also know what it's like to want to forget the shit that fucks with my head. So I never push. And while I want to give this girl everything she could ever want—even a last-minute wedding for her sister that may involve the douchebag that started all the shit back in her hometown—I also want to protect her from anything that might make her break down like that day on the floor of the Brew office.

Seeing her shutdown undid me like only one other thing has in my life. That I didn't beat the shit out of that fuck is a testament to the work I've done to control my temper. How he is the best friend of Via's fiancé I don't get. She and Ryan are the epitome of chill. That their two best friends are drama whores doesn't track. Still, if putting up with them means my girl gets to do a nice thing for her sister, I'm in. With a smile on my face. The event will be on our turf. They don't have any power here, imagined or real, and I'd be a liar if I said I didn't relish the idea of showing off the life we've made here together to the assholes who tried to break her. My sweet, exquisite Ever, who doesn't even realize how fucking brave and strong and incredible she is.

We FaceTime Via and Ryan when we arrive at Brew. It's late in the day, almost sunset. Pete and Shelley join us.

"We can totally pull this off," I say confidently to the screen, Pete, Shelley and Ever all adding noises of agreement. The happy couple want to do it in the beginning of October—less than a month away—but because it's going to be small and intimate, all involved parties agree it's doable.

"Oh my God, Julian. Thank you so much for being willing. All of you. We don't need much. I promise." Via is trying not to cry as she says it, but Ryan chimes in, pushing his face into the frame.

"Well, I'm high maintenance. I want a bunch of special shit to make me happy." He succeeds in making her laugh, though a few tears spill down her cheeks as she does.

They really are super chill. They want a simple, natural event that celebrates not only who they are, but the area they are celebrating at. With a headcount of twenty at the most, we'd be able to make it perfect.

"Of course, Ryan, we'll get you hair and makeup for the big day," Ever teases him. "Seriously, Via, it's going to be perfect. We've got this. I even predict an epic sunset to end the day."

Ever's excitement is contagious. I want it to be perfect for them and her.

***

For the next three weeks, every waking moment is spent working at Fit and planning the wedding. By the time the day comes around, I admit, I'm glad it will soon be over.

"Allie and Ashley are flying in super early tomorrow before the ceremony. A one-day trip is all they can manage." I hand Ever the last strand of string lights and hold the ladder steady as she drapes them over the hook in one of the freestanding planters we placed around the garden area. "Ashley has been on my ass to get back to SoCal for more content and business-related things. I keep putting him off because of the wedding."

"Well, I'm glad they're coming since my mom can't. Maybe we can go back right after the wedding for a couple days," she offers. She steps off the ladder and studies my face. Her brows pull down, making an eleven between them.

I smile, but she's not easily fooled. To Ever, I play it off as wedding prep and work stress, but inside, if I'm being honest with myself, I'm spiraling a little about the asshole friends coming here and possibly upsetting her. I'm sure there's some projection psychology in there my therapist would have a field day with—protectiveness, blah, blah, blah. I do want to protect her with everything in me.

She reaches up and wraps her fingers around the tufts of hair forever falling onto my forehead and pulls my face to hers. Her nails scrape deliciously over the top of my head and curl around my neck while her lips kiss mine so light and sweet.

Logically I know the shit with that group of so-called friends isn't life or death. I know there is no danger, but my nervous system doesn't see the difference. I've grown so attuned to my girl that I know it has her keyed up too. We both pretend her kiss distracts us from what we're not saying. This irrational part of my brain wants to save her from every bad thing or die trying. And that's the core of the issue. That I possibly could've done more three and a half years ago to save a young girl I loved from an irreversible fate. *Fuck, I really am projecting.* It's the unconscious lens I see everything through. *Will that ever go away?* I remind myself for the millionth time that Ever isn't Taya and this isn't life or death. It's a wedding. A celebration. A few hours out of our lives celebrating her sister and soon-to-be brother-in-law.

"Let's get through the wedding and see." My eyes bounce back and forth between hers before I touch my lips to hers again. Catching the sinking sun over our beloved Blue Lake behind her, I make myself take some deep breaths. I tell myself that everything is fine. Good. Great, even. Smiling at her, I turn and survey all we've done to transform the marina into a fairy tale.

"It's perfect," she utters. The twinkle lights everywhere, the arbor, the mason jar candles. Even the new white Adirondacks around the fire pit. Simple, yes. But enchanting. Her arms sneak around me from behind and sneak under my folded arms across my chest.

I lift one and start to turn, but she ducks under my arm and snuggles into my side, looking up from under my chin. The playful, almost childlike grin flips my stomach in the best way.

"We did it." Her flushed cheeks and breathless words trip my heartbeat. She swivels around me until we're face-to-face, locking her arms around my hips. She rocks side to side and stares up at me.

I meet her gaze for a few moments and then turn us back to the sunset show. "It's another good one tonight." I toss my head toward the ombré sky.

"Mm," she agrees, but she's tracking what I'm not saying. "To borrow your line, what's going on in there?"

"Just reflecting. Making sure we've got it all ready for the big day."

"It'll be perfect."

"You already said that," I tease, quoting her. I'm rewarded with the sweet lilt of her laugh.

"They're refreshingly easygoing and it's exactly what they want. Small, simple, intimate," she elaborates.

"In that case, I think it will be perfect."

She accepts my words without pressing further, even though I'm sure she knows there's more.

My low-maintenance girl. I sigh, squeezing her. I'm so lucky.

***

Olivia and Ryan paint a perfect picture kissing in the frame of the arbor Pete and I built for their big day. It felt good to work with my hands like that again. Pete and I even discussed using it for small venue weddings in the future while we built it. Blue Lake's sunset tonight glows around the happy couple and takes my mind to places I never dreamed of—me standing just like that with a gray-eyed, chestnut-haired girl, looking at me like I am the key to her happiness. I catch her eye as the small crowd claps. Hers brim with unshed tears and as her lips curve, one glistening stream runs down the apple of her cheek. Pressure builds behind my own eyes. I clear my throat and stand with the other guests and begin moving chairs to the tables we set up in the courtyard.

Once everyone takes their seats, Ever steps up to the bride and groom table and taps a butter knife to her champagne flute. As the hush falls, Ever begins to speak, her voice shaky with unshed tears. "Via, Ryan, you know Mom wanted to be here. Since she couldn't, she sent you these." She hands an envelope to Via who whips it open and produces two plane tickets. "She's in Hawaii now and wants you to join her before she leaves to the next destination." Via holds the two tickets above her head, dangling them for the guests to see, and it's met with appropriate *oohs* and *ahhs* and applause.

Allie and Ashley couldn't attend at the last minute due to a fire at one of his locations. They also sent an invitation to bring the newlyweds to Malibu for a weekend of their choice. The pressure is back behind my eyes as Everly hugs her sister, then Ryan, and tells the group to raise their glasses. These sisters amaze me with their ability to roll with life and take it as it comes, happiness dripping off them. Chase stands as Everly returns to her seat next to me. I drop my arm across her shoulders and press. It dries up the misty affection behind my eyes and replaces it with a swirling heat in my belly.

Dropping my lips to her ear, I whisper, "I'm just going to check with Pete, see if he needs anything." I ignore the question in her eyes and smile, taping a light kiss on her lips. "I'll be right back." She nods with a soft smile and turns her gaze back to the happy couple and Chase's speech. The guy is being nice enough, polite, helpful. Everyone is on their best behavior. I tell myself that stepping away in the middle of his speech *is* the polite thing to do. Glaring daggers at him while he talks is unnecessary, but something I'm not sure I can avoid. It takes every coping trick I know to keep the feral tendencies caged at the thought of someone hurting my girl. I can't think too much about where those tendencies come from. When I do, I don't feel worthy of someone like her—or anything good.

Chapter 15

EVERLY

Tears prick my eyes watching my sister kiss her husband. The day went perfectly. The sun is just starting to dip into the lake, and it couldn't be a more spectacular end to the day if we special-ordered it. I take another longing look at them as they sway to music on the makeshift dance floor we constructed. And by we, I mean Julian.

Via pulls me aside before the last song and hugs me so tight. "Thank you, sister. Everything was perfect." She wipes a lone tear from her cheek.

"It was all Julian." I give him all the credit because he really did the heavy lifting—literally and figuratively. My heart swells just thinking about it.

Ryan sneaks his arms around her and nuzzles into her neck. "Can I have the last dance, wife?"

"You can have them all." Olivia beams at me, fresh tears sparkling in her eyes. She squeezes my hand she was holding and lets Ryan lead her back to the makeshift dance floor.

Turning, I walk quietly to the beach and slip off my sandals when I hit the sand. Yes, the events of the day went perfectly, but the day itself was kind of weird.

Chase was on his best behavior. Not only that, he also showed up sans Kendall. Via didn't bring them up at all, so I didn't ask. It was her day, hers and Ryan's, and we could all get along for their sake. But for some reason, Kendall isn't here. And Chase is oddly quiet—like he's trying to blend into the background. He and Julian didn't speak unless necessary, but when they did, Chase was all humble respect. Like when we moved the ceremony chairs to the tables.

"Hey, Julian, let me get those for you." Without being asked, he took it upon himself to move all the chairs while Julian helped Pete bring the food out.

"Great. Thanks, Chase. Ev, would you help me?" Even Julian is a little weird today. Strangely quiet and distant but keeping me close. He's all smiles and forehead kisses like nothing is wrong. He's the epitome of smitten boyfriend as far as anyone is concerned. And he's getting all the accolades for setting up the perfect day on such a crunched timeline. As he should. I can tell he's acting a little off—keyed up and hovering.

I just need a couple minutes alone to ponder all the weirdness. I may have smiled, laughed and happy cried my way through the day, but my nervous system isn't so easily indulged. By the end of the day, I just need to take a breath. It's all so fucking weird. Did I already say that? Blue sunsets never disappoint or fail to settle me though. Tonight's is using all the colors. It's so painfully beautiful, it brings tears to my eyes. I draw in a deep breath, but the exhale comes out shaky.

"Everly?"

His voice drops my stomach. I irritatingly flinch, and the hairs on my arms stand up despite the warm evening air.

Chase places a hand softly on my shoulder and immediately apologizes for startling me. "Oh, I'm sorry. I didn't mean to scare you."

"You didn't." I say it too quickly, too forcefully. I try again. "I just didn't hear you. Thought I was alone."

"Sorry. I can go." Apology Chase is weird too. He half turns to go before I stop him.

"No, it's fine. Did you need something?" Uber Polite Me is weirder, especially when it comes to Chase. I tilt my head toward him and meet his eyes, almost opaque in the sunlight.

"Yeah, I wanted to talk to . . . to apologize. To you." Yeah, super weird. But also humble and looking much younger in his sincerity.

"Okay." I drag out the last syllable, then take a deep silent breath and wait.

"Kendall and I broke up." At my raised eyebrows, he rushes on. "That's not what I came down here to say."

I nod as if to say I'm listening.

"I'm . . . Can we sit down? And talk?" He motions to a couple nearby beach loungers with an umbrella between.

I nod again, trying to calm my racing thoughts and heartbeat.

"Thank you." Again, the sincerity.

After we sit, I face him squarely and snap, "Look, Chase, just spit it out, okay? Whatever it is, just say it."

It's his turn to nod. He takes a deep inhale and blows it out through pursed lips, then runs his fingers through the hair flopping onto his forehead, pushing it back to no avail. It flops right back over his forehead and most of his right eyebrow. "I'm sorry I didn't speak up and tell everyone it was bullshit. That you didn't come onto me." He fidgets with his hands, looking down at them.

When I don't respond, he stops and looks up into my eyes, squinting a little in the waning sun.

Something in his eyes calls to that place in me—that heartbroken place that knows the pain and doesn't want anyone else to ever feel it. But the hell I went through fights with my soft, forgiving side. It's trying to win. "Yeah, why didn't you?" I don't trust myself to say more.

His cheeks puff with an exaggerated exhale. He looks back down at his hands. One reaches up to rub back and forth across his forehead. "The short answer is I'm a pussy."

I smirk at his frank honesty, the begrudging side of me losing ground.

"The longer answer is that Kendall and her family have a way of convincing you they own you. Right after we started dating in high school, it's like the rest of my life had already been planned out for me." He begins fidgeting with his hands again, head bent low.

"So, what changed?" I'm genuinely curious. I'm not quite ready to forgive and forget but hearing that Kendall may have treated him like shit too sways me further.

"Via didn't tell you?" That sideways, squinted look again.

I shake my head, meeting his gaze directly, waiting for him to continue. But my breath is a little shallower, my heart rate a little faster. My fingers curl around the edges of my seat as my lips press tightly together.

"It's an even longer story that I don't have to bore you with, but the short version is that Kendall faked her suicide attempt." He stops fidgeting to stare at the palms of his hands, then begins rubbing them together.

It was all a lie. I let his words sink in. The surge of outrage seizes my chest within seconds. *It was all a lie.* I scoot to the edge of my chair, still gripping the sides, and hang my head. I try to take deep breaths. I can't get enough air into my lungs. I claw at my chest.

Chase flies off his chair and kneels in front of me. "I'm sorry, Evvie. Fuck, I'm so sorry. I didn't know. I swear." He doesn't touch me, but his hands brace on either side of my chair, locking me in.

It only adds to the panic rising in my throat. "I can't . . ." The more I try to catch my breath, the more out of breath I feel. My hand clutches my chest. The darkness creeps in at the edges of my vision. My fingers and toes begin to tingle. Chase suddenly disappears from before me. He flies back onto the sand about five feet in front of me, landing on his back with another figure landing on top of him.

Julian!

My vision clears.

Julian clenches Chase's shirt in his fists, lifting the top half of his body off the beach while he straddles the lower half.

What the fuck?

"What the fuck? You've got about two seconds to explain yourself before I make you really fucking sorry you ever set foot on this beach." Julian jerks Chase's face to within an inch of his as he hisses his threat through clenched teeth.

The good news is it rips me out of the throes of my panic attack. The bad news is Chase is seconds away from Julian beating the shit out of him. And I have no doubt he will.

"Julian," I screech and lunge at his back. Hooking my hands onto his biceps, I pull back with all my strength. It doesn't budge or faze him in the least.

Chase's hands are raised on each side of his head in surrender.

"Julian," I plead his name, still pulling uselessly at his arms. "Julie," I whisper-cry into his ear.

The tension in his muscles eases a little under my curled fingers.

"I wasn't going to hurt her, man, I swear." Chase lowers his hands to the sand, trying to gain some leverage to right himself.

"You shut the fuck up." Julian shakes Chase by the shirt as he says it before shoving him back onto the sand and releasing him. "What the fuck, Ever?" He turns his blue eyes on me, although almost none of the blue shows around the dark, angry pupils taking over. He lifts his body off Chase, kicking sand as he stalks to the water's edge. He stands in the darkening glow of the sunset with his hands locked on top of his head. Frustration oozes off him like lava.

"Chase?" I swivel my head from Julian's silhouette and say over my shoulder. "We're not done, but I . . . I need a minute."

He nods and pushes himself up off the shore, dusting off sand as he stands. "Sure. I'm just gonna . . . go find Ryan. Come find me when you're done . . . if you want."

I nod and turn toward Julian, who's now standing with his hands in his pockets still facing the sun, which is now just a thin orange line on the horizon. Over my shoulder, I add, "I want to hear it. That's what I want. I'll be up in a minute." With that, I take the few steps to Julian. I want to put my arms around him, but I don't. Despite the calm façade, I see the rigid line of his jaw, the crease between his brows. I stand next to him, watching the fading orange line.

He doesn't look at me when he says, "What the hell just happened? What'd he do?"

"Nothing," I answer back quickly. Too quickly.

"So what? You forgive this guy now? You're what? Friends again? Because it didn't look friendly. You looked like you were about to black out."

"I don't know. We didn't get that far before you decided to throw him across the beach."

"Oh, my bad. You're looking all kinds of distressed while this guy ambushes you alone on a beach. Didn't realize intervening made me the asshole."

My nostrils flare with my deep exhale.

He looks sideways at me. "What do you want from me, Ever? I'm supposed to stand by and watch you have a panic attack? Watch some douche from your past corner you?"

"No. I didn't say that." I clasp his bicep. The right corner of my mouth lifts in a half smile. "Actually, you throwing him across the beach stopped the attack, so . . . thank you?"

He reaches for me and pulls me into a bear hug. "Fuck, you scared me."

I stay still in his arms, mirroring the rise and fall of his chest and feel his body settling. The calm washes over me like a baptism. It starts where his jaw rests on my temple, travels down my neck, shoulders, spine and settles in my chest. The butterflies in my stomach land. It rolls down my legs into my heels and toes. I want to stay in the cocoon of his arms forever—where nothing can touch me, and if it tried, he wouldn't let it. But I want to hear what Chase has to say. I want to know about the lies that derailed my life and changed its trajectory forever.

"He, uh . . . wasn't cornering me. He was apologizing." Without letting him go, I arch my neck back to look up at him.

"Hmph," is the only response I get.

I lower my head again and stay still in his arms. I count his heartbeats that I feel in my own chest. This man is the sun and I'm in his gravitational pull. My hands creep into his shirt to touch the muscled skin of his back, and his heat seeps into my fingertips. If I could bottle and sell the sanctity I feel in this space, there'd be no need for therapy. Feeling blue? Have a dose of this. Down, depressed, angry, sad? We got you. Take two of these and you won't need to call us in the morning. God, I fucking love this man. I stopped counting heartbeats, but I haven't stopped curling my nails into the taut skin of his back, softly clenching and unclenching to the beat. My human stress ball. Then I hear and feel the baritone of his voice against the side of my face.

"Go get your apology, closure, whatever you need. I'm not leaving though." He pauses. "Do you want me to leave? Wait at home?" His questions drip with incredulity.

Calling it home flips my heart. I shake my head before the words come out. "No, no. Wait here if you want. But I'm not scared. I just . . . It's just a lot to go back there in my mind. But I already told you, I wouldn't take it back, because it gave me you. Us."

He squeezes me tighter and kisses my temple. Once. Twice. The third time he just rests his lips there before he lets me go. Taking a step back, his fingers wander down my arms and twine with mine. He swings them back and forth, knocking our hands together. "See you soon?" He says it like a question.

I nod in answer. "Wait. The wedding party?"

"Everyone, especially the bride and groom, were ready to leave. Pete and Shelley finished the clean-up details. I helped."

"Okay. It really was a perfect day for them. Right? They were happy?"

He nods in agreement.

I mirror his nod.

"I'll come to the apartment as soon as I'm done."

He nods again, pinning me with his stare, his lips curled inward in a thin line.

I know he's not happy letting me go alone, but I want to know. I need to know. Chase isn't going to go there with Julian breathing down his neck.

***

A shiver rolls over my body, and I hug my knees to my chest. I'm still in the clothes I wore for the wedding, and the warmth of the sun is long gone. Chase is sitting with his elbows resting on his thighs, looking down at his hands. Seeing me shiver in his periphery, he turns to offer me . . . comfort? Warmth? I'm not sure even he knows.

"Are you cold? Can I . . ." He reaches his arms out, then abruptly drops them. "I can go find a blanket . . . or a towel? I didn't bring a jacket." He holds his hands out, palms up in apology.

"Chase? It's fine. I'm fine. Just tell me the rest, please. Get it over with." I rest my cheek on my curled knees, face turned to him, in feigned calmness that doesn't reach my bones or match my words. I dig my fingers into the flesh of my calves, willing myself to wait for him to speak—say the part I'd been dreading.

He already told me his cousin, the unit secretary of the emergency department at Oak Valley General, saw the files. "No evidence of ingesting substances in a deliberate attempt to self-harm." The files also noted that there was no clear indication of recent vomiting, though they couldn't determine it conclusively.

"Nothing added up. She never went to one class or therapy session. She acted like her old self as soon as they released her from the hospital. Unless we were around other people. Then it was the victim show. I didn't want to believe it, but I think I always knew."

As Chase speaks, I nod, not looking at him. Just stare down at my hands.

Who would do that? Who does that? It was all a lie. She ruined my life, and it was all a lie. *But she didn't ruin it.* I don't want to ask because I'm not sure I want to know, or if he'll even be honest with me, but no one made him tell me as much as he already had, so maybe . . . And if we're going there, might as well go all the way. Rip the whole bandage off. "What happened that night? Between us?" I say it while looking at my hands, then turn my bent head sideways to look up—to face him.

He doesn't look at me. Instead, he rubs his hands over his face. He starts shaking his head slowly, drops his hands and looks sideways right into my eyes. "I don't . . . I don't really know. I was pretty drunk." He holds up his hands in surrender, like he expects me to argue.

I don't say a word. I'm not sure I even take a breath.

"That's not an excuse. I'm just saying it's all kinda fuzzy—even now."

I nod faintly in agreement.

He continues. "I think I came in to take a piss and I heard you. I think you were asleep or passed out, but I heard you, so I walked over to you. Fuck, Evvie, I don't know. I want to believe I didn't take advantage of you. I don't think I'm that guy."

A tear slips down my cheek at his words. I don't try to stop it. I just keep staring at him, trying to bring the night back, even though it makes my heart slam in my chest and my belly churn. "I thought it was a dream. I thought I was kissing someone else, then it was you." Another tear falls. "Did we . . . Did you kiss me?"

It's his turn to nod slowly.

Another tear. This time the surge of anger lifts my hand to swipe it away.

"I thought . . . you reached for me. When I heard you, I went to check on you. I said your name. You reached for me. I thought . . . you wanted me. Fuck! I feel sick to my stomach right now."

"That makes two of us."

"Listen, I'm not here to make excuses for myself. I've felt like such a fucking creep since that night. And a pussy for not speaking up, if I'm being honest. Shit, if I'm being honest, I've been a pussy since I started dating Kendall." He lifts the side of his mouth in a self-loathing smile and shrugs one shoulder.

I can't help it; I let out a breathy giggle—more exhale than laugh. But his self-deprecating realness touches me. I don't speak because I sense he has more to say, and I find I want to hear it. All of it.

"I saw the way you looked at us. Like we were the perfect couple with the perfect life. And I knew we weren't. I knew I'd been bought and paid for. I'd marry her and work for her dad and fall in line. I'd never felt less like a man—or myself. Probably why I started drinking so much." His shoulders sag as he talks—like the words are heavy to carry, let alone speak.

Still, I keep quiet, wanting to let him get it out.

"When you reached for me, maybe I wanted to be that guy I saw in your eyes—even in my drunken state." He holds his hands up, palms out. "Again, I'm not saying it was your fault. Not even. I just hope you can believe I'm not a monster who tried to take advantage of you." He puffs his cheeks and blows out a long breath. "God, I don't even recognize the person I'm talking about. But it was me—I was that guy." He shakes his head. "I fucking hate myself."

He stops talking again, and I stuff my hands under my legs to keep from reaching out—to . . . I don't know . . . pat him on the arm in some attempt at comfort. I hate *myself* a little that I'm such a pushover—that I want to comfort *him*.

"Anyway, when I thought what we'd done—what I'd done—caused Kendall to try to . . . to attempt suicide, it was easy to get swept along in the current of all that. I didn't know how bad it was for you. Kendall never mentioned any of the bullying shit to me. I swear. Ryan did though. And when I'd try to talk to Kendall about it, she'd just have a dramatic meltdown and accuse me of horrible shit until I caved and dropped it. I became even more of that bought and paid for pussy until I could barely look myself in the mirror. When my cousin let it slip at my grandparents' anniversary party that Kendall faked it, I lost it. I broke up with her right then. I took her to my car, drove her home and told her it was over. It was ugly and dramatic, and I've never been more sure of anything in my life. Except how sorry I am, Evvie. I'm so fucking sorry for the hell you went through because of me. And her. You didn't deserve that. Any of it."

When he pauses, it's my turn to exhale through puffed cheeks.

My heart rate is slower, normal. I feel calm. I feel relieved. All the bad memories in Oak Valley are floating above my head like the bubbles we blew as little kids. They're floating and popping as they rise and disappear. "Thanks for telling me all this," I say, because I don't know what else to say.

"Thanks for letting me—for listening."

I nod again, looking at my toes over the top of my bent knees. A breeze picks up my hair and swipes it across my face. I pull a hand from under my legs and brush the locks behind my ear, then turn to look at him again, my head tilted sideways. "I don't hate you, Chase. I think I did at one point. But mostly I hated those girls and the lengths they went to to torture me. I'm glad you got away from that. It's crazy to think it was all a lie and could've been so easily avoided. But—"

"I'm so sorry I didn't speak up sooner." Chase cuts me off.

"I know. I believe you. And I accept your apology. That's what I wanted to say. Yeah, it was bullshit, and it sucked what they put me through. But I'm happy. I'm really happy now."

"I'm so happy to hear that. For real. If anyone deserves it, it's you." He offers a tentative smile.

I offer one back. The breeze picks up again and puts goosebumps across my arms and legs. "We'd better head up. I'm getting cold." I stand, slipping my feet into my sandals.

"Of course, yeah. I, uh, hope Julian is cool. Maybe I should say something . . .?"

"Don't worry about it. I'll talk to him."

He nods in response as we head up to the Brew courtyard and parking lot.

When we get there, we stand looking at each other awkwardly. After an uncomfortable few seconds, I give him a light friendly hug. As Ryan's best friend, and no longer Kendall's boyfriend, I can see this guy being in and out of my life without it being a constant reminder of shitty times. We just have to start somewhere—like with a platonic, friendly hug goodbye. "See you around, Chase. Drive safe down the hill." I use the term all the locals use for driving down into the valley and smile to myself that it rolled off my tongue so unconsciously.

"Thanks, Evvie, for . . . Thanks." He looks relieved as he says it.

I nod and wave as I turn to walk to the apartment in the dark and find Julian. Facing him sets my heart racing again; in a good or bad way, I'm not entirely sure. I've never seen him lose his shit like that before. I count my breaths as I climb the stairs.

Chapter 16

Julian

Pacing the floor in the tiny living room of my old apartment is giving caged animal vibes. Restless is an understatement. I want to hit something, and I don't have a speed bag or a hanging bag of any kind. Hitting a wall is just going to make more work for me later when I have to patch it. I left the pull-up bar attached to the bedroom door for Noah. He asked me to. I pace down the short hallway and begin doing pull-ups until sweat slicks my arms and drips down my temples and back. It's not working. I pace to the wall of windows and open the slider. I stand in the cooling air, regulating my breaths.

As they become calmer, quieter, I can hear the murmur of their voices—Ever's and Chase's. I can't make out the words, but the soft tones, I tell myself, mean the conversation is calm. I hope it's calm. I really only hear a male voice with an occasional mix of Ever's lilt that I'd be able to make out no matter how faint.

With the chilly night air drying the sweat, goosebumps take its place. I turn from the doorway but leave it open and drop to the floor, doing push-ups until my arms shake—to ward off the chill, I tell myself. Grunting through the exertion drowns any hope of hearing their murmurs. When I can't lift my body off the floor, I roll onto my back and start doing crunches. The fluff of the area rug doing nothing to cushion my spine as it rolls up and down on the floor. I welcome the pain and the sting of the sweat running into my eyes. I'm panting now, but I don't stop. Once my spine is bruised from the floor, I curl my legs and back into each other and twist from side to side, dropping my joined hands on either side as I do. The burn in my abs has me clenching my teeth and audibly panting, but I press on.

Collapsing on my back, chest heaving, I allow myself a minute to recover, my arm draped over my forehead, one leg bent. My mind won't stay blank though. The low-key panic is there in my chest. The irrational fear that I won't be able to save her has my palm rubbing the empty heart tattoo. I roll over and force my body into downward dog and allow my hands and feet to sink into the floor. I push my heels back and breathe through the stretch. The ache in my chest eases with every breath. *Allie would be proud.*

After a few other poses to stretch out my torso, I wander into the kitchen and pound a full glass of water and half of the refill. Gripping the edge of the countertop, I hang my head and will my mind to settle. I decide on a hot shower for my next coping trick. I strip off my sweaty clothes as I pad down the hall. I don't wait for the water to heat up and step into the icy spray, welcoming the tiny needles of shock. Within seconds, the frigid needles are replaced with soothing warmth. I hang my head in the steamy spray, bracing my hands on the tiled wall in front of me.

She's fine. She's safe. She'll be here soon.

The pounding water is helping. It's soothing not only my skin and body, but inhaling the steam is calming my racing thoughts.

Shutting the water off some minutes later, I slide the frosted glass door aside and reach for the towel hanging on the wall rack. My eyes freeze on the figure leaning on the door jamb. My shoulders sag, my exhale audible. "Hi, pretty girl." It comes out on a sigh. I dangle the towel low in front of me, my dripping naked body forgotten at the sight of my girl standing so casually in front of me.

"Hi, beautiful boy." The smallest dimple flashes with her half smile. Her gray eyes rake down my body and create a stir in my gut. "Just grabbing a quick workout?" She smirks as she asks.

"How'd you know?" I grin as I towel off, not bothering to cover my junk.

"You mean other than the jacked arms and chest? Maybe the chiseled abs or the veins in your neck. What the hell happened up here?" She's grinning big now, enjoying herself.

I shrug, wrapping the towel around my hips and stepping to her. "Just distracting myself, I guess. How are you?" I tuck a strand of hair behind her ear and leave my fingers there, curled lightly around the shell. Her skin feels chilled to the touch.

She nods before she utters a sound. "Good, actually. I'm glad I heard him out."

"And...?" I duck my head a bit so we're eye to eye as I rub my hands up and down her arms to warm them up.

"Should we go ahead and have this conversation in the bathroom doorway, with you in a towel? Or...?"

"Fair. I left some fresh clothes in the bedroom." I kiss her forehead as I squeeze past her and trek the seven steps to the bedroom and slide on a pair of gray sweats and a white T-shirt I stashed here after Lilly and Noah left for college. I find her leaning against the open living room sliders gazing out into the night. With almost no moon, it's pitch black—barely a glisten off the water in the distance. I place my hands on her arms, the skin chilled by the breeze pushing against her. "You're cold. There's a change of clothes in there for you too if you want. Or we can head back to Allie's—home."

She leans back into my chest, her hair tickling my neck, the smell of her shampoo swirling around me—sweet sunshine. She nods against my chest. "I'll change. Let's just stay here."

As she moves down the hall, I close the slider and pour us some champagne from a leftover open bottle. When she returns, I'm sitting on the couch with my legs crossed on the coffee table—the two glasses bubbling next to them. She raises an eyebrow when she spies them, walks around the table and sits, cozied up to me, tucking her bare feet under her legs. I reach for the flutes, hand her one and wrap my empty arm around her shoulders.

She takes a small sip with me. "Mmm, are we celebrating something?"

"How about the end of a long but beautiful day?"

"Okay." She drags the word out like she's waiting for me to elaborate.

"I'm glad we got to do that for them. I think they had fun. And . . . I'm . . . sorry I lost my shit on the beach." I take another sip, trying for casual.

"It's okay, Julie." She sets her glass down and turns her body into me, tucking her hand between my thighs.

I set my glass on the side table with my left hand, dropping it down on my thigh after.

She picks up my hand, flattens her palm against mine and laces our fingers together. "I get it. I do," she continues before I butt in. "Just like I kinda get now what happened with Chase."

"*Get* as in forgive?" I can't hide the doubt in my voice.

"Yeah, I guess. Does that surprise you? Upset you?" She's playing with our joined hands as she asks.

"Why don't you tell me how the convo went, and we'll go from there." I sulk silently for the next ten minutes while she lays it all out for me. About halfway through, when she gets to the part where she's passed out on the bed, she lets go of my hand and starts picking at invisible lint on my sweats. I clasp her hand in mine and bring it to my lips. I rub it back and forth against them. The delicate skin gliding across my lips soothes me, and I hope her too. It must because she continues the story until it's done—until she says she hugged him goodbye and came to find me.

"You're incredible, you know that?" I drape her arm around my neck and pluck her off the couch and onto my lap, grunting a little with the effort.

Her bent knees settle on either side of me as her butt plops down on my thighs. "I mean, duh. But you can still tell me."

"I love you, sassy girl. I love your heart. Your capacity to forgive." I place small kisses on her lips with each declaration.

"Hmm, what else do you love?" Her eyes turn storm-cloud gray.

I love it when she's playful, confident in her allure, but I keep it to myself. Instead, I grip my hands under her thighs and flip her onto her back along the couch and brace myself above her using my forearms.

I feel the burn in my overworked abs. I must grimace too because I watch her brows crease as her eyes bounce back and forth studying mine.

"Are you hurt?"

The concern in her voice has me shaking my head quickly. "No, no. Just went a little hard on the crunches." I chuckle to drive home my denial. I settle into the space between her legs and watch her eyes darken again. I dip my head and rub my lips softly against hers.

She parts hers right away and tilts her head to fuse our mouths, and we devour each other.

Yes, I was low-key losing my mind with her out there alone talking to that douchebag, but she doesn't know that. Does she need to? I don't think so. She explained to me why she wants to forgive him, why she did forgive him apparently, and that he didn't act maliciously, that he was manipulated and lied to by Kendall also. Would I have forgiven so easily in her shoes? I don't know. As a guy, I don't know if I could accurately answer that. That she is okay is my main concern. I do worry that she may compartmentalize so completely that she doesn't give herself permission to feel all the things. Maybe that's why I want to make her feel good this way. Or maybe I'm just crazy in love with her and, because I am, I want to show her how much—like all the time. I'll never get enough of watching her body respond to me so completely.

After a few moments, I pull back and take in her glazed eyes and swollen lips before I say, "I love the way you kiss me."

"I love the way *you* kiss *me*," she throws right back, her chest still rising and falling with her mounting desire.

"Yeah? What else do you love?" I play her game.

Looking at me from under her lashes, she hesitates and decides to play it coy. "I'm pretty sure you know what I love by now."

"M-hm, I do. But maybe I wanna hear you say it."

This makes her squirm under me and squeeze her legs against my hips. She closes her eyes and parts her lips to speak but doesn't say anything. I second-guess taking things to a *physical* level. Maybe we need to have more talking. We are insatiable for each other. It's never enough. But I make myself chill, wanting to track how she's really feeling before our desire drowns out everything else.

"I love your hands." Her shy admission pulls me out of my pondering. Sucked back into her, us, I nod, my eyes boring into hers. "On me," she adds, her pupils taking over her irises.

I dip my head till my lips are right at the base of her ear. "On you where?" My tongue snakes out to skim her lobe before drawing it into my mouth, sucking lightly.

"Anywhere. Everywhere." Her reply is breathy as her pelvis rises to meet mine.

"Yeah?" I ask. I don't wait for an answer when I ask, "Here?" I slide my hand over the thin, soft fabric of her T-shirt and seize her breast. I feel her head nod against my lips, still kissing and sucking on her ear and neck. I slip my hand under the cotton and tease her nipple already hardened and begging to be touched.

She arches her chest into my hand.

I pull the hem of the fabric up and replace my fingers with my lips, kissing and sucking while my hand slides lower. The elastic band of her sweats gives without any resistance. I smile at the easy access. Gliding my hands past the lacy edge of her thong, I find her so slippery with excitement I almost forget our game. I pull my lips off her nipple with a pop. "Here?" I barely breathe the word when I feel her head nodding again, and it's all I need. I plunge two fingers into her sweet spot.

Her exhale is long, part moan, part answer. "Ughhh huh." With my thumb driving her crazy on the outside and my fingers driving her crazy on the inside, her thigh muscles are taut and want to clench shut, but my weight between her legs won't allow it. Her eyes are pinched shut and her head tosses to one side, then the other.

"I got you, Ever. I know what you like. What you love." I keep the pressure going—slow circles, my thumb and finger meeting through the sensitive velvet skin at her apex. Just as she's about the come, I capture her lips in a kiss, suctioning her mouth to mine.

When her orgasm hits, she bites down on my bottom lip as I swallow her crying moan.

While the spasms subside, I slowly slide my fingers out, eliciting a tiny moan from her at the vacancy.

"Mmmm. Yeah, I like that," she rasps, her voice husky with desire.

A delighted laugh rumbles through my chest. I kiss her again, loudly smacking her lips.

"That too," she adds after my kiss, but she's squirming a little under me. I don't make her wait.

Lifting myself off the couch, I shove my sweats off my hips and down my legs, then peel her top up over her head and drop it next to our growing pile of clothes. She lifts her hips as I hook my fingers in the waistband of her sweats. I slide them down, along with her thong, and swipe them off her feet to pool on the floor with mine. I quickly settle back between her legs. I kiss her just as quickly—deeply—and as our tongues tangle in their familiar dance, I guide myself into her and sink my hips down all the way.

She lifts her knees, giving me deeper access, and wraps them tight around my ass.

God, she feels so good. Her walls encase me perfectly, snugly. I can't stop the deep moans as I sink into her again and again. "Ughhh. Ughhh."

She rises to meet me and sets the pace, all thoughts of our game long gone.

In fact, I'm not sure I can form words right now. I'm trying not to come before her, but she feels so goddamn good. She's safe, she's here in my arms and she's coming undone for me. She doesn't always say it with words, but she loves me. She says it in so many other ways, every day. I find my voice. "Are you close, Ever? Come for me?"

Her walls tense around me, and I know she's close.

I'm shaking with restraint, driving into her, my face buried in her hair, her neck, her scent. Then I hear her voice, hoarse with desire, and I feel her lips, breath against my ear.

"Yes, Julie. Ugh, fuck, I love you."

I feel the dampness on my cheek, her tears. I feel the shudder of her orgasm around my dick, and I can't stop myself if I wanted to. I bury myself in her deeply and come in an orgasm I feel in every cell of my body. Spent, my body aching from the murderous workout I gave it, I want to collapse. The couch is too narrow to lie next to her unless we rotate on our sides. Coiling my arm around her, I grunt as I lift her and twist us so we're facing each other.

Her frown tells me she tracked the unusual exertion that took. "Did you hurt yourself?" She lays her hand gently on my cheek, pinning me with her stare.

"Not intentionally."

Her eyes go wide at my response. "Like, just now?" Her lips stay parted in surprise. My chest vibrates with my chuckle.

"No, sweet girl, not now. Before, when you were outside . . . talking." I don't say his name. I'm not sure I can yet. If she's okay, I should be too. I'm just not one hundred percent convinced she is.

"How?" She pauses, then answers her own question. "Working out." She rolls her eyes a little as she says it.

"I was just distracting myself while I waited."

She pets my face, almost absently curling her fingers into the stubble thickening on my jaw. "You already said that," she teases. "Did it work?"

Her cheeky question pulls another chest-vibrating chuckle from me as I shake my head slowly. "Not even a little." I'm not sure any of my coping tricks would've worked this time. Which makes me wonder if I need to revisit therapy. I did it for a while when I first came to Blue Lake—online because it's so remote out here. Besides, even if they did have a therapist or two here in town, everyone knows everyone. I'm not sure I'd relax enough to use said therapist to its full potential. What's the point of going to therapy if you're not going all in? But why aren't all my tricks working anymore? I mean, they are . . . were . . . until they weren't. Violence has never been my MO. I grew up watching my parents beat the shit out of each other. I learned quickly how to disappear—literally leaving the shitty trailer as quiet as a mouse. The few times I tried to hide inside, they'd spot me and I'd be dragged into their addiction-fueled tantrums. So I learned to get the fuck out of the trashy little box as soon as shit escalated.

Therapy is exhausting, but I'll start it again if I need to. I'll never be what my parents were. I never want someone I love to see that part of me—that anger that lives inside me. I never understood all the tantrums, screaming and violence. Sure, they'd always make up the same way they got pissed—in some inebriated state—but they'd be covered in bruises and scratches for days after. Stupid.

"Let's go sit in the hot tub. It'll make you feel better." Ever climbs over me to stand up from the couch. "I'll grab the robes after I use the restroom." She disappears down the short hallway—unaffectedly naked.

When will I start to believe I deserve the magic of this precious girl? She's so comfortably herself around me now. God, I love her so much it hurts. Like every time this thought hits me, the pain in my chest follows. I can't survive losing her. I rub small circles on the hollow heart tattoo with the flat of my palm out of habit. I roll up to a sitting position to join her, wincing at the strain on my abs. The hot tub will most definitely help my screaming muscles. I smile to myself that she knows this now too.

Chapter 17

Everly

"We make a great team, you know that?" Julian plants a loud kiss on my lips, his hand possessively on my ass, drawing me to him.

I let him pull me in because I want his arms around me. I don't want to let him go or say goodbye. More content filming and branding meetings down south with Ashley this weekend for him and I've got too much homework to join him. I'm pouting on the inside and trying to hide it from him on the outside. I hate when he's gone. I know that logically we can't be together all the time, and that healthy relationships need space to survive, but still, I feel untethered when we're not together. I'm sure there's some therapy term for it, like codependency or separation anxiety or both. But I'm not ready to admit there's something *wrong* with the way I feel about him or us. We're just better together.

"We do make a good team, which is why you should stay here with your *teammate*." I say it without conviction because I know he has to go. And I know it's important for the future he's building. I'm proud of him and proud to be with him. "Kidding," I add, dragging the word out so he doesn't think I'm guilt-tripping him. I'm really not. I love what this opportunity Ashley's giving him means—for him, for us, if we stay . . . a team. I squash that last thought.

"Miss me." He says it like an order and plants another fat kiss on my lips, lifts his bag off the ground and turns toward his Jeep.

"Always." I watch him from the doorway and wave as he backs out.

Just before he drives off, he looks back and winks at me with those stunning blue eyes.

My stomach flips, and I wonder for the umpteenth time if it will always be this way. Will he always make my stomach flip? I close the door and already feel restless without him. Even though I have plenty of homework, I entertain the idea of diving into a new book while he's gone—a fictional world to lose myself in. Lately though, picking a book is like picking a movie to watch—more time spent browsing than watching. I browse and browse and in the end decide on nothing. I fear my deliciously handsome *teammate* has ruined my love of romance books and book boyfriends. And the next thought that occurs is the usual—I need to swap my love for romance to another genre. Suspense, maybe? Thrillers? Something sans swoony male main characters. None of them holds a candle to the one I've got in real life.

Flopping onto our bed, I open the Amazon app to peruse new book releases. Homework be damned. Before I can spiral down that rabbit hole, Lilly's face takes over my phone screen. I tap to answer her FaceTime call.

"Oh my God, Lilly. I miss your face so much."

"Yeah? Well, you're about to see a whole lot more of it. Open your door."

"What?" I bound off the bed and race down the stairs, then throw open the front door. There in the place of Julian's Jeep is Lilly's old Ford Bronco, with her standing beside it tucking her phone into her jeans. I leap off the three steps in one hop and throw my arms around her. "What the hell are you doing here?"

"Long weekend. Came home to see the fam. And you, of course."

"No Noah?"

"No, his fraternity has some bro shit to do so . . . here I am." She throws her arms out wide.

"Oh my God, this is so perfect. Julian just left to go down south for work."

"I know, I passed him turning onto your street. We stopped in the road and chatted for two seconds. He told me you were gonna freak out. He looked way too happy I was gonna surprise you. Could you guys be any more sickening? I mean cute." She rolls her eyes on the last part.

"Get in here. What are we doing first? Wanna go for coffee? Want me to make you some breakfast?"

"Is Pete around? I'm dying for one of his breakfast burritos. College food sucks."

"Yep, he's already shut down on the weekdays but still does Friday through Sunday breakfast for a few more weeks. Wanna drive or walk?"

"Let's walk. I miss home."

***

"**S**o, when are you moving back?" I loudly slurp the last of my iced coffee through the straw.

"When are you coming with me?" Lilly tosses a napkin on her empty plate and stretches her arms over her head as she leans back in her chair.

"Well played." I smirk. I miss her so much.

While her retort was a joke, it sobers me a bit. The tug of war in my head between feeling like I'm missing out by not having gone away to college and not wanting to be away from Julian is strong. More so when it hits me in the face, like now, seeing Lilly talking about her life on campus—especially when her life in San Luis Obispo sounds perfect and similar to life here. Trade the lake for the beach and you're there. Cal Poly was one of my top school choices. But just like Pepperdine, I never applied. Maybe if I'd applied before all the shit went down, I'd be away at school right now. But that would mean I may have never met Lilly. Or Julian. My stomach drops on that sobering thought—makes me tuck that longing and sadness away. I wouldn't go back and redo it. *I wouldn't.* Sometimes I just need to take a walk down What If Lane to remind myself of that.

"What'd you have planned while your man's away?" Lilly pulls me out of my pity spiral.

"Homework. Boring." I shrug and stand to clear our plates and take them to the kitchen.

"Okay, I mean I have some too. Can I sleep over and we'll do it together?"

"For sure! I'd love that."

We say our goodbyes to Pete and take the trail back to Allie's—home. *My home. With Julian.* Lilly entertains me the whole way back with stories of campus life and Noah's fraternity adventures. She says she's not the sorority type.

"Same," I agree. After the mean girl nightmare I went through in OV, you wouldn't catch me willingly signing up for that shit.

"Okay, I gotta jet to Southy and see the fam. Might stay for dinner. Wanna come?" she asks as she stands next to the open door of her Bronco, ready to hop in.

I shake my head. "Nah, I'll get a head start on my assignments while you're gone. Are you sure they'll let you leave once you get there?" I laugh, knowing how close they all are.

"I gotta spread the Lilly love around while I'm here. They'll have to deal." She holds her hands out to her sides in a cocky stance.

"Oh, okay." I toss my chin at her. "Well, I'll see you when you get done signing autographs." I hear her giggle as she closes the door and starts her engine. Ambling up the steps and into the entryway, I can't stop smiling. God, it's so good to have Lilly home. *Home.* Will I ever get used to calling it that?

***

"**G**irl, I can't believe I missed the Chase drama." Sitting in the cool air on the deck, layered in hoodies, sweats and blankets, we recline on the loungers in the dark. The full moon casts a glow on the night.

"To be fair, it was more anti-drama. Felt kinda bad for the guy, if I'm being real."

"Yeah, I guess. But sometimes you're too nice, Davis."

I smile without answering and hug the throw pillow to my chest. Agreeable Everly. That's been my identity since I can remember. Never rocking the boat. It's clear to me why I lost myself in books ever since I could read. The characters, especially the female ones, were always strong and outspoken and fierce. I always wanted to be more like those girls. Sometimes now I feel like I am like them. I feel bolder than I ever have, and I think a lot of that has to do with Julian. I feel brave and safe around him. Like I can just be me and he's not going anywhere. The weird thing about people leaving you when you're young is that even though you're repeatedly told it's not you, it feels like it's you. Like if you'd done something different . . . been different . . . they would've stayed. After years of therapy and simply getting older and . . . wiser, I know logically that's not true. Emotionally, though, that default setting can still fuck with my head.

"Love looks good on you, Ev." Lilly pulls me out of my head.

"It feels good." When my response causes her to grimace at me, I add, "Eww, not like that. But . . . well . . . okay, like that." I giggle and push the pillow to my face.

"I mean, I figured. You can't have a body like that and suck in bed." She giggles.

"Right?" I don't recognize the forward girl talking boldly about sex, but I love her. And I love that I have someone like Lilly I can be that girl with. "And, like, we do it all the time. Like all the time. Do you and Noah?"

"I think we did at first. Maybe. But now . . . I don't know. Maybe we're in a rut. Or just busy with school. I don't know."

"Hmmm. That's two I-don't-knows in the same breath. What's up, Lill?"

Lilly bursts into tears. "I think we're breaking up." She presses the pillow to her face now.

"Oh my God, Lilly. Holy shit, why didn't you say something? Or tell me to shut the fuck up about Julian and all the sex."

"No. It's not like that. I wanna hear about you guys. I'm happy for you. Really! I just . . . I don't even know how to not be with Noah. It's been almost five years. Since freshman year of high school." She sniffs and wipes her cheeks with the backs of her hands. "It started getting weird over the summer when we moved into the apartment. We became more like roommates. Now in college, it's like we're best friends or . . . brother and sister." She shudders on the last part. "We still have a lot to talk about and catch up over lunch at least four times a week. Or dinner if he doesn't have frat stuff. But the frat is like his new family." She chokes up again. "I'm happy for him. I want him to have fun. To belong. All the things. I just don't know where I fit in anymore. Or if I want to."

"Like you guys outgrew each other?" I offer this softly, wondering.

"Yeah, maybe." She sniffs loudly. "I've never seen Noah so animated as when he's talking about his BPΩ bros. Especially his new BFF, Seth. Taught him how to surf and now that's his whole personality." She's picking at invisible lint on the pillow now. "I went from being his whole world to the audience of his highlight reel. And the weirdest part is I'm not even sure if I'm sad about Noah or about not knowing who I am without him."

"Do you like school, living in SLO?" Picturing Lilly alone at school makes my chest feel heavy. It reminds me of when I first came to Blue Lake. How alone I felt.

"Yeah." With a heavy sigh, she adds, "Yeah, I do." Lilly hugs the pillow, one knee bent to her chest.

"For real, though? Or like 'that's what I'm supposed to say?'" I push, but gently.

"Mostly, yeah. It's beautiful there, being so close to the beach. But . . ." Her heavy sigh says more than her words ever could. "I miss home. But like more than the place. I miss the feeling. I don't know if that makes sense."

"No, it does." I cut her off. I know exactly what she means. It's more than Blue Lake for me. It's Julian. It's Fit. Brew. But mostly it's the way I feel about myself when I'm here. "I like who I am in Blue Lake. And I'm not trying to make this about me. I just mean . . . this place—which includes you—feels like a part of me now."

"So, you get it." She turns her head, resting her cheek on the pillow, and pins me with her watery, milk chocolate stare.

I nod, feeling the pressure build behind my own eyes at seeing my bubbly, confident friend breaking down.

"But I'm not a quitter." She blinks her eyes a couple times and tosses the pillow off her lap. "C'mon, I need ice cream. Got any?"

***

As the bright blue Bronco backs down the driveway, I lean against the open doorway, waving until Lilly turns onto the highway and disappears. We stayed up all night talking. I worry she's too tired to drive, but she insists she'll be fine. She promises to fuel her four-hour drive back to campus with plenty of caffeine. I low-key want to go with her, to be her hype girl while she's going through the weird shit with Noah, but I'd rather keep her here than go there. One thing that listening to Lilly describe college life did is make me grateful for my online journey. I get to keep my happy safe place and get my degree. It's clearer to me now what I want to do.

Maybe Blue Lake and Julian have become *my whole personality*, but is that a bad thing if I love it? The way fitness changed my life makes me want to learn more about it and contribute to Fit in a way we don't yet offer. I want to talk to Allie and Julian about it more, but I'm leaning toward majoring in some kind of exercise psychology. The way fitness plays a key role in dealing with trauma intrigues me. Maybe Ashley can find a way to incorporate that expertise into the McKay Method, offer it to clients as part of the packages—if Julian is into it. Another maybe . . .

Am I still trying to make his life mine? It doesn't feel that way. I'm truly interested in pursuing this major. Although I'm not exactly sure what that major would be—Sport, Exercise and Performance Psychology (SEPP) perhaps. Mostly I just want to find a way to help build this life we love in a way that feeds my love of learning and passion for peace in the face of trauma. I hope Julian is excited about it like I am. Why are there butterflies swarming in my stomach at the thought of telling him? But Lilly is proof of what the right environment and mental state can do in the face of stress. After two short days at home full of fresh air, exercise and connecting with people who love her, she felt empowered and ready to face her life back at school. This is what I want to contribute to Fit and the McKay Method.

This decision is like a giant exhale. Like I will finally have a light at the end of the college tunnel to focus on and work toward. My love of and passion for writing will always be there, and who knows? Maybe

I'll write a book about the psychology of fitness. The thought puts a glow in my belly where the butterflies used to be. My smile takes over my face as I step back inside and close the door. Combining this new passion with my lifelong one is giving me all the feels. Julian will be home soon, and, with a racing heart, I can't wait to fill him in. To placate my nerves, I go for a run. I do some of my best thinking while running.

Chapter 18

JULIAN

As soon as my Jeep leaves the freeway and reaches the meandering highways of home, the weight leaves my body. I roll the windows down. Despite the cooling temperatures, my lungs welcome the air that chills my face. I inhale the smell of home—soil-rich fields, woodsy oaks, and a hint of something ancient and quiet. The rolling golden hills of dry grass and sprawling alligator-skinned oak trees as far as the eye can see embrace me. My anticipation grows the closer I get to Blue Lake and my gray-eyed girl. I've missed her so much. Especially since early feedback shows the algorithm favors clips with Ever as much as those of me alone. Proof we're better together. It's also true what they say. Sex sells. And she's sexy as fuck on camera. I'm eager to tell her. Mostly because I'm so proud of her. But I'm nervous how she'll respond to the growing interest in her. She's private and still hasn't reactivated her social media since leaving Oak Valley.

Opening the door, every cell in my body exhales. The faint and steady patter of water hitting tile trickles down the stairs. My girl is in the shower, which immediately sends blood rushing south. I drop my bags at the door, swing the wood shut behind me, and ascend the stairs two at a time. Steam fogs up the mirror so I can't see her in the reflection as I approach the open master bathroom door. I stop in the doorway and lean on the jamb, watching her sluice water off her hair, head tilted back in the spray, eyes closed. She must sense me there, because her eyes fly open and pin me with her smoky stare.

Straightening from the doorway, I yank my shirt over my head as I'm kicking off my Dunks and sliding my joggers and boxers down my legs. I'm already hard in anticipation. I step through the sliding doors and reach for her.

She snakes her heated arms around me, molding herself to me.

"Hi, beautiful girl." I kiss her wet lips, sucking on them slightly until she opens and presses her tongue against mine.

She quickly sweeps in and out, closing her lips again on mine. "Hi, beautiful boyfriend."

"I missed you, Ever." I peck her lips again.

"Yeah? How much?" Her smoky eyes grow dark like a thunderstorm.

I don't answer her with words. Instead, I curl my fingers around her thigh and lift her leg, placing her foot on the tiled seat. Taking her hands, I lace our fingers and pin her arms to the shower wall above her head and drive into her without warm-up or warning.

"Augh."

The cry that rips from deep in her chest gives me pause. I freeze for a moment. Did I hurt her?

She presses into me. "Don't stop, Julie."

So I don't. I swivel my hips and thrust into her again. As I drive into her, she bears down on me in a fevered rhythm that rivals the heat of the shower. When I feel her muscles tighten, her walls squeezing me, I don't stop. Her eyes are shut, her breaths labored and still I plunge. I'm close. I know she is too.

"Fuck, I missed you. I want you to come, Ever. I'm so close. Are you close?" I've never come before her. I reach between us and use my thumb on the bundle of nerves.

"Yessss." The pressure drags the word from her throat. Her free hand grips my neck; her nails dig into my skin.

"Good girl. Come for me, Ever." Her walls convulse around me as I still my thumb, pressing it hard against her pulsing clit. With one last thrust, I come so hard I brace myself with my arm outstretched, palm flat against the tile wall.

Once the convulsions stop, hers and mine, I bury my face in her neck and rain kisses behind her ear and along her jaw until I capture her lips. I pick her up, her legs wrapping around me instantly, and kiss her until we're both breathing hard. *Did we ever stop?*

Panting as our lips separate, Ever giggles breathlessly. "Wow, I guess you did miss me."

"Yeah, sassy girl, I did." I squeeze her ass playfully as I release her, snag a loofah off the hook, pump a blob of body wash onto it and begin rubbing it on her arm to create a lather.

Taking it from me, she says, "Me too," and begins soaping my chest and torso. "And I'm already showered so . . ." She trails off and continues spreading the suds over my body.

I turn and let her cover my back. Her slippery hands on me feel too fucking good. I reach up and rub the bubbles covering the tattoo on my chest. Whatever I did to deserve her, I don't take it for granted. She's beyond what I ever hoped to have in this life.

When we're drying off, Ever says she has a surprise for me. My heartbeat trips and thuds a little quicker. I'm not sure I'll ever like surprises. But I smile and raise my eyebrows askance.

She takes my hand and leads me into the bedroom and begins throwing on her oldest softest sweats. "Just throw on something cozy. It's in the garage."

My heartbeat doesn't calm down as I pull on my baggiest joggers I wear for lounging around and a T-shirt from a drawer without caring which one.

She twists her hair up into a wet knot on her head and grabs my hand to lead me downstairs.

As soon as she opens the garage door off the laundry room, I hear the little mewling sounds coming from the laundry basket. Her angelic smile spreads as she tracks my expression. The thudding slows and a smile takes over my face. Anything that can make my girl's eyes shine like that is okay with me. Apparently, it's three somethings. One orange, one gray and one "everything."

"I found them just off the trail when I went for a run today. There was no momma that I could find. Just them. I couldn't leave them out there to get eaten by the CCS." She pleads her case while I laugh at her remembering our nickname for the "crazy country shit" that might incidentally eat kittens in Blue Lake—coyotes, mountain lions, and hawks to name a few.

"Okay." I look at her beaming face and tuck a fallen wet strand of hair behind her ear.

"Okay? We can keep them?" Her smile creases the corners of her eyes that have gone almost opaque in her excitement.

"What if we keep them at Brew?" We need barn cats to help keep rodents out of the storage garage.

"So, garage cats?" She looks worried.

I nod in answer. "It's a thing out here. Another aspect of the CCS. Barn cats keep the rodent population down, which keeps the snake population at bay. Let's call it the Blue Lake circle of life."

"But how do we keep them safe?" Her eyes, like saucers, plead with mine as she points to the laundry basket.

"We'll keep them inside until they're fixed and big enough to defend themselves. Besides, I think Pete and Shelley will be thrilled to have them policing Brew." She looks dejected they won't be here with us. So I add, "I'm not an expert, but I think these types of feral cats will be happier hunting." She nods once, twice, but her eyes are sad. "C'mon, let's go inside and text Pete about them."

Pete and Shelley are beyond thrilled about the abandoned litter. Their old cat, Smokey, just "crossed over the rainbow bridge," and their boys have been sad about it. This information brings the light back to my girl's eyes. Knowing she's giving a gift to those boys trumps her longing to keep them. I'm relieved because, as much as I'd do anything to make my sweet girl smile like that, raising three kittens is not the move. With traveling down south and her carrying a full load for school, plus our regular jobs, I don't see how we'd manage it. Fuck, I sound like a grown-up. When did that happen?

Almost two hours later, we're back at home preparing dinner together. Between going to the local feed store for kitten supplies and bringing them and all their necessities to the DeLucas', I'm now starving. But Pete, Shelley and the boys were ecstatic with the little fuzz balls. Seeing the boys with them made Ever so happy, she doesn't seem at all sad about not keeping them. I'm relieved because I want to bring up her role in the McKay Method—which, if she's into, will mean a lot less time for things like kittens.

We decide on camp tacos for dinner, which was just her dad's way of saying taco salad. I grill chicken while she dices the vegetables. Now we're taking turns tossing it all into a giant bowl when I decide to spit out the idea and hope for the best.

"Ever?"

"Julie?"

We speak at the exact same time. Then we both half laugh in unison, which makes us laugh again.

"You first," I say, wiping my hands on the towel and giving her my full attention.

"No, you go," she offers. I'm already shaking my head like I insist. "Okay," she adds when she sees I'm not budging. "I've been thinking," she continues timidly. I wait while she works her way around to saying whatever it is she's struggling to say. I ignore the increase in my heart rate. "I think I picked a major." Her gray eyes look unblinkingly into mine.

My heart rate settles. "That sounds like good news. What is it?"

"Sport and Exercise Psychology." She smiles as she says it but looks like she's holding her breath waiting for my reaction.

"Wow, Ever. That sounds amazing. And . . . kinda perfect." I reach for her and wrap my arms around her. "Like you." My wheels are spinning. For her and where this could take her. And us.

"Or I could just get the degree in psych with a minor in health and wellness. I want to use it to help people. Teach them to use exercise and fitness to deal with trauma. Like offer that at Fit. Or . . . at the

McKay Method." She says the last part quietly with her cheek against my chest.

I pull back and can't keep the smile off my face.

When she looks up at me, she steps back from my embrace and mirrors my smile. "What?" She looks skeptical, like I'm up to something.

"You're not going to believe how perfect this is, but . . . okay, promise you'll hear me out before you react."

"The disclaimer doesn't exactly scream 'perfect.'" She folds her arms over her chest and waits for me to elaborate.

I offer what I hope is a reassuring smile. I'm beyond hyped by her news. I want her to be hyped by mine. I'm seeing our future roll out in front of me, and I almost can't contain the excitement, foreign as the feeling is. I've never really looked forward to my future like this. At least not the way I am now. If someone would've asked me even a year ago where I thought I'd be at almost twenty-two, this wouldn't have even made the radar. "It turns out people love you. The videos of us together are getting way more views and interactions than the ones of me alone." I hold my breath and wait for her reaction.

Her eyebrows are up, her eyes wide and round, smile crooked, lifting on one side. She exhales through puffed-out cheeks. "Are you serious?"

I nod, grinning. She mirrors my expression. I don't want to bring up socials and wipe it off her face, but she needs to hear it all to make the best decision for her. "People love *love*. That's how Ashley's team puts it. They want you to activate your socials." I look down at my hands as I say it, but I raise my eyes to hers again when I add, "I told them that may not happen. It's totally up to you, Ever. Whatever you're comfortable with."

"I know. You always make sure I'm okay." She reaches up and runs her nails through the hair on my forehead and pecks my cheek with a soft kiss. "I don't love the social media part but considering where I'm at with my degree and career idea, it could be kinda perfect," she concedes.

After catching her up on the rest of my meetings with Ashley, Ever reluctantly agrees she might need to activate her social accounts again. I can tell she likes the idea of taking a more active role in the McKay Method. I'm so relieved she's on board. Maybe we can even find a way for her not to have her own social presence but a business one that's managed by an assistant instead. Whatever my girl needs to feel calm and secure. I want our life to be a happy, peaceful one. And I'm cheesing like an unhinged weirdo as my brain thinks in terms of *ours*. The best part is her expression mirrors mine. I rub the spot on my chest, in happy anticipation this time.

Chapter 19

EVERLY

Roaming the Malibu farmer's market is one of my favorite things to do when we fly down for business. Julian always tries to make time to take me. If we lived here, I'd be loaded down with local food items. Since we fly home tomorrow, I'm content to simply indulge on the spot. Sinking my teeth into the sweetest peach I've ever eaten sends my eyes rolling back, my lids closing and throat humming with a deep "mmm."

"I couldn't agree more." The timber of Julian's voice is low, for my ears only.

I open my eyes to see him watching me, his eyes a deep ocean blue. "Wanna taste?" I offer the peach to him.

He nods, never taking his eyes off mine. Ignoring the fruit in my hand, he leans over and more sucks than kisses my lips. Then, leaning till his lips touch my ear, whispers, "Delicious."

I can't help the giggle that bubbles in my throat and the heat that swirls in my belly.

"Aren't you Julian McKay?"

Our heads swivel simultaneously toward the voice, a striking young woman accompanied by two others just as striking.

"Hi. Yep. Nice to meet you." Julian extends his right hand and smiles. I can tell he's embarrassed, though he fakes it well. Encounters like these are becoming more and more frequent. He reaches down with his other hand and clasps mine as he greets the women.

Since I agreed to join him on the McKay content, Callie's team has been setting up my "brand." They're teasing the McKay Method on socials, creating buzz, building curiosity. And thankfully, her new team created social accounts for me that I don't have to manage or even look at so far. Julian and I have flown to SoCal twice to film content since I signed on officially. This trip will be the last before we hard launch his company on his birthday, which is coming up October 22nd. They picked the day strategically—a psychological draw. Ironically, I'm learning all about this in class right now. My psych course though is framing it as manipulation. Ashley promises this launch will not be that. Just using psychology to market strategically, he assured. *Noted.*

ASH seems to have a bottomless ocean of resources to make shit happen, and Julian and I are being swept up in the current. It could easily get overwhelming, but Ashley runs ASH just like he lives his life—with kindness and generosity. For a whirlwind it's been pretty stress free. I haven't panicked once, which I'm counting as a win. Of course, I'm still living in anonymity for the most part. But Julian is now getting recognized when we're out in public, especially in ASH territory. I'm not sure who gets more uncomfortable with the encounters—him or me.

Considering it's mostly young, beautiful women approaching him, it might be me. But Ashley is even coaching him on handling that with grace. I'm merely taking notes from the sidelines. I want to be proud and supportive, not shallow and jealous. The fact that my green flag of a man doesn't have one ounce of interest in his *fans* beyond being grateful for their support goes a long way in helping me in that role.

"This is my girlfriend, Everly. She'll be running the performance mindset part of the company for us." Julian handles the group of women with impressive charm.

"Hi, ladies. Great to meet you. Will you be joining the McKay Method when we launch? Lots of fun giveaways to the first ones."

McKay Method will include a free birthday merch box for the first thousand people to download the app and sign up for the premium package. The merch box will include things like water bottles, hats, stickers and the sore muscle cream Julian and Allie made, Blue Heat—which is also being commercialized and sold now. If a member refers a friend and they sign up for a premium package, both members get a free month of membership. If the push is a success, they may extend it through his "birthday month" and try to get 10k downloads in the first month.

My pitch is met with enthusiastic yesses and other affirmations. Their excitement is contagious.

I catch Julian's bright blue eyes over their heads, and he winks at me, which never fails to make my stomach flip. I'm so proud of this beautiful man. He deserves all of this so much. That I get to help him realize this level of success is just a bonus. As we wave goodbye to his fan club, he laces his fingers through mine, and we turn and walk toward the parking lot to our borrowed car.

***

"**S**o, what are you doing for your birthday? Shall we have a celebration? Like a launch party?" Allie asks as she hands Julian a beer.

"No." His reply is as instant as mine.

"Yes." I lock gazes with him on our simultaneous conflicting replies. "Oh, c'mon. Let's celebrate your birthday. Would we do it here or in Blue Lake?"

"Who would we even invite? I'm not big on celebrating my birthday."

"This is different though. It can just be about business if you want to look at it that way," Ashley chimes in, then takes a sip of his beer.

Julian rolls his eyes at me and Allie and reluctantly agrees. "Fine. But let's do it at Blue Lake. In fact, let's do it at Brew and ask Pete and Shelley to join us. Lettie."

"Done," Allie and I say at the same time, which makes us both giggle.

Julian just shakes his head, resigned.

Flying home the next morning, Julian brings up the birthday celebration again. "Maybe Lilly and Noah can come home for it—a quick weekend. Since Allie and Ashley won't be able to fly home for it."

"Yeah, I'll ask," I say, nodding.

"Why do you sound less than thrilled by that?"

"No, it's not that. I think there might be trouble in paradise."

"What? Nooo." He swings his wide-eyed stare toward me.

"Maybe it's freshman year growing pains. I don't know. She said he's spending a ton of time with the frat guys. Mainly one named Seth. Taught him how to surf, and according to Lill, it's now 'his whole personality.'" I use my fingers as quote marks.

Julian doesn't respond, just raises his eyebrows in wonder.

I change the subject. Because if a couple as seemingly solid as Noah and Lilly are struggling, it doesn't bode well for the rest of us. "Ya know, I've always wanted to learn to surf. Have you ever done it?"

He shakes his head, smiling. "I'm not sure I'm a strong enough swimmer. Out of respect for the ocean, I think I'll stick to cliff jumping in Blue Lake."

"Fair." I smile back. Meanwhile, my mind drifts back to my friend. I check my signal and decide to text her while we're in the air.

Me: Hey Lill. How's everything?

Three dots appear right away. I drum my fingernails against the back of the phone, antsy for her reply.

Lilly: Long story. New development, I think we're just friends now. □

Lilly: I'm surprisingly okay. It doesn't feel much different than it's been for a while.

Me: Wow. OK. That's a lot. Landing now. Talk later? □

Lilly: For sure. Love you.

Me: Love you too.

"How's Lilly?" Julian doesn't look up from his laptop when he asks. And I wonder for a moment how he knew. Not like I was hiding it, but I didn't say. Does he just know me that well? The thought has me smiling to myself and feeling a twinge of guilt over my friend and her situationship.

"Weirdly okay. Lilly is a G. Just a badass. Ya know?" I roll my head on the seat to look at him.

"Like someone else I know." He taps his index finger on my nose and leans over to place a soft peck on my lips.

I feel the pressure build behind my eyes, and I blink a couple times to clear it. *How'd I get so lucky?* I blurt out the thought in my head. "How'd I get so lucky?"

"Mmm, you've got that backwards, sweet girl. I'm the lucky one."

"Can we just agree it's a tie?" I roll my eyes.

"Kiss me, sassy girl, and I'll agree to whatever you want."

"Ooh, this just got interesting."

"We're landing. We don't have time for this."

"And you call Via a cockblocker."

"That sass is gonna get my bookish girl a plot twist."

A giggle bubbles in my throat. "Ooh, I see what you did there. Promise?" I lower my gaze and look up at him under my lashes. I'm so turned on by the shift in our conversation, I clench my knees together. Julian lowers his gaze to my legs, tracking the slight movement. His eyes are deep indigo, pupils wide when he brings them back to mine. His visible swallow drops my eyes to his throat. My tongue swipes across my dry lips.

"You're right, you are lucky. Lucky this plane just landed. But I predict that luck runs out when we hit Blue Lake."

"I guess that depends on your definition of luck." One eyebrow quirks up in challenge.

"You're not wrong." His deep baritone chuckle follows me down the aisle as I try to walk like I'm unaffected by our banter.

Chapter 20

Julian

The drive from Oak Valley Airport to Blue Lake takes forty-five minutes. Everly's hands fidget in her seat as soon as we're settled in the Jeep, and I can't keep the smile from my face knowing what's got her so keyed up. Looking over my right shoulder to back out of the parking spot, I track her eyes. They're hungry. She reaches up and lightly pokes her finger in the dimple near my mouth, which makes me cheese even harder.

"I like your dimple." She says it so sweetly.

"Yeah, pretty girl? What else do you like?" My eyes are now looking forward, navigating the airport lot. But I know her eyes are a dark, storm-cloud gray, and her cheeks are flushed. That I know her body so well has my pulse jumping in my wrists and the front of my joggers tightening.

"Everything," she says earnestly. "Everything I know so far."

"So far?" I quirk my brow and snag a quick look at her before casting my eyes back to the road. "What don't you know that you want to know?" I see her body turn toward me in my periphery.

She curls one leg up on her seat. "I don't know. Everything?" A short chuckle escapes her throat like she's nervous to admit she wants to ask.

"Ask me anything." And for the first time in my life, I mean it. I want her to know me because I'm finally proud of who I am.

"What were you like as a little boy?"

Her question stops me cold, like a needle dragged off a vinyl record. When I don't jump to answer, I see her smile falter out of the corner of my eye. I want to be so open with her. I just don't want to relive my life before her. I swallow and prepare to answer her as honestly as I can. "Hmm, well, nothing like I am now."

"That's vague and uninformative."

"I know. Okay . . . I . . ." I push a long breath from puffed cheeks. "My mom and dad fought a lot. And made up a lot. They drank and stuff. Mostly I just tried to stay out of the way." She lifts her hand to her mouth. From my side vision, it looks like she's chewing on her fingernail. I reach for her hand and bring it to my lips. "They weren't great. Neither was my house. A trailer in a shitty trailer park—the only trailer park in South Point. But it's why I'm so focused on now and what we're building. It's a long way from that kid who hid from his parents' drunken bullshit." I take a quick glance at her, hoping I've steered the conversation to something I want to talk about. A tear trails down her cheek. "Ever . . . don't cry. I'm good now." I kiss the back of her hand again and catch her swiping her cheek with her other hand.

Squeezing my hand in hers, she quietly asks, "So when did you meet Taya?"

My brows shoot into the hair dipping across my forehead. A half laugh, half exhale escapes my lips. "We're really going to cover all the topics right now." I don't say it as a question but as a foregone conclusion. "Okay." I blow another breath out. She doesn't retract her question or offer to change the subject. And she has been so transparent with me about her own life, I want to match that energy, even if it means ripping a bandage off an old wound. She deserves to know me. If I really want this thing to go the distance—and I do—I've got to let her. *I can make her happy. We can make a life together.*

"I . . . When I was fifteen. I worked for her dad. On their ranch."

"Did you . . . Were you . . . Did you date the whole time?" She stumbles over her question, and I hate it.

I bring her hand to my lips again, rubbing the soft skin against them, wondering how best to answer her. I want to answer her, and I can't be afraid to tell her the truth. With that thought, Ever's words she once said slam into my brain: *It seems to me it's the shortest route to getting to the point of a thing.* I audibly exhale and snug our joined hands into my lap. I'm gripping her hand too tight, but I don't loosen my hold. "We never really dated. No one knew we even knew each other."

"You didn't go to the same school?"

"I missed a lot of school growing up. Either because my parents didn't get me there or I couldn't get to the bus on time. When I got old enough to get myself to the bus on time, I also started realizing that being independent meant less time in that house, around them. Then we had a global pandemic, and remote learning became a thing. We all, my family, took advantage of that. I never went back to school and stayed remote through graduation. As soon as I could, I wanted to work and make my own money. At fifteen, Bennick said he liked my initiative and hired me full time."

"Bennick?"

"Taya's dad. Rusty Bennick. He's like the unofficial mayor of South Point. He even agreed to pay me cash so my parents didn't have to sign anything, since I was only fifteen. I thought he was a nice guy."

"He's not?"

"Taya's family was kinda fucked up like mine, just with more money. Her mom died when Taya was sixteen. Accidental overdose. She took medication for depression and anxiety, and I think she combined a lethal dose of pills and alcohol one day and OD'd."

"Oh my God, that's awful."

"Yeah, after that, Taya just . . . She and I got closer. But we had to hide it from her dad. After her mom . . . He got even more protective, more controlling. So no one knew we were friends, especially her dad. She said it was best if he thought I was just a hired hand."

"That didn't bother you?"

I feel her staring at my profile, but I keep my eyes on the road. The weight on my chest makes it hard to breathe. The foothills of home roll in the near distance, so I focus on them like a beacon. "Besides a Little League groundskeeper and my mom's father, the few times I saw him, no one ever gave a shit about me until Taya." I see her lips part, hear her sharp intake of breath. I release her hand and rub the spot on my chest.

She leaves her hand on my leg and curls her fingers into the thin fabric of my joggers.

"So no, I guess it didn't bother me. I didn't know any different. That she gave a shit was enough."

"Julie . . ."

"It's fine." I make myself grab her hand again and rub circles on the back with my thumb, the repetitive motion on the smooth skin soothing me. "I'm fine now. Good. Great even." I swing a quick smile her way and meet her eyes for a second to hopefully reassure her. We're into the foothills now—officially in Cavern County. I let go of her hand to slide the sunroof open. The air is cool, but the smell is home. "What is it you said to me? 'I would've never met you. And I wouldn't take that back.' So, it's all good, Ever. Really. Don't be sad for me, okay?" I grab her hand again and squeeze.

Her head nods. She leans over and plants a soft kiss near the corner of my mouth, and her smell wafts around me in the swirling air. Ever and home. I close my eyes for an instant and inhale deeply.

Chapter 21

Everly

"Thanks for telling me all that, Julie." He doesn't answer me, just squeezes my hand again. "Is there anything you want to ask me? I'll answer anything."

"I know, sweet girl. You're so willing, and I love that about you."

"So ask me." I trace circles on his knuckles with my free hand.

"I . . . uh . . ." His brows are drawn together in thought. "What's your favorite plot twist?"

"In books?" I warm to the topic.

"Sure. Let's start with books." His dimple is winking at me, and I sense he means something else.

"No, what do you mean? Like movies, shows?" My brain floods with all my favorites.

"I mean like our discussion on the plane."

"Ohhh." My cheeks feel hot. I face forward in my seat. The leg I had curled under me straightens and presses into my other leg. My palm slides up and down my thigh as I resist burying it in my lap to ease the throb. I know he's switching topics to avoid getting too serious, and I get it. Despite my body's reaction, I can't ignore the train of my thoughts. "Can I ask you something first?"

"Always."

"Do you think everyone has sex like us? Like as much as we do?" As soon as the question leaves my mouth, he barks a sharp laugh.

"God, I hope so." His dimple deepens with his smile. I pinch his thigh and wait. He sobers immediately. "I don't know, love, but I really do hope so."

"I mean, I'm pretty new at this and I just . . . well, I kinda want it . . . you . . . all the time." I let my free hand press into my lap now—my body unconsciously responding to the sex talk and the new term of endearment. It crosses my mind to wonder if it's weird to talk about it. But Julian doesn't make it awkward. Or . . . more awkward. He's the opposite. Deliberately encouraging, whether it's in conversation or physically.

"Ever . . ." He drags out my name like he's about to say something significant, and I hold my breath. "This is new for me too." He reaches for the hand on his thigh and pulls it to his lips again, takes a quick glance at me and continues. "I've never let anyone in before. Only you. Always you. And we don't have to make this conversation about sex. We can talk about anything you want. I mean, I like our talks whatever the topic. Pick one."

His words have me blowing a long sigh out through puffed cheeks and pressure building behind my eyes. I decide to use his trick to distract myself from the emotions hovering on the brink. "So . . . plot twists . . ."

I'm rewarded with his deep, rumbling sexy little laugh. "I'm all ears. And your timing is perfect. We're home."

I look out the windshield as we cruise into the driveway. My heart thuds in anticipation.

We drop our bags inside the door, and I kick off my shoes next to them.

Julian is right behind me and does the same. With bare feet, he pads the two steps to me and snakes his arms around my waist, drawing me back to him. Tilting my neck to unconsciously invite his kiss, he obliges me by nuzzling the sensitive spot behind my ear with his nose. He places small kisses there before he whispers, "Tell me, Ever, what would be your favorite plot twist right now?"

My heart pulses in my neck. His lips must feel it.

"I . . ." His lips steal my words. I try again as my hand travels up his neck, along his jaw, up to the longer hair on top of his head. Running my fingers through it, I grab a handful and tug his head away from my neck. So I can think straight. I still feel his breath where his lips used to be, but I try again. "I . . . think . . . the best . . . plot twist is . . ."

"M-hm." His breath flutters across my skin. He urges me, "Is . . .?"

"The one you don't see coming." I release his hair, the pull on him, so that his lips fall back onto my neck.

He kisses the pulse there once, twice. Then, without warning, sweeps me off my feet, flips me over his shoulder and smacks me hard on my leggings-clad ass. The sting sends a shock straight to my center, followed by a flood of moisture. He doesn't speak but carries me toward the stairs, the bedroom.

My mind screams *plot twist*.

He tosses me onto the bed and yanks the waistbands of my leggings and thong down my legs in one fluid movement. He leaves my shirt on but whips his over his head before he leans his hands on the bed at my feet and begins inching his way up my body. His blue eyes are dark, almost black, and never leave mine as he closes in on the vee of my thighs. His warm breath hits the bundle of nerves a second before his lips. A soft kiss, then another. Then he stops.

I open my eyes that closed at first contact and look down.

He's watching me, waiting for me to look at him. He pushes his hands under my thighs and scoots me farther onto the bed so my upper body is propped against the pillows. Stretching out between my legs, he purses his lips and blows softly on my sensitive bud, still watching me with dark hungry eyes. My knees are bent on either side of him and press in with the intensity. He smiles and shakes his head slowly, moving his hands to my inner thighs and pressing them down, spreading them.

Moisture slips down into the crevice below my opening. I clench the comforter in my fists and curl my toes. "Fuck, Julie. Don't tease me." I squeeze my eyes shut, arching my back, begging him with my body to give me what it wants. Each expanse of breath creates friction between my T-shirt and nipples. They strain against the fabric, drawing Julian's attention.

"Want me to stop?" He places a soft kiss to my center after he asks.

"Uh-uh. You know I don't."

"Lose the shirt." I raise my eyebrows in question, and he nods slowly like *you heard me.*

I reach for his head, to pull him tighter to me, to make him give me what I want. Like a lightning strike, his hands snake under my bent knees and clamp onto my wrists, pinning them to the mattress. This holds my thighs up and apart while keeping me from touching him. I can't use anything except my words, so I do.

"Please, Julie. Ohmygod. I can't. I need . . ."

"Tell me, baby. Tell me what you need and I might give it to you."

"Kiss me. Ugh. Put . . . your . . . lips . . ." I raise my hips off the bed, trying to reach his mouth. His grip on my hands pulls my body like a bow, and I arch off the bed.

"Right here?" His lips surround the hardened bud and suck softly.

"Yesssss," I hiss. "Don't stop. Please."

But he does stop. "You want my hands on you, Ever?" He's kissing me, sucking me again.

"I do." I push my body down as much as I can into his face. My hands are squirming in his grasp to be free.

"I'm going to let you go. Take your shirt off and put your hands on your tits. Show me how you want me to touch you."

I meet his eyes and nod my head. I can't speak. As soon as he lets them go, my hands fly to the hem of my shirt and whip it over my head, then I plant my palms on my breasts, my nipples jutting between my spread fingers. I squeeze my index and middle fingers together, rubbing back and forth along the hardened nubs obediently, hoping it gets his lips back on me.

"Good girl, Ever. Feel good?"

Words trap in my throat. I want to thrash my head from side to side, clamp my eyes shut, but I keep watching him for some sign he's going to give me what I want.

"Answer me, Ever."

"Uhhhhh," I try to say, but it comes out a moan. And another, "Huhhhhh." My eyes are shut so tight now, they water.

"Pinch your nipples for me."

I comply.

"Harder," he commands.

I do it.

"Yes, baby. Good girls get rewards." He plunges two fingers inside me and scrapes his teeth along the sensitive bud before sucking it into his mouth.

I can't help the scream that rips from my throat or the tears that trail past my temples and into my hairline. My muscles contract around his fingers as they slide in and out of me. My breathing sounds like panting sobs to my ears.

Then he's there, his face next to mine a second before his hard length fills me thoroughly.

I suck in air at the sweet invasion.

He's kissing my ear, whispering to me. "I got you, Ever. My sweet Ever." His words begin to match the rhythm of his thrusts. "Ugh." *Thrust.* "So good." *Thrust.* "So sweet." *Thrust.* "Good girl." *Thrust.* "My girl." When my orgasm subsides, he slows his strokes and his lips kiss the tracks of tears on each side of my face. His body shakes with restraint. Still inside me but not moving, he touches his lips to mine. "Hi, pretty girl."

"Hi, Julie." My voice is hoarse.

"You feel good?"

I nod my head in answer, not trusting my voice.

"Yeah?"

I nod again.

"I love making you feel good."

More nodding, but I find my voice. "Are you . . . Did you . . ." I'm tracing his heart tattoo with my fingernail while my other hand floats up and down his back along his spine.

He shakes his head slowly, pinning me with liquid blue pools. He twitches inside me, still rock hard.

"Oh." My brain registers *plot twist,* right before he pulls out and flips me onto my stomach.

He's on his knees between my legs, pulling my hips up so my ass is off the bed while my face slides off the pillow and onto the mattress.

"Ready for another plot twist, sassy girl?" Before I can answer, he drives into me as he pulls my ass to his groin with a slap of skin on skin.

The moan it rips from my throat sounds feral.

He pounds into me with one hand on my breast and another reaching between my legs to circle my center.

I can't take all the sensations as my legs give, my lower body inching toward the mattress.

"Uh-uh, Ever. Bring that ass back to me." He slides his hand from my breast to my hip, pulling me back up and into him to meet his long, slow thrust. He freezes there, though it costs him. His arms tremble. "Be a good girl and take it, Ever. I know you like it. You're dripping for me. Tell me you like it. Tell me to fuck you."

"Fuck me, Julie. Fuck me till you come." I'm panting again with the force of his long, slow glide into me. Too slow. I want more. I fleetingly wonder if people ever hyperventilate from sex. The thought vaporizes with the circles he's drawing on my clit. His finger is slippery. So am I.

"Uh-uh. One more time, Ever. Come for me, baby. Then I will." As if on command, my walls start convulsing around him. He drives in harder. The hand on my hip holding me up slides around to my ass, and I feel his thumb dip into my slick opening where he's sliding into me. Slicking it with my come, he draws it back up slowly until he finds my other opening. He pushes his thumb softly against it, swirling it, moistening it, then harder.

It's like shock waves. So many nerves. My whole lower body clenches up and shudders. And still he drives into me, pulling all the way out and plunging in. His other hand circles my clit. All the sensations, the trembles, the animal moans—I can't control my body. It belongs to him. Every nerve ending is so heightened I feel a drop of sweat from his face hit between my shoulder blades like the prick of a needle just before his final thrust sends his body into its own shudders.

He finally allows me to sink to the bed as he does too, his body covering mine. He rolls onto his side, pulling me with him. His lips are parted on my shoulder, his heavy breathing making the spot warm and wet. As his panting slows, his lips press together, kissing my skin repeatedly. "God, I love you, Everly Davis." His arms tighten around me. His lips press against my shoulder again.

"I love you, Julian McKay. Plus, you're really good in bed, so, go me," I tease.

He smacks my ass loudly and rolls me to face him, pulling my thigh up to drape my leg over his hip. "Did I just hear you ask me for another plot twist? Because I might need a minute to accommodate my needy girl." He kisses the corner of my lip.

I crook my eyebrow in challenge.

Chapter 22

JULIAN

Everyone is making a big deal about my birthday, and it's got me a bit crazed. No one has ever made a big deal or even cared about my birthday until now. Except Taya a couple times after she found out. After twenty-two years, yeah. It's giving awkward self-importance vibes. Although Allie has tried the last couple of years to make me celebrate, even that was meager. I mostly indulged her because it was easier than protesting. She's all about energy and signs, and now that I'm with Ever, I've got to admit her logic tracks.

As a Libra, Julian, it's important you have strong social connections. It's in your nature. Your sign is ruled by Venus, the planet of love. You're drawn to love, beauty, harmony and relationships. Let people love on you.

So I'm letting these people of Blue Lake, that I love, love on me, as cheesy as that sounds. I only hope it's low-key. Plus, if it's going to be good for business and the brand, I'll suck it up.

"Hi, boyfriend." Ever bounces into the kickboxing room as my last class files out.

We're less careful now about PDAs. Mostly because everyone in a town this size already knows we live together at Allie's, which will soon be ours and kinda already is.

She wraps her arms around my sweat-drenched muscle-shirt-clad torso and kisses me on the lips.

"Hi, girlfriend. What can I do for you?"

She kisses me on the lips again, ignoring my sweaty skin.

I love that she isn't grossed out by sweat. In fact, I think she kinda likes it. I focus my eyes on her face and ignore the pull in my groin. *God, I hope we always want each other this way.*

"I need to know your favorite cake." She's enjoying this way too much.

I roll my eyes. "Cake too?"

"Duh. It's a birthday. There's always cake."

"What if I don't like cake?" I nuzzle her ear, inhaling her scent.

"You have to have cake." She reaches up and twists her fingers into the longer locks of hair on top of my head and tugs softly—her favorite thing since our *plot twist*. I let her pull my head away from her neck and look into her almost opaque eyes. "Or some kind of birthday dessert," she insists.

I ponder for a moment. "Can I have donuts?" I smile and peck her lips.

"Absolutely. I'll call Glaze of Glory tomorrow morning."

"My girlfriend is the best."

"I agree." She plants a kiss on me and turns to leave.

"Hey," I call out, stopping her. "Any plans for dinner tonight?"

"No. I actually have a couple big assignments due by midnight."

"Okay, cool. Pete asked if I'd swing by Brew and have a beer with him. Talk party details. It's weird I'm weighing in on my own birthday, isn't it? It feels weird."

"It's also the McKay Method launch day. Maybe think of it as your launch party. Either way, go hang out with Pete. I'll crank out my assignments and maybe enroll in the certification program."

"I thought you wanted to wait for summer break to do that."

"I think I can handle it. School isn't as hard or time-consuming as I thought. Especially now with Brew shut down till spring."

"Okay, Einstein. Knock yourself out. You riding back with me? I'm done for the day."

"Yep. I'm good to go when you are."

The domesticity of the entire conversation has me grinning like a lovesick puppy. It lasts all the way home. I shower quickly, change clothes and drop a kiss on Ever's head on my way out to meet Pete. With her earbuds in, books and laptop littering the coffee table and her butt planted on the floor in front of the couch, she barely looks up, blowing a kiss in my general direction. That she's locked-in makes me proud. My lovesick smile is back as I swing the door closed behind me.

***

"I think simple is always better." Pete takes another swig of beer and sets the icy bottle neatly on the coaster. Brew is empty, so we're sitting at a table in the center of the dining room. The view beyond the glass wall of windows is pitch black. We walked through all the details, including how to mirror Ashley's Zoom Room onto the big screen so the launch party from down south can be part of the birthday here in Blue Lake. Everything he mapped out looks tasteful but keeps the vibe of lake town.

I'm gratefully relieved. "See? This is why I need you running the show. You won't let this thing get out of control."

My answer is his low laugh. But he promised he'll keep it low-key. "Sometimes the celebration *for you* isn't *about you*. Sometimes it's about the people that care about you needing to show it. And in that case, it's up to you to find a way to let them because you care about them too." Pete quietly picks up his beer again and takes a long sip, staring into the darkness.

I don't know what to say, so I don't say anything. I just sip my beer too and wonder if Pete moonlights as a therapist. His words perfectly worm their way into my soul. I'd do anything for the people I care about—including indulging them in this birthday party, I guess. Downing the last of the hops from my bottle, I pick up Pete's empty bottle and drop them into the recycle canister. Shaking his hand, I say, "I appreciate you, Pete. And I'm counting on you to keep this thing small. If you can do that, I can let them . . . care about me." I say that with a wink so he knows I'm being sincere and not a smart-ass.

"You got it. You still coming by tomorrow?"

"Yep, after my Fit sessions. I've decided to keep the apartment. I want to expand it and use it for people that fly in and need a place to stay."

"Love that idea. Let me know if you want help. I love a good reno project."

"Will do. Have a good night, Pete. And thanks again." I push through the glass door and step into the pitch-black parking lot. It's later than I'd planned to stay. I wonder if Ever is still awake as I hop into the Jeep and steer toward home, my thoughts already consumed with her.

***

Although I have no solid reference or comparison, the birthday party was perfect—low-key but festive. Kicked back in the dining area of Brew, I swallow the lump in my throat as I reflect on the night.

"Did you have a good time tonight?" Ever wraps her arms around my neck from behind as I sit staring into the night, sipping the last of my beer like I had two weeks ago with Pete.

"I did." Setting my bottle on the table, I reach my hands up and rub them along one arm still curled around my neck.

With her other she reaches for my beer and tilts it to her lips. Once she takes a long sip, she returns it to the coaster and plants her cold lips on my neck. Almost everyone is gone now. I still hear Pete clanging a few dishes in the kitchen. Snaking one of my arms around her waist, I swing Ever onto my lap sideways. Covering my cheeks with her hands, she brings my face to hers for a lingering kiss.

Ever is bolder and more confident in our relationship now than she was even two weeks ago. It's like our *plot twist* dissolved any lingering shyness. She asks for what she wants or takes it, like now. Her kiss is hungry. Her tongue is cool, tangling with mine, and tastes like malt. I like it. It doesn't stay cool for long though. The kiss itself is heating my whole body and hers.

Pete clears his throat from the swinging doors of the kitchen behind us. "Goodnight, lovebirds. I'm out. Only thing left is to lock up."

We don't startle or separate immediately. Not anymore. We just stop kissing. I crank my head to look back, and Ever looks up over my shoulder. She's the first to respond.

"Thanks for everything, Pete."

"Yeah, man, it was perfect," I add.

"You bet. See you guys. Have a good night."

Ever returns her gaze to me and says, "It was perfect, wasn't it?" She's pushing her fingernails through the hair on my forehead and dragging them up along my scalp deliciously, making it hard to concentrate.

I nod as my eyes roll back, my lids drifting closed. "Mmm, it was. I'll give you ten years to stop doing that." I groan again at the lulling strokes of her nails.

A giggle bubbles in her throat as her lips find my neck again just before her whispery voice, raspy from all the talking, fills my ear. "Ready to go home?"

I nod, enthralled, her husky voice alone affecting me. This young woman owns me and I'm not sure she even realizes it.

"Okay, I'm going to get the leftovers from the kitchen. Two minutes . . ."

I nod again as she lifts herself off my lap and pushes through the swinging doors of the kitchen. I take the empty beer bottles from the table, stand and swivel to place them in the recycle canister just as the bell over the front door chimes. Expecting Pete, I turn and open my mouth as the word *hey* dies on my lips and the bottles in my hands slip and shatter to the floor.

"Hi, Jay." My jaw feels weighted, being pulled toward the floor. My eyes are tracking the blonde hair, a little darker and shorter than I remember, the face a little leaner. The eyes are the same. The lips. My ears prick. Her voice is the same.

How? "Taya?" My head is already shaking back and forth in disbelief. Every nerve ending tingles like a near-miss collision. My mind screams it's not possible. "How . . ."

"Sorry to just show up like this." Her smile is timid, but it's the same. It's hers.

What the fuck? *How the fuck is she here right now?*

As if in a trance, I step to her and reach out. Once my hands touch her arms and she's real, my fingers clench around her biceps. I squeeze and pull her to me with a slight shake. "How are you here right now?" My eyes are blurring and welling, the pressure behind them making my head pound.

"Jayce, you're hurting me." Her words snap me out of my trance.

I blink once, twice.

Then *her* voice hits me like a slap back to reality. My head pivots to the sound.

"Julian?" Ever steps into the dining room from the kitchen, arms full of containers. For home. *Home.* "Jayce? Who's Jayce? Who is this?" Her expression morphs from uncertainty to suspicion, then betrayal at the next words spoken.

"She doesn't know?" Taya's voice swings my head back to her, then back to Ever.

My head feels like it's stuck in a vice. Each heartbeat like a hammer to my temple. "Ever . . . I . . ." I track her deer-in-headlights look. I haven't seen it in a long time. It breaks me.

She slowly, deliberately sets the containers on the nearest table and begins backing toward the swinging doors—like she backed away from me that first day at Fit. She's spiraling. I can see it in every fiber of her being.

So am I, like I'm about to implode.

"What's going on, Julian? Who the fuck is this?" She braces her hands on the swinging doors behind her, still pinning me with saucer-wide eyes—eyes that start to swim with unshed tears.

"Taya." I release one of Taya's arms and hold my hand up to stop Ever's backwards steps. "But . . ."

"Taya, who died? So, what? You fucking lied?" She's pushing the doors open with her back as the first tear spills down her cheek, then another. She tilts her head and swivels it from side to side as she asks, "And why did she call you Jayce?"

"No. Ever. Don't." I hold my hand up to stop her as my foot takes a step toward her. "I didn't lie." I turn back to Taya. "I thought . . . He said you died." The swoosh of the kitchen doors whips my head back to where Everly stood, but she's gone.

"Stay," I command, releasing Taya's other arm, holding my hand up like a stop sign, and dash through the swinging doors. But I'm too late. The back door is wide open, and Everly is gone. Then I hear the Jeep motor start out front. I mentally curse this small town and that we leave our keys in our vehicles.

Coming back into the dining area, Taya hasn't moved. She's still here. Standing inside Brew. Very. Much. Alive. I stop just inside the swinging doors, just as Ever did moments ago, and watch her watch me. I must look like a dog that hears a weird sound. I even tweak my head sideways as I study her face.

Then she speaks again, snapping me out of the trance. "You thought I was dead?" It's her voice. It's really her. And she's moving toward me. "This whole time?" Her welled-up sea-glass eyes spill. Another step toward me. "That's why you never called, never came."

Like the streaks on her face, my legs turn to liquid. My knees sink to the polished concrete floor with a thud that sounds painful. I feel nothing. I reach for her. My fingers dig into denim-clad legs and pull them to me. Two shuffling steps and the denim brushes against my cheek. The smell of horses and hay and coconut, *her smell*, drops my mind back into the Bennick barn, transports me back in time, almost four years ago. The day Rusty Bennick discovered us half-naked in one of the horse stalls and threatened to kill me. The last time I saw Taya.

Her fingers threading into my hair just like Ever does snaps me out of my memory spiral. *Ever!*

Swiping my damp cheek across the leg it rests on, I stand and find my voice. "I have to go find her."

She nods slowly, her haunted liquid eyes never leaving mine. "Don't ..." My eyes scan the room like I'll find all my answers there. "Can you stay? Fuck. I feel like I'm unraveling here. This . . . It's too much." I hold my forehead in my hand and take one deep breath, then speak again. "Taya, I need to understand this. But I have to find Everly."

She nods. "Go, Jay. I'll wait for you."

Now I'm nodding. Relief flooding through my veins that I will get to Ever. I take her arm without asking and guide her through the glass doors and into the parking lot. "Those stairs . . ." I point toward my apartment stairs. "They lead to my apartment. The key is under the mat. Wait there. I'll be back as soon as I can."

She's swiping her cheeks with both hands—familiar hands.

"Taya, please don't leave."

She's nodding. "I'll be here. Promise." She gives me a sad smile and turns to walk up the stairs.

That I am clear-minded enough to lock up Brew reassures me I'm not going batshit crazy or in the throes of some delusional psychotic break. Once both the front and back doors are locked, I take off running. I make it back home in thirteen minutes. It felt like thirty. My Jeep is parked in the driveway. The front door is unlocked. Once inside though, the silence tells me she's gone before I confirm it for myself. Taking the stairs two at a time, I burst through our bedroom doorway. Her drawers are slightly open. Her bathroom things are gone. My breathing gets shallow as I race back downstairs, through the kitchen and laundry room, but I already know. I fling the garage door open. It's empty. Allie's 4Runner is gone.

Reaching into my back pocket, I swipe up to open my phone and check her location. It's off. *Fuck.* I call her, but I already know she isn't going to answer. It goes straight to voicemail. My heart rate thuds slower, my shoulders dip as I slide the phone back into my pocket. I don't even rub the raw ache in my chest. This is familiar. This is what Jayce Keller is, what he deserves. Nothing and no one. I slam the door shut, the sound of it rattling on the hinges satisfying. I slap both palms on it once, twice, repeatedly until the sting in my hands goes numb.

With my palms stretched above me flat on the door, I hang my head and struggle to collect my thoughts. She probably drove to Via. It's past ten o'clock. I don't want to call or text her this late. And what if Ever didn't go there? Then I worry Via. Where else would she go? Lilly is four and a half hours away. She wouldn't drive there right now. She's never been to SLO. She wouldn't do that in the middle of the night. My logical, level-headed, smart girl wouldn't. But that isn't the girl that ran out of Brew and turned off her phone. I've never seen her like that. I don't know what to do. Tapping one fist against the door while the other drags through the hair dipping onto my forehead, I beg the gods or the universe or whatever holy entity exists to keep her safe and bring her back to me. To me, *Julian*, and our life here. The life that is just getting started. The new business venture that is already setting records and promising to be not only lucrative but fun.

Why didn't I tell her about changing my name? It never came up. And that guy, Jayce Keller, is nobody. Nobody that matters. Julian McKay matters. He has a life and a career. Friends and a home. And a woman he loves, who loves him. *Right? She loves me. She'll come back. She'll talk to me. She'll understand. I don't even understand. Taya . . .*

I bend over, rest my hands on my knees and take three deep breaths. Standing, I walk back through the kitchen and into the living room. I look for my keys on the entryway table. Not there. I walk out the still-open front door and check the Jeep. They're inside. Removing them, I quickly lock the front door and slide into the driver's seat to go back to Brew. To Taya.

Chapter 23

Everly

"C'mere, sis, I got you."

"Don't hug me or I'll fall apart, okay. Just let me in. I gotta pee."

"For sure. First door on the left."

Once inside the tiny bathroom with the door closed, I let myself lose it a little. Just a little though. I turn the sink faucet all the way on so the water gushes into the sink just as a sob slips out. I pee quickly because I wasn't lying. I did have to pee badly. There were no open rest stops for about the last two hours of the trip—at least none without a high sketch factor. So I held it. It's now three a.m. and I'm mentally and physically exhausted. I don't want to play twenty questions with Lilly. I just want to sleep—if I can—and try to forget the last six hours of my life. Or maybe wake up and realize it was just a dream and I'm back home in Blue Lake with Julian. *Julian.* Who even is Julian? Taya called him Jayce. *Taya.* What the fuck even is my life right now? Another sob slips out.

My brain wants answers. My heart doesn't. If life had taught me anything, it's that nothing lasts. Especially the good things. And if Julian isn't Julian and our easy, happy life is over, I'd rather not know. I'd rather disappear and pretend like it never existed in the first place. Kinda fucking pissed I left my Kindle at home. *Home.* Do I even have a home anymore? That thought rips another sob from my throat.

"Davis, don't make me come in there."

"I know. I'm coming. Peed for like ten minutes." I open the door, and Lilly is leaning on the opposite wall, arms folded across her chest.

"What happened?"

"Can we just go to sleep and talk about it in the morning?"

"Yeah, okay. Whatever you need." Lilly slings her arm over my shoulder and walks me the three steps to her bedroom doorway.

"Nooo," I protest. "I can totally sleep on the couch."

"Nah, babe. I told you. I got you. Behold, the one-bedroom guest hack." She sweeps her hand wide like a game show host.

Her room housed a double bunk bed and was decorated in the coziest beach theme of blues, greens, burnt oranges and golden yellows. She used the space well. Every inch invited you to take a deep breath and relax.

So I did. And was again overcome with exhaustion. I didn't even unpack pajamas. Just dropped my clothes and crawled up the ladder and in between the sheets in my T-shirt and thong.

"Love you, Davis."

"Me too. Thanks, Lilly."

"Of course."

***

Sunlight streams through the window, hitting my face and blinding me. Not my window. Not my bed. I shoot up and almost smack my head on the ceiling. Then it hits me. It all comes crashing back through my brain. I flop back onto Lilly's top bunk and pull the covers over my face. *I want Julian.* A sob bubbles up in my throat. My eyes sting.

He's not even Julian, my mind screams.

This is what I get for thinking life can be like the books. In eight months, I'd gone from a virgin who'd never kissed a guy to living with one, thinking he's some real-life Prince Charming sent to earth for me alone. That he was perfect. That we were perfect. And I don't even know his real name. Is the story he told me bullshit? Some of it must be. His first girlfriend isn't dead like he said. I saw her. She called him Jayce. Not Julian. Another lie. Another sob erupts on a shaky breath.

What the actual fuck is happening?

"Chica? You awake?" Lilly's voice penetrates my rabbit hole spiral.

"Yeah, barely." I fling the covers off my head, tucking away my looming meltdown as she comes around the corner into the tiny bedroom.

"I got the whole weekend free. What are we doing? Drinking? Double homicide? I gotta know what to wear?" Classic Lilly pulls a smile to my lips.

It doesn't reach my eyes though. I want to laugh, but my heart stops it cold. The pressure is back behind my eyes. I'm fighting to keep it at bay, which makes me instantly furious. I'm not doing this. I'm not wallowing. I'm tough. A military brat. I let this supposed fairy tale make me weak, vulnerable. This is why I don't let myself depend on people. People leave, lie, hurt you. My about-face comes quickly. My resolve locks in. Whatever the fuck—whoever the fuck they are . . . I can't finish that thought. I won't let myself picture him. Her. Them. *Just no!* "I'm hanging on by a thread here. Can we just pretend I'm here for a friendly visit, ignore my drama for now and have some fun?"

"Hell, yeah, we can. I got you, girl. Let's go surfing."

"Wait. You surf? Lill, I can't surf."

She's already throwing off pajamas and digging through drawers for a change of clothes. She throws a pair of shorts and a hoodie at me. "Don't worry. I got an extra wetsuit, and we'll ask Noah and Seth to bring you a board."

"Great. So it's all figured out then." My sarcasm is impossible to miss.

She ignores it. "Exactly. Let's go, Davis. Move your ass. Negative ions, baby."

***

Pismo Beach is everything I need right now. And apparently fall and winter is peak weather—especially for surfing. Seth Koa, Noah (and Lilly's) new bestie, is an excellent surfer. Growing up on the island of Molokai, he's been surfing since he could walk, and it shows. Pismo waves are hardly a challenge for him, but it's a great beach for beginners. Noah has taken to the new sport . . . like a fish to water. My punny assessment raises the corners of my mouth for a hot second. Seth is a thing of beauty though. I wish I had my phone to capture what my eyes are seeing. But I've left it off so I can pretend—for now—that I can disappear from things I can't wrap my head around. I'll have to face it all eventually. But not today. Not right now.

Seth is walking in from the shore, his board tucked under his arm. Lilly and Noah are floating on their boards just beyond the break.

"You ready to give it a try, Davis?" He sets his board down and unzips his wetsuit, peeling the top half from his body to leave it dangling around his waist. The water droplets on his cinnamon skin are glistening in the morning sun, his pecs and biceps jacked from the wave he rode in. Even someone dead inside like I am right now can't miss it. This specimen of a man is smiling at me with perfect, straight white teeth and full pouty lips. I can see the draw and appreciate the simple earthy beauty in a detached way.

I lick my lips and squint up into his face, shielding my eyes from the sun with a hand to my forehead. "I think I'll be the spectator of the sport."

"Aw, c'mon. Pismo's perfect for beginners. Trust me. I got you."

His words transport me back. I feel the contents of my stomach, only coffee so far this morning, rising in my esophagus. I quickly roll onto all fours and crawl a couple feet before I hurl it onto the sand.

"Oh, shit."

I hear his words behind me as I swipe the back of my hand across my mouth. Twisting and planting my butt back in the sand, next to my vomit, I use my hand to swish sand over it. "Okay, that's embarrassing." I take a couple deep breaths through my mouth, not looking at him. "You know what, fuck it. Let's go surfing." I stand and reach behind me for the zipper on my borrowed wetsuit and pull. I look up then and meet his eyes—like melted chocolate with gold flecks that seem to sparkle in the sun.

He's nodding and smiling like he's proud of me.

That transports me too and pisses me off. I turn away and focus on the extra board lying next to his. It's big. And blue. *Like his eyes.* I shake my head to lose the image. Standing next to Seth in the wet sand, I ask, "Can we just practice the paddling part? I don't think I wanna try to actually stand up. I just . . . want to be in the water."

"Totally. I got you. Attach the leash right here." He motions to the line attached to the end of my board. "And we'll take the boards out about waist deep."

I nod, bend and attach mine like he demonstrates.

On the ten-minute drive here, Lilly told me Seth teaches surfing to tourists, which helps him pay for college. He's a good instructor, patient, thorough. I briefly wonder if he'll end up teaching for a living. He'd be perfect. Dr. Franklin's face pops into my head—my favorite teacher from Oak Valley, though not a teacher, a counselor. Still, she probably taught me more than anyone there. Maybe my brain is taking me back to when things felt simple, easy.

"How's the water?" Seth's voice brings me back to now. We're standing in the foam, the water swirling around my hips, swaying the board.

Nodding, I make myself focus on his words, the waves rocking against my torso. "Good. The wetsuit helps."

"Stretch out on the board while I steady it for you. Oh, wait." He tilts his head to look beyond me. "Check out Noah. Snagged a clean one."

We watch as Noah rides a wave in. He's fluid and impressive. I can see why it's become *his whole personality*, as Lilly claims. It's majestic to watch, even an amateur.

"Wow, he's so good." I shimmy myself onto my board as Seth steadies it with one hand while straddling his own.

"Right? My dude is a natural." He pumps his fist in the air to Noah, who copies him.

Folding my body in half, I lay my head down on the board, my hands tucked under it like a pillow, feet dangling on either side in the salty sea. Seth holds his hand out to me. I don't lift my head up and instead look at it like it's a snake ready to strike.

"C'mon. I'll get you beyond the break so you can float. The good news is Pismo is a great beginners' beach." He already said that, but I don't mention it.

"What's the bad news?" I side-eye him quickly and return my focus to the water and my board, still not taking his hand.

"No bad news really. Just paddling out isn't really a first step. You got me breaking the rules, Davis." His smile has a dimple winking at me. He drops his hand, lays down on his board and begins to demonstrate form.

I try not to zone out on the dimple and the images it conjures. Before I start to paddle, Lilly catches a wave and rides it for a few seconds before she falls. I feel my smile in my whole face this time. I close my eyes for a long blink. When I open them, Seth is watching me. We lock eyes. I wet my bottom lip and roll it into my mouth with my teeth. He tracks the movement. I turn my head back toward the sea and the waves rolling in, ignoring the weight on my chest and oscillating my hands through the water.

More than an hour later, my skin feels toasty, my eyelids heavy. A perfect day on the coast. Seventy-five degrees and clear. My arms burn from paddling, but in a good way.

"Anyone else hungry? Let's get breakfast burritos from the taco truck." Noah is stretched out between Seth and Lilly, arm flung over his eyes, not moving. In answer, my stomach growls.

Next to me, Seth quietly chuckles. "Davis wants one." He tilts his head toward me.

I track it in my periphery but don't turn my head. "I'm in," I say with forced pep I hope sounds natural. As the words leave my mouth, my stomach churns in protest. I hope food will help settle it.

"You'll love these, Ev. Best burritos ever." Noah stands and starts rummaging through his cinch sack. "C'mon, my treat. Who else?"

Lilly and Seth both raise their hands, not opening their eyes or otherwise moving from their flattened positions on their towels.

"Come help me carry them." Noah holds his hand out to me.

I clasp it tightly as he pulls me to my feet. We walk barefoot to the parking lot, where the taco truck serves a line of at least six wetsuit-clad surfers.

"Tell me a story, Davis." Noah parks a few feet behind the last patron and turns to face me, arms folded over his bare chest.

Swinging my hair as I shake my head side to side, I ask lightly, "Can we just pretend I missed you guys and wanted to see your new life? Besides, Lilly is the storyteller, not me."

Nodding slowly, like he's considering whether to push me on it or not, he wraps one arm around my neck in a half hug/half choke hold and kisses me on the cheek. "Okay, babe. Get ready for the best burrito of your life."

"I'm ready. Starving actually." And I am, I realize. Noah and Lilly meeting me where I'm at, no third degree, is calming my nervous system. But my cynical mind knows it's the calm before the storm, because I can't hide here forever. Still, I'll take my calm while I've got it.

Returning to our spot on the sand, the universe confirms it. Lilly holds up her phone to me, display showing an unread text from Julian. Or Jayce. Or whoever the fuck he is.

"Don't open it," I plead.

She inclines her head, pursing her lips in a tight thin line.

"Can we just eat our burritos first?" My voice sounds damn close to a whine, even to my own ears. And I don't whine. I clear my throat and add, "I don't want to ruin the best burrito of my life."

Lilly's heavy sigh and Noah's grinning nod give me my answer. She drops the phone on her towel and unwraps her burrito. Seth takes it all in but says nothing.

After we eat, Lilly doesn't waste time and circles back around. "I gotta respond. I can't just ignore him. What do you want me to say?"

Noah and Seth already paddled back out and float beyond the break, waiting for a set.

I guess the thirty-minute break after food that adults hammered into our brains isn't a thing. "I wouldn't ask you to lie for me. I just . . . I don't know. Fuck! How is this my life right now?"

"What the fuck even happened?"

"I don't know how to explain it or even understand it myself. But he lied to me. That much I know. I'm not sure I even know who he really is." Lilly's eyebrows shoot up, and I know she assumes this is a metaphor when I mean it quite literally. "Can you just say I'm here visiting for the weekend? What'd he text anyway?"

"'I'm sorry to put you in a weird spot, but is Everly with you?'" She closes the screen she read from and sets the phone face down on her towel, raising her eyes to me in question. I don't speak, but my eyes must beg for me because she concedes, "Yeah, I can say that." Picking her phone up again, she slides it open and reads her text out loud to me as she types.

Lilly: Yeah, she showed up last night to spend the weekend. I got her. Don't worry.

To me, she says, "Cool with that?"

I nod and blink away the pressure behind my eyes.

"Good. Don't make me a liar too. Let's make it a weekend for the books, yeah? I think the BRΩs are having a party tonight," she informs me, referring to Noah's unofficial fraternity. Her phone buzzes in her hand, making my heart jump in my chest. I don't have to ask. She reads it to me, then sets it back down.

Julian: Thank you.

"I guess I better turn my phone back on and text Olivia before she flips her shit. Or calls my mom. Or Allie. Fuck my life." I dig into my bag and draw my phone out with a shaky hand, pulse jumping in my wrists. I hold the button down to power it on, blowing out a long exhale through pursed lips, and watch as the notifications load one after the other.

Seven missed calls, one voicemail and a handful of texts. All from Julian. *Or Jayce.* I throw my phone down on my towel, pop up and stalk toward the wet sand just as Seth rides a wave all the way in.

He picks up his board and strides toward me and the shore. "Ready to try it again?" He shakes his wet hair loose, sending drops flying, and smiles at me with those straight white teeth, brighter against his tan skin.

"Ready to float again, maybe. The water feels amazing. Not sure I'll ever be ready to surf for real."

"Try a few pops. See if you get it enough to give it a try out there. You can use my board." He flops his board onto the sand and begins demonstrating the move. "First, do it on the sand a few times. Then switch to the board."

I follow his instructions and do about ten *surfer burpees* in the sand until my legs and arms quiver with the effort. I stand, shaking out my arms and kicking my legs a couple times.

"Impressive. You must work out. Wanna try the board now?"

I nod and ignore the comment about working out—mostly because of where it takes my thoughts. I straddle his board and plank on top of it before collapsing my full body weight. After a few deep breaths, I repeat the burpees on the board. Afterwards, I roll onto my back in the cool, wet sand and catch my breath.

"Going hard. I love it. We can rest before we take you out."

"No, I wanna go now." I spring up off the sand and walk back to our spot on the beach to grab my borrowed board.

Lilly squints up at me as I approach. "You gonna answer those?" She tosses her head toward my phone that's buzzing on the towel.

I shake my head before she's done asking the question. "Not right now. Right now, I'm going to surf. Coming?"

Shaking her head and smirking, she says, "Yeah, okay, Davis, let's go catch a wave."

***

Euphoric. After two hours in the water, I mastered standing up—three times. Only for a few seconds each, but I did it. I ate shit way more than three times. And now muscles I didn't even know I had hurt, but I don't even care. It was fucking incredible. Now I'm showered, changed and ready to go to my first frat party. Ish. Beta Rho Omega, or BRΩ, is a rogue fraternity, not recognized by the university. Mostly, it's just a bunch of wicked smart beach bums who like to drink beer and surf, which is why they call it BRΩ. Seems like a fuck you to traditional fraternity and sorority life, but they're too nice to be true assholes. More like an irreverent sense of humor. This I respect. I borrow clothes from Lilly. In my reckless haste, I grabbed handfuls of whatever was on top of my drawers and shoved them into a duffel bag and ran out the door. Mostly workout clothes because that's my life. Or was. Nothing matches or even makes sense.

Lilly is shorter than me but about the same size, so she lends me a pair of jeans that are long on her that work perfectly on me. With my Dunks and a cropped Guns N' Roses tee, my fit is on point for a frat-*ish* party.

Chapter 24

JULIAN

"Ever!" I wake with a start, her name a croak on my lips. It takes me a full seven seconds to remember where I am. I'm flat on my stomach. On my old couch. In my old apartment. I feel the indent of the cushion seam on my face. Squinting against the sunlight streaming in through the oversized glass slider, I sit up. It's later than I ever sleep. I can tell because the sun is high enough to light up the lake beyond the deck. It's blinding. My eyes burn. But that could be as much from lack of sleep as the glare.

"Jay?"

I drag my hands down my face and look up into a face I haven't seen in over three years—except for last night. One I thought I'd never see again. She's standing in the opening between the living room and the kitchen.

"Tay . . ." My voice comes out a gravelly whisper. I clear my throat and try again. "Taya. How'd, uh, you sleep?"

"I imagine same as you. Not good. But I found your coffee. Want some?"

I nod. I don't trust myself to speak. The last twelve hours have me clinging to my sanity with a death grip.

"Still black?" she asks from the kitchen.

"Uh . . ." I clear my throat again. "Yeah, thanks." I can't get my bearings. I stand, stretch once and walk the ten steps to the bathroom to take a piss. Inside the guest bath off the hallway, I splash cold water on my face and rinse my mouth in place of brushing my teeth. I'm a zombie going through these motions. I'm afraid to think about things too much, that it might break me. Again. But one thought won't stay down. *Ever!*

Throwing the door open, I stalk to the couch and retrieve my phone from the coffee table. Sliding it open, I scroll my texts until I get to Lilly.

Me: I'm sorry to put you in a weird spot, but is Everly with you?

I see the bubbles pop up immediately and wait. Then they disappear. I drop the phone onto the wood surface with a thud.

Taya moves into my periphery and extends a steaming mug to me. "Did you find her?" She sits down in the chair to the left of the couch and sets her mug on the table just as my phone buzzes.

Shaking my head in answer, I snag it off the surface and set the mug in its place.

Lilly: Yeah she showed up last night to spend the weekend. I got her. Don't worry.

My exhale is shaky. I sink to the couch and hastily type "thank you" in reply and drop the phone next to me on the cushion. With my elbows propped on my knees, I press the heels of my hands to my eye sockets and wait for the pressure building there to subside. I blow a couple deep breaths out through puffed cheeks and dropping my hands, I say, "She's with her best friend, Lilly." I don't meet her gaze but see her nodding in response.

"Will you go to her?" Taya is leaning all the way back in the chair, looking all kinds of relaxed. I know that can't be true. After everything we both discovered last night, there's no way. I've spent three years learning to channel my anger and sadness in a better way, and I'm barely hanging on. My knee is bouncing my elbow. My knuckles are white holding the mug of coffee. It's burning my palm, but I don't care. "I don't know. I don't think so." I look at her squarely now. "Lilly said she's visiting for the weekend. Maybe she didn't tell her anything. Maybe she's coming back in a couple days. Fuck. I don't know. I don't know what to do. With any of this."

"I know, Jay. Me either. I'm sorry I just showed up like that. When I found out . . . when I saw my dad's files—he kept tabs on you—I kinda lost it. Just got in my car and came here. To the address he had written down."

"I'm sorry for your loss." I say the words robotically. Then I hear Ever's words in my head. *You fucking lied?* I'm a lot of things, but I'm not a liar. "I'm not sorry he's gone," I add. "Honestly, I might've killed him myself if he weren't already dead."

Her eyes fill as she slowly nods. "I know. God, Jay, I'm so sorry. I can't imagine what that must've been like for you. I thought . . . He said you took money. That he paid you to leave. That if I tried to find you, he'd have you arrested. For rape."

"I know. I remember it all from last night. Can we not relive it? Especially the part where you didn't come find me after you turned eighteen. When he didn't have a say."

"You know the statute of limitations in California extends till I turn forty, right?" Her sass takes me back, haunts me, and reminds me of the sassy girl with gray eyes that's crushing my soul right now, making it hard to breathe. *My girl.* "But I did try, Jay."

Her voice brings my eyes back to her face. Yanks me out of my head and the storm-cloud eyes I see there.

"Your phone went straight to voicemail. Texts didn't deliver. No social media. You became a ghost."

"I crashed my bike the night he told me you died. Smashed my phone, my head and a few ribs. Jayce Keller sort of died that night too. Started going by my middle name and my mom's maiden name. So he'd leave me alone."

She's nodding again. Her eyes are sad, but at least the tears are gone.

"Actually, that's a lie. It wasn't conscious or calculated. It just came out. Julian. When Allie—my business partner—asked my name the night I crashed."

More nodding. "Wow, Jay. Business partner. It's incredible what you've built for yourself." She's smiling now, but it doesn't reach her eyes. It's a sad smile that pulls at my heart.

I involuntarily start rubbing the spot on my chest.

I don't acknowledge the compliment and rudely ask instead, "What will you do now?" Part of me asks because I want her to go away so I can pretend my life didn't just burn to the ground with her reappearance. Part of me wants to help her make sense of the bomb that dropped on us both.

She spreads her hands wide and shakes her head, then she rakes her fingers through her blonde hair, the gesture so familiar I watch as if in slow motion. Her being here in my old apartment close enough to touch, smell, is fucking with me. It's playing with my mind and my memories. Every tug on my heartstrings is superimposed with an image of my life with Ever. *Ever!*

I'm thanking whatever superpower that's in charge that I didn't text or call Via. If Ever wants to tell her sister anything, that's up to her. I know Lilly is loyal to Ever and will take care of her at least. Via would likely involve their mom and maybe Allie. I have nothing to hide. I just don't know what Ever's thinking and I don't want to have to explain this to everyone we know. Hell, I don't want to explain it to myself. This is beyond insane. And maybe that's the crux of it all. Rusty Bennick was certifiable. Controlled everyone around him with his power and money.

"Part of me wants to burn it all down. Literally set fire to the whole goddamn house. I really didn't know the depths of his twisted control. Through the lens of a kid, it came off like he was just an overprotective, over-religious father of an only daughter. What an asshole." Her laugh is humorless.

I laugh despite the heavy topic. "That he was."

"Maybe I'll put the place up for sale. I'd need to find a home for Sugar and Cookie."

"Oh my God, Sugar and Cookie are still around?"

Her laugh is real. The same as I remember. "Uh, yeah, Jay. Horses live like twenty-five to thirty years."

"Right. I knew that." I didn't. "Do you still ride?"

"Law school doesn't allow me much time, but yeah. Occasionally."

"Law school." I don't say it like a question, but I'm curious.

"Yeah, I guess all his threats and control took me down a rabbit hole of curiosity-turned intrigue-turned-career choice."

Her explanation shoots my brows into the hair dipping onto my forehead. The domino effect of one man's control masquerading as love. It sends my thoughts literally crashing into my life as I know it. Ever's words slam into my frontal cortex. *I would've never met you, Julie. And I wouldn't take that back. Not even to erase all that.* The day she told me that, I realized I wouldn't either. But now here it is—my past, Taya, alive and well and in my present—and Ever is gone. For good? I can't let my brain go there. I can't breathe if I do. She'll come back. It's just the weekend. I can distract myself for three days—the three days we took off. For my birthday. See? My birthday is nothing to celebrate. But I am grateful Allie and Ashley will not need me or otherwise miss me for the next three days. Maybe by then, everything will be back to normal. Who the fuck am I kidding? Normal has left the building and possibly the stratosphere. Despite the alternate universe we seem to have dropped into, I reach for normalcy. "Are you . . . hungry?"

"I could try." She says it like she's trying to get the right answer on a test. "I'm more curious than hungry. Can I . . . Will you show me your life?" Her smile, though still sad, makes it to her eyes and lifts her cheeks.

It makes my chest ache for what we lost, then spirals me right back into what I stand to lose, and might lose, now. Everly floats through my mind like an apparition—smoky eyes, pixie nose, pouty bottom lip, wisps of chestnut hair that smell like sunshine, long fingers that wrap around my neck and graze the fade of hair behind my ears, legs that wrap around me so perfectly. Rubbing the spot on my chest, I stand. "Let me change and I'll show you the fitness club. Do you need

. . ." I note she's wearing the jeans and tee she showed up in last night. "Want a change of clothes?"

"I mean, I wouldn't say no to a pair of sweats."

"Ever has . . ." I trail off. What am I doing? Am I really acting like any of this is normal?

"No, Jay, it's fine. I'm fine." She stands too.

"No, it's all good. I'll be right back." My politeness kicks in again. "Oh, there's a spare toothbrush, toothpaste in the front bathroom. Extra toiletries for guests. Help yourself."

She nods as I squeeze past her and the coffee table and disappear into the bedroom to change out of the clothes I slept in. I close the door and zero in on the made bed. The bed she slept in—on—last night. Taya slept here. Taya *is* here. Alive. And *here*. And Ever isn't. *Just breathe.* I brace my arms on the edge of the bed, hang my head between them and count my breaths. Once my breathing returns to normal, I snag fresh joggers, boxers and a shirt from the dresser. Then, I take out leggings and a tee from the drawer of Ever's clothes. I can't help it. I press them to my face and inhale. They're clean and smell like laundry. Not sunshine. God, I miss her.

Chapter 25

EVERLY

Music vibrates my chest and pulses in my ears. The BRΩ house is at capacity. Really, it's just a regular house that a handful of guys share, but it looks like every movie image of a frat party I've ever seen. Bodies everywhere holding solo cups, a kitchen littered with half-full bottles, a small crowd gathered around a keg and another around a heated game of beer pong.

Lilly, Noah and Seth move like a single unit through the bodies and sweep me along with them. Lilly squeezes my hand she's holding as Seth presses a foaming solo cup into my free hand. Noah hands one to Lilly, and she taps her cup to mine. We take a sip together.

The beer is refreshingly ice cold. I take another bigger gulp. Seth tracks my swallowing as he downs half his cup in one gulp. I can't tell if it's the beer or his stare that makes my stomach feel twirly. The adrenaline spike has me gulping more beer though. In two swallows, my cup is empty. I hand it to Seth, who fills it back up with a nod and a grin. We're standing at the kitchen island. Noah and Lilly are greeting the girls currently concocting some pitcher of bright pink liquid. Noah snags four Jell-O shots off a tray and passes them out to the three of us. I down it without hesitation. I want to dull my nervous energy. And I don't want to think about my life back home. If I even have one anymore.

As the familiar guitar riff of AC/DC's "You Shook Me All Night Long" erupts through the house. I grab Lilly's hand again and cry, "Let's dance." But she's already shaking her head.

"You go. Noah and I are about to school these clowns in pong."

"I'll dance with you, Davis." Seth slings his arm over my shoulder and steers me toward the living room, crowded with several jumping, swaying coeds shouting the lyrics word for word.

Draining my solo cup, I toss it back onto the kitchen bar and move with him, my head beginning to buzz. We join the group, moving to the beat, shouting the lyrics too. The DJ must love old-school rock because AC/DC flows right into "Patience," my favorite Guns N' Roses song. As old-school rock goes, this isn't a common choice.

Seth slides his hands up and down my hips and pulls me close.

I let him, even though it feels wrong. His touch is wrong. His smell is wrong. It's all wrong. But tonight, wrong is better. No piercing blue eyes. No fingers that curl around my ear. No lips that—

Axl Rose's voice interrupts my doom spiral.

"I love this song," I lean in near Seth's ear and blurt over the music and noise. "It reminds me of my dad."

"Does he like GNR?" he asks loudly to be heard.

I'm smiling, but I shake my head. "He did. He died in Afghanistan when I was twelve."

"Fuck, Davis. I'm sorry."

"No, it's okay. I'm okay. I like that I have this reminder." I keep swaying with him, smiling, my wrists resting on his shoulders.

His eyes, golden in the dim lights, lower to my lips. His lashes are long, dark and curl perfectly.

Why are lashes like his always wasted on guys? He's so pretty. A total thirst trap. Because I'm thirsty. A giggle bubbles in my throat at my train of thought. I lick my lips, craving another beer, liking the buzz in my head.

With the slightest pressure, he pulls my hips toward him.

I close my eyes and lean in just as the song ends. I open them and he's watching me, our noses almost touching. Realizing what almost happened, I step back and blink, breaking the . . . whatever that was. I'm getting dangerously drunk, but this level of numb feels so good. "I want another beer," I announce and step out of his arms.

"Anything for you, babe." He steps back too but takes my hand and turns toward the kitchen.

Lilly and Noah are still at the pong table. She's standing in front of him, his arms around her. Noah cheers loudly and kisses her on the cheek. It makes me smile, but my cheeks feel rubbery.

"Looks like they're winning," I say over my shoulder as Seth fills another solo cup for me.

"Yeah, it's what they do." He holds his cup in salute to Noah.

Noah puts his hand to his forehead like a military salute in response.

Lilly and I make eye contact, and she tosses her head to me like "You good?"

I toss mine back in confirmation. Even in my beer haze, I love that we can communicate without words. She's the best friend I've ever had. The only friend. I shake off the sad turn my thoughts take. No sappy bullshit tonight. Just beer and fun and forgetting.

"C'mon, let's go check out the firepit." Seth snags a bottle of clear liquid off the bar, takes my free hand and leads me through a slider into the backyard.

***

"How'd you end up with a house like this? On the beach?" It's just us in the backyard now, sitting in two of the plastic Adirondacks around the fire pit. I stamp down the image it conjures of the Brew fire pit. Brew's chairs are wooden, heavy. The view is a lake. But the parallels are undeniable. I sip more beer to blur it. The beer is almost too warm to drink now. I reach for the bottle Seth brought out and read the label. Casamigos Blanco Tequila. *House of Friends. Appropriate.* It makes me smile. I zero back in on Seth's voice.

"It's a VRBO my parents own, but they rent it to me for college. I charge these feral fuckers"—he waves his hand toward the house—"and easily make my rent."

"That's a sweet arrangement." I twirl the bottle in my hand, watching the liquid swirl.

"Can't complain. It's a clean setup. Close to school. Close to surfing." He nods his head thoughtfully. "Yeah, a damn good flex."

Reaching for the bottle, Seth's fingers brush mine as he takes it from my hands. He twists the top off with a plonk and takes a healthy swig. Swallowing with a grimace, he hands the open bottle to me.

Bringing it to my lips, I inhale through my nose first. It smells surprisingly light and clean. Tequila usually smells more like nail polish remover. I take a tentative sip. *Smooth.* I take another bigger sip. It warms my throat and my belly when it lands. Swallowing a few more times to relieve the slight burn, I pass it back to Seth, who's watching me with those golden tiger eyes.

Pressing the cork back on the bottle, he drops it to the grass and holds out his hand. "Let's go to the beach." He stands as he says it.

I take his hand and allow him to pull me out of the chair and lead me down to the shore. The path is dark, but the moon is almost full and lighting our way. Once we're standing on the sand, I slip off my Dunks, then my socks and stuff one into each shoe. Seth kicks off his flip-flops, leaving them where they land, so I set my Nikes next to them. Even the dry sand is cool between my toes, causing a shiver to roll up my body.

Seth peels off his hoodie, plops it over my head and pulls it down to my hips.

I push my arms through the sleeves and reach up to pull my hair out of the neck at the same time he does. He lets his hands fall to my shoulders and pins me with a hungry stare. That hunger brings Julian's face to mind.

I close my eyes to block it out—an accidental invitation. When I do, Seth's lips touch mine. They're cool, soft. Different. Not Julian's. I don't pull away. Like a weird test or comparison, I let him kiss me. Once. Twice. He tastes like tequila. Not like Julian. I've only ever kissed *him*, so this feels wrong and reckless, dangerous even. I'm glad it's different. I don't want to think about Julian. *Or Jayce.* Or Taya. Or liars. I lean into him and tip my head slightly, invite him to deepen the kiss. He does. His mouth opens, and I feel his breath on my lips.

His tongue brushes my lower lip before it slips past it to caress mine. Soft like his lips. With his fingers in my belt loops, he pulls me to him and wraps his arms around me.

My hands reach up to tangle in his hair. It's wrong too—long, parted in the middle and dipping just below his ears. I pull on it lightly, fusing our mouths tighter together.

It elicits a low moan from his throat. The sound is off. It's not the voice that makes my tummy flip, but it flips all the same.

Sliding his hands down, he cups them under my ass and lifts me. My legs instinctively wrap around him. It's not *his waist*. We don't fit the same. He's strong but slender. *This is wrong.* My hazy brain is screaming at me through a vortex. It dimly registers but not enough.

He drops to his knees with me in his arms and lays me back on the sand, covering his body with mine.

The swift swinging motion makes my head spin. Lying flat doesn't stop the spinning. His face closes in to kiss me again, but I halt him with both hands on his chest. I shove him hard and roll over just before I lose the contents of my stomach. Again.

"Shit," I say after heaving and catching my breath. I note that Seth is holding my hair. "Sorry. Again." I turn over and plant my butt next to his in the sand in an all too familiar scenario. *Great. I'm the barf girl.* Sweeping sand quickly over my upchuck spot, I sit up, prop my elbows on my bent knees and hold my head in my hands. After a few quick gulps of salt air, my stomach settles.

"Yeah, what is it with you and beaches?" He opts for humor, and I'm grateful for it.

"It might have more to do with the tequila this time. Or all the beers. I'm not really a drinker."

"Special occasion?" That he keeps it light is the only thing staving off the hysteria bubbling just below the surface, threatening to take over.

"Something like that." Still holding my head, I turn it sideways to look at him.

He's resting his cheek on his knees, arms wrapped around his calves, watching me. Half of his face is in shadow, the other illuminated by the moonlight. "So what's your story, Davis?"

I can see half of his close-mouthed smile. "Hmph," I snort. "It's not a good one, Seth. In fact, I came here to forget about my life. For a few days anyway. Cool?" He nods in response, so I add, "Help me forget." His eyes go dark with unmistakable hunger, and I realize my inadvertent invitation. I quickly amend my statement. "Lilly said you grew up in Hawaii on Molokai. What's that like?"

His smile is kind, understanding. I lie back on the cold sand and stare up at the black sky littered with stars. He stretches out on his side and props his head in his hand, facing me. "Small." His laugh is a deep rumble in his chest.

It makes my stomach twist because it reminds me of another deep laugh. One I love. I squash it. "Tell me stories, Seth. Help me forget." I fold my hands over my stomach.

One of his hands reaches out and rests on top of mine. It's warm. Then I hear his voice. It's warm too.

"What do you want to know?"

I ignore the pressure behind my eyes. "Tell me about the first time you learned to surf."

"I was three." His fingers trace slow circles on top of my clasped hands, warming them.

His voice is like a melody. It soothes me. I stare at the stars and hang on every word.

Chapter 26

JULIAN

"It's incredible, Jay. Or should I say Julian? I mean, you're kinda famous." Taya is standing in the middle of the kickboxing room at Fit and turns to smile at me. "Proud of you."

"Thank you." I smile back. My first genuine smile since she showed up, even if it doesn't reach my eyes. Seeing her here in my space, in the life I created, being able to show her what I've made of myself, hearing her say she's proud of me, is like the validation I didn't know I needed. I don't have parents showing up to tell me they're proud of me. No one from my past is even part of my life now, not that there were many—or any. She's pretty much the only person who knew me when I was a kid—a teenager, anyway—and ever made me feel like I mattered. It feels nice and . . . normal to have someone in my corner who knew me before.

"Hey, Julian. What a nice surprise." Sylvie's voice pierces the moment. She's leaning half her body through the glass door of the kickboxing room. "You teaching a surprise class today?"

"Hey, Sylvie. Nope. Still taking the weekend off. Thanks for coming to the party last night." I try to sound normal, then turn back to Taya to hopefully end the conversation. No such luck.

"Of course. We wouldn't have missed it," she replies with her lip-sticked smile, referring to herself and the rest of my clients that came. "And who's this? A new member?"

Closing my eyes while still facing Taya, I start to turn to answer when Taya speaks up.

"No, I'm an old friend from high school, just passing through. Wanted to see the place."

"Oh, how nice, dear. Well, enjoy the tour. Gotta get to my workout." She wiggles her fingers in goodbye and dips back out the door.

Taya bursts into a tinkling laugh once she's gone, which makes me laugh.

For a second or two, I forget. I feel the laugh in my chest. Then *her* face slams into my head. The reminder of what a shit show my life has become overnight. "C'mon, let's get out of here before I get hit up for questions or demos."

"Or autographs?" Taya teases.

"Nah, I'm not famous here," I deadpan.

She rolls her eyes and laughs again.

The sound sends a warm glow to my gut. *Taya's alive and here.* I'm insatiably curious about her life. I guess the feeling is mutual.

Once we're out the front doors of Fit and settled into my Jeep, Taya asks, "Will you tell me about the rest of your life?"

"What do you want to know?" Not in the habit of oversharing, I fall back on my default of answering a question with a question—what my old therapist would call deflection or avoidance, something I guess

I learned from my childhood. I amend it with, "I'll tell you whatever you want to know." And I mean it. I want to know everything about her too. That she's had a life to live the last three years is inexpressible. It makes my heart hurt but in the best way. I rub my chest with my palm as I drive one-handed.

"I want to know about it all, especially the girl. But start with where we left off and don't stop. But . . . can we just drive? Hey, wanna go see Sugar and Cookie?" She turns sideways in her seat. "I bet they miss you."

I grip the steering wheel with both hands, knuckles going white. She tracks the tension.

"He's gone, Jay. It would just be us and maybe Mitchell, the caretaker my dad hired a year ago." She's looking at me to gauge my reaction.

I nod slowly. I'd probably agree to whatever she wants right now. "Okay."

"Okay? Really?"

"Yeah, Taya, we can go." Her name feels foreign in my mouth but familiar. My grasp on reality feels tenuous. I wonder, not for the first time, if it's too early to drink—and I don't drink. Speaking of drinking, I decide to start there. "After he caught us . . . found us that night and threatened to have me arrested, I tried calling and texting you. When you didn't respond, I knew—"

"He took my phone."

"Yeah." I nod and resume my death grip on the steering wheel. I see it in my mind like it's yesterday, but I haven't pictured it in years. "After trying to reach you by phone for almost twenty-four hours, I went back to your house and banged on the door. I had some half-cocked idea I'd just bust in there and take you away." One side of my mouth quirks up as I quickly glance over at her in the passenger seat.

The windows are down, and her golden strands drift across her face. Her green eyes look sad.

I turn back to focus out the windshield so I don't have to see them.

"He sent me to boarding school that day. Didn't give me a choice. Said he'd have you arrested if I didn't go." She tucks her hair behind her ears, but it still swirls across her lips and nose.

I swipe my hand down my face and drop it into my lap. When I blow a heavy sigh out through puffed cheeks, Taya puts her hand on top of mine and squeezes. Nodding, I say, "I know. I, uh, I kinda lost it after that. Got shit-faced drunk. Stole the alcohol from my parents and drank in one of the empty stalls until I passed out."

"One of our stalls?" I see her eyes go wide in my periphery and nod.

"He found me there the next morning. That's when he started threatening me with words like statutory rape. I left so he wouldn't call the cops—left my bike there and walked home. For the rest of that week, I stayed drunk. At the trailer. If my parents noticed, they didn't care. It must've been three or four days. When I finally went to get my bike, I went to the front door first. I had some wishful thinking that he'd calmed down and would tell me where you were. That's when he told me you weren't coming home. That you took a bunch of pills, and it was my fault. That if I'd never come to work for him, he'd still have a daughter." I stop to take some deep breaths.

Taya's hand covering the back of mine is gripping it so tight that her knuckles are now white.

I look down at her hand and turn mine over in hers. Our fingers intertwine and we both squeeze. I don't want to tell her the next part—mostly because I don't want to relive it. I take one more deep breath and begin. The short version.

"I took off on my bike, drunk. I stopped and got more to drink and just kept going. I was going too fast, taking turns, and I think I was . . . trying to die." I see her swipe her other hand along her cheek. "I crashed in front of Allie's house. She helped me. She gave me a job. I learned everything I know from her. I owe everything I am to her." I hope the CliffsNotes version will suffice.

She pulls our joined hands into her lap and covers them with her other. "What an asshole," she breathes, like she's shocked.

I laugh because it's such an understatement for the evil he did to us. "Yeah," I concur. We pull up to the entry gate of her property. It's a new entrance with an automatic iron gate, a giant iron B on the arch.

She rummages through her bag and produces a remote, taps it and the gate begins its slow swing to allow us entry.

"That's new."

"He installed it right after . . . " She lets the rest of that sentence hang unspoken. She motions for me to keep driving past the house and around to the barn.

It's as picturesque as I remember. I stop the Jeep in front of the wooden picnic table on the side of the barn. It's showing signs of weather and almost ready for another makeover.

She says what I'm thinking. "It's held up well."

"M-hm," I answer absently, lost in time. I open my driver's door almost in a trance, like I'm being pulled through a portal. I step into the shade of the barn, where the lack of sun drops the temperature.

An older man pushing hay and debris through the far doors stops and turns to greet us. He's not as old as I thought. His skin just looks weathered, probably from years of working outdoors. He props the push broom against the nearest stall and moves toward us. "Hey, Taya." He greets her casually as he extends his hand to me. "Hi, I'm Mitchell." His handshake is firm, strong. His eyes kind. He's wearing a ball cap backwards, straw-colored hair curling around the edges and poking out through the hole on his forehead. His eyes look like heavily creamed coffee. As he finishes shaking my hand, his eyes track back to Taya and linger. Too long. His eyes move over her face. His expression softens as he smiles at her.

It raises the hairs on the back of my neck and sends a surge of . . . jealousy . . . to my gut. Who is this fucking guy? *The ranch hand. Like I used to be.* I dislike him immediately, despite his welcoming kindness.

"Jay—uh—Julian," I reply late, awkwardly.

Taya speaks up, "He's my . . . An old friend . . . from high school."

"Nice to meet you, Julian." Mitchell smiles at me, but it fades as he notes my expression.

I can feel the frown between my eyes. I intentionally relax my features and smile back. "You too, Mitchell." I make myself say his name and look him squarely in the eye, exactly like I'd address a client or business acquaintance. He's not my enemy or my competition, I remind myself. So why am I acting so territorial?

"C'mon. Let's go see your girlfriend. I'm sure she missed you."

My heart drops into my shoes. Ever's face swims before me like a mirage. I know Taya means her horse. I refocus my brain on the now, my eyes on the familiar stall, and move my feet toward it.

"Jay used to work here in high school," Taya calls back to Mitchell as we move through the barn.

"Yeah? And which one is your girlfriend? Wait. Lemme guess. Sugar." His words are met with Taya's affirming giggle. "She's such a flirt."

"She's such a flirt." Taya and Mitchell say it at the same time. Then laugh together at their timing.

I feel out of place. Like a third wheel. I rub the spot on my chest as I move to Sugar's stall.

"Here, try these."

I turn at the sound of Mitchell's voice behind me as he pulls a couple carrots from his back pocket. I take them and nod a thanks, not trusting my voice. I don't know if Taya and Mitchell are a thing, but I know that look. The one on his face. Because I used to have it too. I place my hand on the top of the stall.

Sugar pauses her grazing and eyes me. Trotting over to the gate, she whinnies and tosses her head. She nuzzles my hand. Then she drops her head over the top of the gate, trying to nudge me.

I offer her a carrot and rub her soft nose. "Hi, pretty girl. You remember me?" She tosses her head at me again as if to say yes.

Behind me, Taya and Mitchell softly laugh.

"I think it's safe to say she does." Taya steps next to me and scratches behind the ears. "Right, Sugar? We didn't forget."

She says "we" not "you" and it makes my heart bleed, my eyes sting. I turn and stalk out of the barn and around the corner to the old picnic table. *My* picnic table. I sit on the surface and prop my feet on the attached bench, resting my arms on my thighs. Staring across the rolling hills of their pasture, I take a few deep breaths, but I can't stop the pressure behind my eyes. I press my thumb and forefinger to them to try. Pinching the bridge of my nose, I once again attempt to wrap my brain around this reality. The one that doesn't feel real but is right here in front of me.

Then I feel her hand on my shoulder, her hips sliding next to mine on the table, her body heat. "Hey. You okay?" She leans toward me, her hair swinging forward, brushing against my arm.

"No, Taya. I'm not," I add pointedly. "Are you?" I drop my hand and turn my head to look at her. We're so close I can count the freckles on her nose. My body reacts to her on its own. My pulse speeds up, her pull undeniable, but it's not me, Julian. It's me, Jayce. Eighteen-year-old Jayce Keller. Young and in love. It's like I've found a time machine or fallen through some portal to the past. Being this close to her, in this place, fucks with my head. I lift my hand to her face.

Her eyes close and she exhales through barely parted lips. Her breath kisses my lips.

"Jay." She says it like a plea. "We can't. You love her. I saw how much."

"I loved you too. I think I still do." A tear slips down my face.

She traces it with her finger, then cups my cheek in her hand. "Not like you love her. Maybe you love the memory of us." She drops her forehead to mine. "We didn't deserve this, Jay. But we aren't those kids anymore."

I close my eyes and, in the middle of my exhale, feel her lips touch the corner of mine. I reach my other hand up to cradle her face. Her cheek is damp like mine. I want to kiss her back. But it's not me now, it's time machine me.

Mitchell clears his throat behind us, breaking the spell. We don't spring apart like we're caught. We just separate. As Taya said, we're not those kids anymore.

"Hey, Mitch." Taya turns her head toward him and rests her chin on her shoulder.

"I saddled them up like you asked. I'm going to head out now if that's all."

"Thanks." She turns her face back to me, one eyebrow lifted, and says, "You remember how to ride?"

Yeah, thanks, Mitch. Man to man, your timing couldn't have been better. What the fuck are you doing, Julian? Lock it the fuck up. I rub the spot on my chest as I try to mirror her grin. "I think so. Not sure joggers and gym shoes are the right fit for it, though." Still, I hop off the table and follow her into the barn.

Chapter 27

Sitting up, I drape the bottom of Seth's hoodie around my drawn-up knees. The coldness of the sand is seeping through the butt of my jeans, making me shiver a little.

Seth notices and stands holding his hands out to me. "C'mon. Let's head back in and see what 'Nolly' are up to." He uses air quotes on the nickname for Noah and Lilly.

I giggle and take his hands, letting him pull me to my feet. "Is that what we're calling them now?"

Seth drapes his arm over my shoulders as we aim toward the house.

My head is clearer now. The buzz likely dwindling from vomiting. I want to rinse my mouth. I ask Seth to point me toward the bathroom once we're back inside. The house is quieter now. Music is still playing but it's background noise. In the bathroom, I find toothpaste in a drawer and use it to rinse the taste of barf and alcohol out of my mouth. I can't stomach the idea of more alcohol, and my body is mentally and physically exhausted from the shit show of the past twenty-four hours. I wander down the hallway to the master bedroom, Seth's, he told me earlier. Sitting on the edge of the mattress, I flop back, stretching out sideways, dipping my head over the side and looking upside down at the ceiling. Finally ready to look at my messages, I pull my phone from my back pocket.

Thirteen texts now. All from Julian. He must not have called my sister. Or Allie. For that, I'm grateful. I listen to the voicemail first.

Everly, please answer. It's not what you think. None of this is what you think. Please.

I open my texts next.

10:36 PM

Julian: I didn't lie to you. I wouldn't.

11:02 PM

Julian: Ever, please answer me.

11:38 PM

Julian: Please text me back. Or just come home.

11:45 PM

Julian: I love you.

Julian: Please come home.

10:02 AM

Julian: Lilly said you're with her.

Julian: Please be safe. Please.

Julian: I swear I didn't lie to you.

Julian: I love you, Ever.

It's been over twelve hours with no new texts. Part of me expects him to show up here. Another part of me wonders if he's with *her*. He said he didn't lie. If he didn't, then he thought she was really dead. I need to hear what he has to say. Or has he given up on explaining? Is he done trying to convince me to talk to him? Will he be waiting for me at home? Do I even have a home anymore? What we have is real. Right? More real than what he had with Taya? We did rush into everything. I went from my first kiss ever to living with a guy in a matter of months. Who does that? Someone with no life—ready to grab the first one offered to her. That's who. Am I so delulu that I thought we'd be the real-life fairy tale? The one that defies all odds? *Stupid! Naïve! Dumbest smart girl on the planet.*

"Hey, boo. You good?" Lilly's upside-down image appears, her head peeking through the door of Seth's bedroom.

I roll over, phone in hand and smile. "I don't even know. I think I need to go home."

"Okay, but maybe not right now." She walks over and plops onto the bed and stretches out next to me. "Maybe in the morning?"

I nod and roll back over onto my back, holding my phone over my head, staring at the screen.

She adds, "Did you text him back?"

"No, I just finally read all his. I should text him. But it's . . ." I check the display on my phone. "Eleven twenty."

"Girl, don't even act like he would mind. Man is probably crying in his beer waiting for you to call."

"Or he's with her."

"What are we doing, ladies? Crashing out?" Noah ambles into the room looking every inch the drunk frat boy. Seth follows on his heels, steadier on his feet. Noah plops onto the end of the bed next to Lilly, and Seth flops on the other side of me and wedges himself between me and the pillows at the head of his bed. That they all treat this as normal makes my radar. Maybe this is what my life would be like if I'd gone away to college. A coed friend group I feel comfortable lounging on a bed with—in the middle of the night. Noah and Lilly seem perfectly at ease—although that may have more to do with alcohol-lowered inhibitions.

"My girl, Ev, wants to go home," Lilly announces to the ceiling.

"Naw, not tonight. Tomorrow," Seth says as he rolls toward me, snakes his arms around me and pulls my back against him. I'm facing Lilly, who turns toward me as Noah does the same to her.

She pets my cheek. "Tomorrow," she says, smiling drunkenly. Lilly's eyes drift closed, and her breathing becomes rhythmic almost instantly.

Seth and Noah seem to pass out too.

I can't sleep with Seth's warm breath heating my shoulder blade, penetrating the thick fabric of the hoodie, his arms snugged around my middle. I know I crossed a line earlier—with the kiss. But without the alcohol haze, I can't. I only want Julian. *Or Jayce?* My stomach pitches, my chest tightens. I count my breaths to distract myself from the panic, but even the calming trick only reminds me of him. How did I let him become my whole life? Had my parents' story taught me nothing?

My phone buzzes against my chest. I tilt it to see the screen, but I already know it's him.

Julian: I miss you, sweet girl.

Julian: So much.

I want to text him back. But what do I say? *I miss you too, but I don't even know who the fuck you are. Oh, and btw, are you happy your dead girlfriend is back? Do you miss me more than you missed her? Also, would you still miss me now if you heard my train of thought about a girl who supposedly died? Would I still be your "sweet girl"? Or what if you knew I let a frat boy kiss me? That I'm lying in his arms right now?* I blink the sting of tears away and wonder if I can get an Uber this time of night at the beach. I want to go home.

***

Turns out you can get an Uber anytime in Pismo, but the wait was "a little longer than usual." I am on the road back to Blue Lake within an hour. I leave a note for Lilly at Seth's and take my Uber back to her apartment to get my bag. I leave her key (that I took from her bag) hidden under a plant on her doorstep and text her where it is. A perfectly safe practice in Blue Lake. I hope that's true in SLO. I also hope my text doesn't wake her up. It's 12:33 a.m. and my map says I'll be home at 5:01 a.m.—the normal time Julian wakes up every morning. But nothing about right now is normal. Will he be awake? Home? With her?

Cranking the volume button on the steering wheel, my old-school playlist pierces my ears. I take a gulp of the gas station coffee and merge onto the freeway. I'm counting on the bitter black liquid and Bon Jovi, GNR, Aerosmith and about ten others to keep me awake for the next four and a half hours. I'm also counting on the songs I know by heart to keep me singing and out of my spiraling thoughts as I drive. First up, "Runaway." Next, "You Give Love a Bad Name." Is it me or is my shuffle on my ass like a pissed off parent? But then it gives me "I'll Be There for You" and "Who Says You Can't Go Home." That's better. But when Aerosmith serves up "I Don't Want to Miss a Thing," I tap the *next* button on the steering wheel. I can't with that song. Not right now. I can't start bawling driving down the highway alone in the middle of the night.

That sounds like a country song. Arguably not my best plan. But I couldn't stay there either, pretending that cuddling with the new hot surfer BFF was gonna get me any sleep. *I just want to rewind back to when my life made sense. Back to when Taya was still dead? What the fuck is wrong with you? Just listen to the songs. Sing the songs.* A therapist encouraged me to sing or hum songs after my dad passed—when my panic attacks started. She said it stimulates the vagus nerve, which regulates the body's stress response. I guess that was when I started building my old-school playlist—my parents' favorite music. I already knew a lot of the words because they'd always have it on in the garage—my dad's game room.

The last hour of my drive, I struggle to stay awake. My eyelids droop. The cold air blasting on my face almost doesn't work anymore. It's freezing out, but I roll the windows down. The air smells like home. That lulls me more in my exhausted state. By the time I'm rolling into the driveway, I can't stop my eyes from filling. Seeing his Jeep makes my chest ache. I don't take my bag. I just walk to the door and slide my key into the lock. But the door isn't locked. My lips arch in a smile. He tracked me. He knew I was coming home. I swipe the tear that escapes.

The house is quiet when I walk in. I slip off my Dunks in the entryway and pad silently down the hall and up the stairs. I stop in the doorway of the master bedroom. He's lying on his side, facing the door, his phone next to him on the bed. His eyelids are soft, his chest rising and falling rhythmically. I sneak into the bathroom to brush my teeth—the stale taste of coffee bitter on my tongue. When I come back out, he hasn't moved. I swipe the hoodie—Seth's hoodie—over my head and drop my jeans on the floor. As gently as possible, I lie down on the bed, pulling the blanket over me. I want to snuggle into him. I want his arms around me more than I want air in my lungs, but I don't want to wake him. I don't want to have to talk about the circus that has become our life. Not yet. Right now, I just want sleep. I'm careful not to touch him or otherwise disturb the tranquil space. I even slink the blanket up my frame slowly, careful to avoid his body. My heart is pounding so loudly in my chest, I think he must hear it—or feel it. I take deep breaths as quietly as I can and exhale them slowly. My heart rate drops to a steady thud and my eyelids droop within minutes. The last thing I remember is feeling his arm across my ribs, pulling me to him. I can't open my eyes. They're too heavy. He feels too good. With a long sigh, I go under again.

Chapter 28

Julian

After my last text to her at 11:30 last night said "delivered" right away, telling me her phone was on, the text bubble pops up telling me she's reading it. The dots move for a few seconds like she's typing then disappear. I check her location. It's still enabled, so I can see that she's in Shell Beach now that her phone is on. With Lilly. *Phew.* I exhale, relieved. She could've turned her location off so I couldn't see where she is, but she didn't. It gives me hope.

Stretching out on our bed, I place my phone next to my head, turn the ringer up and lay my hand down on top of it. I'm exhausted, but I want to hear it if she texts or calls me back. I can't keep my eyes open any longer. At least in sleep, maybe I won't ache for her and worry if she's safe. I'm physically and emotionally drained. I crave oblivion, a void of nothingness. That's the last thing I remember until . . .

Sunshine. But not just sunshine. Salt. Sand. Alcohol? But it's her. I know it is. She feels the same in my arms. Familiar. She's home. I try to open my eyes, but I haven't truly slept in over twenty-four hours. I feel drugged. All I can do is hold on and pray it's not a dream. I'm not sure who or what I'm praying to, but I plead in my unconscious state for her to stay. And I thank them for bringing her back to me.

Thank you. Mmm. I kiss the spot behind her ear I love so much. I missed you. Wait. I tighten my grip around her. Don't go. Her hand grazes my arm. Stay. I feel her slipping away. No! Ever! Blinking against the bright light, I try to focus, get my bearings. And I see her.

Chapter 29

Everly

His lips on that spot behind my ear wake me up. I'm disoriented and still depleted, but it all rushes back. I'm home. I have no idea what time it is, just that it's later based on the light pouring in through the wall of glass.

His speech is garbled with sleep. "I missed you."

I move slightly to gauge if he's truly awake.

"Wait." His arm draped over me tightens. "Don't go."

Panic wells in my chest. I softly push his hand off me.

"Stay."

I sit up and start to scoot to the edge of the bed.

"No. Ever."

With one leg hanging over the edge and the other curled in front of me, I swivel as sleepy, piercing blue eyes pin mine. Frozen, I watch him watch me for a few seconds that tick like hours.

He drags his body over to me and lays his head on my bent leg. His unshaven jaw scrapes along the tender skin of my inner thigh. "You smell like the beach." His words are barely coherent, his voice groggy and hoarse.

I pet his scruffy jaw. "I . . . I should shower." I gently push him off me.

His head falls heavily to the mattress.

I slide off the bed and move toward the bathroom. I don't look back, but I feel his stare all the way—the pull of it broken as soon as I close the door. I lean on it for a second, then take the quickest shower ever. I towel dry my hair and twist it into a wet knot on top of my head. When I slide the door open, our room is empty. I smell coffee. It churns my stomach. Snagging a pair of sweats and a T-shirt off the top of the folded clothes in my drawers, I hastily slide them on and lie back down on the bed and pull the blanket over me.

When I wake again, my head rests on the soft cotton fabric covering Julian's chest, which is rising and falling in the rhythm of deep sleep. My leg is draped over his, and I'm curled into his side with my hand resting on his taut abs. One of his arms is around me. The other is bent over his forehead. I don't want to move and disturb him, but I have to pee. I softly press my hand on his stomach to begin inching up.

The hand on his forehead comes down on me, and both arms squeeze and drag my body up till we're face-to-face. His eyes are closed, but his lips come down on mine. His hands sweep up my body to trap my face. He rolls us until he's half covering my body, never breaking the contact of our lips.

I let him kiss me for a few seconds, and I kiss him back. I can't not kiss him. But I have to stop him before it goes too far. I need answers. Ones I'm not even sure I want. Still, I need to hear them.

Placing my hands on his chest, I shove a little.

He stops and blinks his deep blue pools once, twice. Then brings his forehead to mine, closing them again on a long exhale. Relief etched in every inch of his face.

I need distance to think straight. Plus, I really do have to pee. "I have to pee." I smile cautiously and scoot out of his embrace. He lets me go. I again feel his eyes track me all the way to the bathroom until I close the door. When I open the door, he's sitting on the foot of the bed, elbows on his thighs, head hanging between them. The longer hair on top of his head is sticking up in messy tufts, like he's been pulling on it.

He looks up as soon as I open it and pins me with eyes that mirror the same unease I feel. "Hi." His voice is gravelly, deep with sleep, his smile barely raising the corner of his lips. No *pretty girl* or *sweet girl*. Just *hi.*

"Hi." My reply is breathy, like I just finished a workout.

"I missed you."

"I know. Me too."

"I didn't lie to you."

"Okay."

"Can I hug you?"

I feel the moisture building behind my eyes because I want to hug him too. But who am I even hugging? As the first tear spills, I swipe it angrily away. "Just tell me your name. Your real name."

He hangs his head again and, with his hands spread wide, palms up, he says, "Julian."

When he raises his eyes back to mine, I quirk one brow and fold my arms over my chest as if to say, "Try again."

"I was born Jayce Julian Keller. McKay is my mother's maiden name. I legally changed it when I moved here almost four years ago." He says all this looking at me squarely, unblinking.

I nod swiftly twice and step to him.

He follows my approach, never taking his gaze from mine. When I stop at the parting of his knees, he reaches his hands to my hips and stands, pulling me into him. His hands make their way to the sides of my face. With his palms resting on my neck just under my ears and his thumbs brushing the shells, his fingers curve around my neck and thread through my hair. His lips touch my forehead, my temple. His thumbs press under my chin to bring my lips to his. He leaves his lips on mine, slightly parted, not moving, and just breathes softly in and out.

My fingers clench the fabric of his shirt at his waist. As soon as I feel his fingers curl tighter into the back of my neck, I pull the shirt to me. His arms scale down my back, over my hips and under my ass, picking me up. My legs coil around him naturally and my lips fuse to his. Our tongues sweep into each other's mouths. He tastes so fucking good. God, I missed him.

We kiss until my lips tingle, until we both need to take a breath.

He sits back down on the bed, taking me with him. "Hi, sweet girl."

His pet name for me is back and has me swallowing nervously, because am I though? If I don't tell him about Seth, are we both liars? But did he even lie? When I don't readily respond with a pet name of my own, I note the subtle frown between his eyes. "Hi," I answer back after a few pregnant seconds. I don't say Julie or sweet boyfriend or anything except hi.

His fingers tuck a fallen strand of hair behind each ear.

I leave my forehead pressed to his to avoid his scrutiny. He keeps circling his fingers around the shell of my ears. It's lulling me. I want to disappear into his touch. I want to forget everything except his touch on my skin.

"Talk to me, Ever. What's going on in there?" He swipes his thumbs over my forehead from the center to my temples. "I'll tell you anything you want to know. I have nothing to hide. I promise."

On the last sentence, his promise to hide nothing from me, I exhale a partial sob. Because now I'm the one with secrets and something to hide. If I tell him the truth, will he still call me his sweet girl? Will he still want me, love me? I don't want to know. And even though I know now he didn't lie, the whole hot mess opened a Pandora's box of noise in my head. Still, I don't know if I'll have the guts to come clean or at least unpack all the shit crowding my brain. What if I do and it makes him never look at me or touch me the same again? I selfishly want to feel his arms around me and feel him kiss me like he always has one more time. Especially if it ends up being the last time.

Chapter 30

JULIAN

"I don't want to talk. I don't want to think." Her dark lashes rest on her cheeks. She won't look at me.

"Ever . . ." I sigh her name. *Is she still doubting me? Who I am? If I lied? Why doesn't she want to talk? What is she afraid to find out?*

"Just make me forget about the last twenty-four hours. Okay?" She swipes a damp trail off her cheeks with the backs of her fingers, then raises her liquid-gray eyes to mine. "Can we just pretend . . . just for now . . . that none of it happened? That we're still us and none of it changed?" When I don't immediately answer she adds, "Please?" She presses her lips to the pulse in my neck.

My body responds instantly, and I lean into her kiss.

As soon as I do, she's tugging the shirt up my body and whipping it over my head. Then she removes hers. She's naked under it and presses her breasts to my chest.

Fuck, I missed her. I know we should talk before we do this, but I also know I won't deny her. I pull her hips into mine where I'm already hard.

Her hands roam up and down my stomach and chest, pushing me back on the bed. She shimmies out of her sweats, again naked underneath, then hooks her fingers into the waistband of my pajama pants and slides them over my hips. She sees the boxer briefs and stops her motion to pull them down with the PJs. Once we're both naked, she climbs back on top as I inch my way farther onto the bed.

Sitting with her moist heat perfectly on top of my hard-on, she leans down and kisses me, swiping her tongue into my mouth expertly, fusing her lips to mine. Without altering the tempo of our kiss, she reaches down and takes me in her hand, guiding me to her opening and plunging down on me with a sharp intake of breath and a cry.

I clamp my hands down on her hips and hold her to me for a few seconds, rocking her back and forth a couple times until I feel her expand to accommodate me. Then I pick her up slowly, drop her back on me with a groan and pull her hips toward me. I repeat it, setting a cadence that has us both panting and her dripping.

When I feel her begin to tighten around me, I stop and roll her onto her back and wait. Her eyes were squeezed tightly shut the whole time she rode me. I hold myself still inside her until she looks at me. I want her to see me, feel me, acknowledge me. I want her to remember us, what we have. Once her thunderous gray eyes find mine, I nod.

"You see me, Everly?"

She stares at me, not answering.

I pull all the way out of her, watch her brow crease in a frown, then slam into her so deeply she arches off the bed, her chin aiming at the ceiling, her eyes rolling back and fluttering closed again. I freeze and wait. When her back relaxes and her chin lowers, she finds my eyes again. I nod. "Good girl. You like that, don't you? Me inside you?"

She nods.

"Tell me, Everly. Tell me who's inside you."

"You." It's more a breathless moan than a word.

"And who am I?"

"Julian."

I reward her answer by pulling all the way out and slamming into her again. "That's right. And I love you. Do you hear me, Everly? I love you."

She's nodding, her chest rising and falling rapidly.

I lower my face to hers and trail kisses along her cheek to her ear. "Say it, Ever. Tell me."

"You . . ."

I pull out.

"Love me."

I slam into her again.

"Ugh." A cry rips from her throat.

"I'll always love you," I growl into her ear and drive into her again.

Her legs are quivering with the buildup, her thighs pinned tight against me, wanting to clench together.

"You wanna come for me, Ever?"

She nods against my lips still pressed to her ear.

"I know. I can feel you shaking. For me." I swirl my hips as I pulse into her a few times. "Tell me."

"Make me come, Julie." She moans it and when she adds my name, I groan into her ear.

"Ugh, yes, Ever. Gonna make you feel so good." I reach my hand between us and roll the hard bead above her opening between my thumb and finger.

She jolts and cries out. Her head is swiveling from side to side. I pull all the way out, and she whimpers. I trail kisses down her neck, take one nipple in my mouth and tease it with my teeth before I pull it into my mouth and suck hard. My other hand squeezes her other breast. Her lower half writhes, begging me to fill the hollowness there.

"I know, baby. I got you." I drop my face down to her center and swipe my tongue along the hard bud and kiss it softly before I pull it into my mouth and suck. At the same time, I slide my fingers into her and swirl. *So slippery.* Curling my middle finger, I meet my bobbing lips from the inside.

"Yes. Fuck yes." She instantly bows off the bed and cries. Her walls pulse around my fingers, and I don't stop even though I know it's too intense.

I keep sucking and moving through her orgasm until she's screaming and crying my name. And when she's done, I don't stop. I pull my fingers out and climb up her body and thrust into her again. Deep, hard, over and over.

Tears drench her cheeks. Her finger is clamped between her teeth. With her other hand she yanks the longer tufts of hair above my forehead and pulls my face to her neck. I nip the pulse there and suck, and she moans deep in her throat. Her legs wrap around me like a vise as her hips rise to meet every thrust.

Within moments I'm ready to explode.

Bringing my lips back to her ear, I thrust once more, deep, and whisper, "I love you, Ever," shuddering with the intensity of my orgasm. I press her tightly to me, not moving except for my heaving chest, pounding heart and convulsing cock inside her. I curl my arms around her and bring her with me when I settle on my side. She's facing me but not looking at me. I tilt her chin up with my index finger.

Still, she holds out, keeping her eyes downcast.

I trail my finger down her nose, along the outline of her lips. God, I missed her. I press my lips to her forehead and swipe my fingers across her damp cheeks. When I pull back, she looks up under her lashes and lifts one side of her mouth, flashing a dimple. But her half smile is sad.

"What's going on in there, Ever?"

Her only response is a shrug.

"Talk to me." Still nothing. I roll onto my back, letting my arm fall to my stomach. My other is trapped under her head, which is resting on my bicep, damp from her tears.

Her fingernail begins tracing the tattoo on my chest. "Where's Taya?" she asks stoically, but there's an underlying menace to her words.

"Seriously?" My anger spikes. "At her house," I snap and hear her make a *hmpf* sound under her breath.

She stops tracing the tattoo.

I place my free arm under my head and prop myself up. She still won't look at me.

"The tattoo was for her, wasn't it?" Her voice is part sulk, part accusation.

"It was for me. A reminder." I can't help the clip of my words. How can she doubt me, *us*, after what we just did? I know she felt it just like I did.

"Of her," she throws back.

"Of the pain. Surviving it actually."

She flops over onto her back, dropping her arm over her forehead.

"C'mon, Ever? What is this? I thought we talked to each other." I'm sitting up now facing her and she's pulling for the blanket to cover herself, sitting up too. *What the fuck happened to my girl?* I feel panicky. My fingers itch to rub my chest and the tattoo. I curl my fingers into a fist instead, not wanting to draw attention to it since it's currently an issue.

"Okay, let's talk. What does it mean that she's back? That she's not dead? You love me. But you love her, too, right? I mean you loved her up until she 'died,' right?" She uses quotes around the word died. "Well, she . . . undied. So, now what?" She throws the blanket off her and stalks to the foot of the bed where she grabs her clothes and yanks them on. My girl is looking for a reason. Any reason. How the fuck did she go from screaming my name to squaring up?

"Now nothing. I was lied to. By her dad. We both were." I brush my fingers through my hair, swiping it off my forehead, only for it to tumble back down where it was. I stand up and retrieve my sweats, not bothering with my shirt. "We've moved on. We're different people now. It's too late." We're standing in the middle of our bedroom like it's a face-off. I don't know how to get her to take this down a notch. To talk to me. She's ready to fight.

"But what if it's not? She's back. She's here."

"Not here. In South Point."

"Technicality," she half shouts.

"What are you doing, Ever? Trying to blow this up?"

"No," she cries. "I don't know. I . . . just need to think. I couldn't do it at Lilly's. I don't want to go to Via's and have to explain. I . . . I'm going to the apartment."

"You're what?"

She turns to take some things out of her dresser. Pajamas, under-wear. She picks up her clothes she wore home and bundles them with her clean clothes—which is weird.

I blow a heated breath through puffed cheeks. I don't know how to reach her. That she is here in front of me is only marginally better than her being gone and not being able to reach her. She might as well not be here for all I can get through to her. "Stop. Ever, please stop."

But she doesn't. She shoves the items in her arms into a small backpack and drops it on the floor to pull on some socks. Snatching it up again, she's moving into the hall and walking toward the stairs, then the front door.

"Why won't you just stop and talk to me? Help me understand." I pull at my hair as I follow her. I clench my fists and shove them into my pockets. The urge to hit something, break something, sends adrenaline coursing through my veins. I know without a conscious thought there's a speed bag session in my future. One of those things my therapist refers to as a healthy addiction. "God damn it, Ever, just fucking stop. I can't lose you." I press my fists to my eye sockets.

"Same, okay?" She spins and hurls at me. "This is why I don't need people. So they don't go away." She's clutching the backpack in a death grip.

I drop my hands as the dots start to connect. "I'm not going any-where." I close the gap between us and rub my palms up and down her biceps, but I don't pull her into my embrace, as much as I want to.

"You can't promise that. You can't know that." She drops her fore-head to my chest, and the smell of her freshly washed hair floods my nose.

My sunshine girl. I wrap my arms around her now. "Okay, fair. But we're here right now." I rest my chin on her head and smile, relieved that this is what she's spiraling about. It's going to be okay. I inhale and exhale. Then I kiss the top of her sunshine-scented head, my dimples pinching my cheeks with the first genuine smile I've felt since before she left. My delight is short-lived.

"I can't need you like this." Her arms move from behind my back to my hips and she's pushing me away.

I keep my grip for as long as I can before stepping back, dropping my hands.

She's staring at my chin.

Why won't she look at me? Nodding slowly, resolved, I say the only thing I can. "What can I do? Tell me what to do."

"Let me go." She's looking at her hands, fidgeting with the strap of her backpack. Her knuckles are white, shaking. Tear after tear slips unchecked down her cheeks. Her body language tells me she doesn't want this.

Dropping my chin to my chest, defeated, I shake my head side to side as if in slow motion, contradicting my words. "Okay." I raise my eyes to her face the same time she raises hers to mine. "Okay, Ever." I hold my hands out to my sides at my waist, palms up. "You win."

On that, she takes a small step backwards, toward the door. One heel bumps her shoes in the entryway. She looks down at them and her sock-clad feet and bends to pick up the shoes. Then she's turning toward the door.

I can't feel my legs. Or my arms. Just a stabbing pain in my chest. Like something is pressing down on it, stealing my oxygen.

"I'll . . . I'll just be at the apartment. Okay?" She doesn't face me when she says it. Her hand is on the door handle.

"Okay? Like I have a choice in this? Do I? Because I choose no. I choose that you stay here and talk to me."

"I just need a minute," she pleads. Ever turns to look at me now, but she doesn't take her hand off the door, like she needs to ensure she can bail.

The deer-in-headlights look is back. It's breaking me. I haven't seen it since I met her. Now I've seen it twice in as many days. I hold my hands up, palms out in surrender, nodding slowly again, hoping it calms her, assures her she has nothing to be afraid of. *Is she afraid of me?* "Ever, I love you." I drop my hands to my sides.

"I know." She doesn't say it back.

Did she say it back earlier, in bed? I don't think she did. Maybe not in words, but her body did. Has she changed her mind? Her body can't lie. *She loves me.* She presses the handle, opens the door. "How long?" I hate how desperate I sound.

"I don't know. I just need to think."

"About us?" I can't help myself.

"About everything."

"Okay." I think I've said that more times in the last two minutes than I have in my whole life. But nothing is *okay.* So why do I keep saying it? What else is there to say? But I can't not try. "Remember when you told me that saying the truth seems the shortest route to getting to the point of a thing?" I don't wait for her reply. "We tell each other the truth. You can tell me the truth, Everly. I'm here. When you're ready to talk."

"I know." She walks through the door and closes it softly behind her.

I stand there and listen to the car start. Listen to it leave the driveway. I stand there long after the sound of her leaving fades. And because I want to hit something, I change clothes quickly and drive to Fit—to take it out on the kickboxing equipment.

Chapter 31

EVERLY

The first thing I notice in the apartment is the slight lived-in vibe. No one has been here since the wedding. Did Julian come here? With Taya? Did she stay here? The bed looks slept on but not in. A couple glasses litter the sink. Were they here together? I quickly throw the dishes into the dishwasher so I don't have to look at them, think about what they might mean. But how can I flip my shit about that when I kissed Seth? I need to talk to Lilly. As if I summoned her, my phone dings with a text from her. Three actually.

Lilly: Got your note.

Lilly: You home safe?

Lilly: Fuck my head hurts.

She sends a string of emojis depicting a hangover.

Me: I'm home. Sorry your head hurts and that I bailed. Had to get home.

Me: When you feel better can we talk?

My phone screen immediately fills with Lilly's FaceTime call.

Lilly: Where are you?

Me: The apartment.

Lilly: Why?

Me: I don't know. Just needed some space. To think.

Lilly: Does Julian know you're back?

Me: Yeah, I went there first.

Lilly: And?

Me: And I don't know. I don't think he lied, technically. He just . . . doesn't share much about the past. But Taya is here, back. I don't know more than that. I . . . How can I grill him about his . . . ex? Is she his ex? See? This is the shit I'm talking about.

Lilly: Why can't you ask him?

Me: I . . . uh . . . kissed Seth.

There's a pregnant pause while Lilly just looks at me through the screen. After a few seconds, she exhales loudly.

Lilly: And?

Me: That's it. But . . . I'd flip my shit if Julian kissed someone else.

More loud exhales and staring at me through bloodshot eyes.

Lilly: Look, Ev, I'm not telling you to lie to your boy, but college is . . . college. And Seth . . . kisses everybody. To be honest, I think it's how the boy says hello.

It's my turn to stare at her. I blink a few times, absorbing this college dynamic she described. Am I making a bigger deal of this than it is? Fuck my inexperienced life. I feel like a toddler trying to walk, fumbling around, crashing into shit. A knocking sound interrupts my mental spiral and sends my heart up into my throat. Julian's here. Only he knows I'm here. A swarm of butterflies erupts in my stomach.

Me: I gotta jet. I think Julian's here.

Lilly: Davis? It's no big deal. Okay? Love you.

I nod because this logic calms my nervous system. I want it to be true. *It can be true.*

Me: Love you.

I hurry to the door ready to throw my arms around Julian and tell him I love him. Tell him that the past doesn't matter. We matter. The two of us. I'm giving myself whiplash with the complete one-eighty. But ghosting my issues, my typical MO, would be so much easier. I ignore the way my brain wants to scream *SELLOUT*, that I'm betraying myself, and swing the door open and freeze mid-step. The past does matter, because it's standing in my doorway. "Taya?" I don't even conceal my shock.

It mirrors hers telling me she's not here for me. "I . . . hi. Everly?" Her polite smile is meager, nervous. Points for finding her manners.

Mine are MIA when I reply, "Julian's not here," sans smile or emotion of any kind.

"Oh, okay. I just wanted to return these and tell him thanks." She hands me a pair of sweats and a tee—*my* sweats and tee.

I look down at them like they're a coiled snake about to strike. *Thanks, Dad, for modeling compartmentalizing.* "Great, I was just about to start some laundry." I take the items from her and stand with my hand gripping the door handle. Manners dictate that I invite her in, offer her a drink. I do neither. I let the charged silence hang between us and wait, not breathing or blinking.

She finally speaks. "Sorry for just showing up like this." Without the clothes in her hands, she's fidgeting with her fingers, then shoves them into the pockets of her jeans. Her awkwardness penetrates my detachment.

"It's fine. Come in. I can call him for you if you want." I turn and move to the bag of clothes I dropped earlier, taking the worn ones out. *Why the fuck did I offer to call him for her?*

"No, I don't want to intrude." But she takes a step inside.

I can't help the smirk. *Don't you, though?* I can't help my bitchy thought, but my manners win. "It's fine," I say again. *But is it?* "Want some coffee? I was just going to make some."

"Okay. Yeah. Thanks."

"Sure. Just, uh, follow me." I move toward the kitchen and hear her close the door behind me. "Have a seat. Just gonna start this load." I drop the clothes into the barrel of the washing machine like they're toxic waste. *Aren't they?* Moving back into the kitchen, I make myself look her in the face. She's so pretty. My opposite, really. "Want me to text Juli—Julian for you?" *Does she call him Julian now? Or Jayce.*

"I . . . Can we talk? You and me? Without Jay?"

Or Jay. Fuck her just a little for using a pet name. "Okay." I turn and busy myself making coffee. I opt for the quicker single cups over a whole pot. Within seconds of removing her from my line of vision, I find myself. The new me I was slowly becoming who isn't afraid to say shit. "But, honestly, none of this is okay. It's fucking weird and it's got me spun. Just wanted you to know that. I'm not normally an asshole. But this is weird."

Taya's laugh is full-bodied and kinda hot, like her. I hate her a little more. But I feel guilty for it because, in our world, mine and Julian's, she was dead until a couple of days ago.

Her reply has me retracting my claws. "Well, I *am* an asshole, usually, so no offense taken. This *is* fucking weird. Until a few days ago, I thought Jay was an asshole too, who took a payout from my dad to disappear. Stayed pissed off through most of college, too, and angry-screwed my way through a few frat houses because of it."

Hmm. Maybe that is just what you do in college—kiss everybody. Or in her case fuck everybody. The way Taya just overshared and nutshelled her side of things is refreshing. And endearing. Maybe it's a girl thing. Except for me. I used to only have deep, stimulating conversations in my head or in my journal that never saw the light of day—until Julian. But I've read that statistically, women talk more than men. Maybe Julian's stoicism about his past is more about his anatomy and less about hiding things. He doesn't exactly *not* talk about it, but only answers what's asked. I give Taya a genuine smile when I hand her a mug of coffee. "Cream or sugar?"

"I'd love both if you have it." She smiles back with her whole face.

Finding my irreverent sarcasm is easy when she's so open. I don't think twice before I say, "Did you off your dad when you found out what he did?"

But her smile disintegrates, and I realize instantly what she's going to say. Asshole status reactivated.

"He died. Of a heart attack. That's how I found out. About Jay. He had files." She fidgets with her hands again, then wraps them around the coffee mug and looks at me with a tinge of anger, darkening the sea-glass green to emerald. "He was an asshole, too. My whole life."

The smile I give her is sad, but I want to somehow unring the bell of my thoughtless comment. "I'm sorry, Taya." Saying her name feels weird on my tongue. "My dad died when I was young. He wasn't an asshole, just gone a lot."

She nods sadly. "It's okay. And thank you. I got over wishing he was something he wasn't a long time ago."

We both sip our coffee in the awkward silence.

Taya speaks first. "Jay—Julian is lucky to have you. Now that I know he's not an asshole who bailed on me, I'm happy he found someone like you to love. I'm sure you know his life growing up was shit. His parents are shit." One perfectly arched blonde eyebrow spikes upward as she goes silent for a second, staring into her coffee mug. I can tell she's not done, so I stay silent as well. When she focuses back on me, her eyes brim with unshed tears. "He really is as good as you think he is. Always has been. He could've turned into an abusive bag of shit like his parents, but he didn't. I'm so happy he has a beautiful life." On the last sentence, one tear spills. She swipes it hastily and stands. "Thanks for the coffee . . . Everly. I'm gonna go."

I nod, following her as she stands and moves out of the kitchen, my mind spinning. I'm searching for the words, the manners, and drawing a blank.

Then she turns back and adds, "And I like your T-shirt."

I look down at my faded holey Guns N' Roses tee. *My dad's.* "Thanks. It . . . was my dad's. It was his favorite band. My favorite band." I fixate on my pinkie dipping through a hole in the bottom hem.

"Mine too." She says it softly, bringing my eyes back to hers. "But I think it's more the moody aggression than nostalgia." She smirks, and I'm transported back to Julian stalking to the sound system that day at Fit and snapping it off. I had "Paradise" turned all the way up. I realize I'm staring at her, lost in the memory.

"Are you sure I can't . . . call him for you?" I don't know why I offer that. *Nice Everly.* "Our . . . This isn't where we live. It's not far though," I finish lamely.

"No. No. It's all good. I'm good. He . . . knows where to find me if he needs to."

I'm nodding again. And following her as she makes her way to the front door. In a trance, I hold the door she opened as she walks through it.

Before she gets all the way out, she turns and puts her arms around me. Without releasing my grip on the door, I awkwardly pat her lower back with my free hand. "Let him be good to you. He will. Always. That's who he is." With that, she hurriedly turns and jogs down the stairs.

I watch her go. I stand there in the doorway long after she gets into her truck and drives out of the parking lot, reflecting on the last hour of my life.

Part of me feels stupid for not seeing the bigger picture—leaning into what I know about Julian. But even if I've completely misread him, Taya is still back—very much alive and . . . here. And what about me? I almost burned everything we have to the ground in less than twenty-four hours with a trip to Pismo. Proof that I am not as solid as I'd like to believe. Trauma is a funny thing. I need to admit to myself that deep down I expect the good things to go away. I was ready to believe it was gone, he wasn't who I thought he was and what we have (had?) isn't real. No matter how much work I've put in or how *fixed* I think I am, healing isn't a one-and-done scenario. Triggers show up unexpectedly and sometimes at the most inconvenient times. My life up till now has taught me that it doesn't matter how good things get. It can change in an instant. I need to know I'll be okay if it ever does go away. I don't want to be my mom, escaping the reminders of what used to be. I'm not sure I've entirely wrapped my brain around the circus of Taya being alive and what it means for us—me and Julian—but as I move through the apartment, doing laundry, thinking, planning, I decide that I'm going to stop waiting in fear for that change to come.

With that decision comes the realization of the path I need to take to ultimately get there. It's not a complete plan, just the beginning of one. My resolve scares me, but I've also never been more sure it's what I need to do. I need to see Julian, talk this through. Not only do I owe it to him to explain it, but I also owe it to myself to commit to it. Before I lose my courage to do it or talk myself out of it, I text him.

Chapter 32

F it is almost empty, thank God. Sundays usually are. I'm not in the mood to be "on." And it's not lost on me that the timing is ideal. I've had this whole weekend off. No traveling. No content filming. And no real work. Considering how things played out, ideal is an understatement. Who could've seen this shit show coming? Not me. Maybe the universe threw me a bone for my birthday. *You can't escape the shit show we've got in store for you, but what if we give you the weekend off to deal with it?*

Blasting my workout playlist through the Fit sound system because I couldn't find my AirPods, I work out until sweat drips into my eyes and my arms and legs shake from exertion. Because the place is all but vacant, no one is bitching about it. Another gift from the gods.

No matter how hard I go, Everly stands center stage in my thoughts throughout my exercises. I know she loves me. Her body tells me she loves me. Every time I touch her. Even if she can't say it right now. I spin into a roundhouse kick, striking the bag to drown out the old self-talk that tries to invade my thoughts. *She loves me. I deserve her.*

Do you? Another kick. *Yes!* Back kick. *She loves me.* Side kick. *I deserve her.* Reverse turning kick.

Panting, I flatten my palms on the bag to catch my breath. *What if I lose her?* The thought slams into my brain with a force that threatens to drop me to my knees. I bend at the waist and brace my hands on my knees and take some slow, deep breaths. *I'll be okay. I'll be okay.* Taya thought I abandoned her, thought I took a payout from her dad to stay away from her, and she dealt with it. *But you didn't love each other like this.* That thought sobers me. We didn't love each other the way I love Everly. The way I think she loves me.

Eminem's iconic intro beat to "Lose Yourself" pulses through the speakers. I move out of the kickboxing room and into the main area and step onto a treadmill. Cardio isn't my favorite, but this is my favorite song to run to. I keep pace with the beat—it's almost a perfect five-minute cooldown run. Just as it's coming to an end, a few of my clients walk in—the cougar club as some like to call them, sans Sylvie. Thank God for little mercies. Except I'm missing my AirPods, so I hop off the treadmill and kill my playlist. I smile and greet the ladies as I swing into the office and cue the gym playlist. I wave on my way to the door, hoping they won't stop me. They don't. Again, maybe the universe is on my side.

Even after the grueling workout, I'm restless—and fixating on my missing earbuds. I storm into the house and begin rummaging through the tray on the entryway table. Nothing. I search the kitchen counters and the junk drawer. Not there. I already inspected my Jeep thoroughly. I take the stairs two at a time, moving into our room. *Our room.* I freeze in the doorway for a second, taking in the tangled sheets, half-open drawers—a reminder of her, in my arms, telling me with her body (if not her words) that she loves me.

She loves me. Right?

Not sure who I'm trying to convince anymore, I storm into the room and begin thrashing through backpacks and drawers. My top nightstand drawer holds lube and condoms, which we haven't used since our first night together. No earbuds. I slam it shut along with the reminder of our first time—her first time. Stalking to her nightstand, I yank it open so hard it falls to the floor, spilling the contents: lip balm, hand lotion, hair ties, pencils, pens . . . her journal. I stare at it like a pendulum. My name at the top of the page might as well be a neon sign. In a trance, I reach for it. I grip it till my knuckles turn white. If the universe decided I'm worth a damn, I'm about to prove it wrong, because instead of closing it, I begin to read. The very first line has me faltering. *This isn't for me.* The second line swells my heart. I want to close it. I know I should. I stop reading, wrestling with my conscience. My desperation wins. Maybe I'm not a good guy and don't deserve her. I continue reading, heart racing in my throat, pulse pounding in my wrists.

Dear Julian,

You're never going to read this, so here it goes.

I want you! I've never wanted anyone the way I want you. I've never wanted anyone—period! That's not to say I haven't had attention from boys before, but they were clumsy and dumb and painfully transparent. They didn't want me. They wanted someone or the experience. I could've been any girl. That didn't exactly make me want to rip my clothes off and have all the sex. Or even kiss. I began to wonder if there was something wrong with me that I didn't want to be with a guy. Now I know it was the guy. Because with you, I want . . . everything. I want you to touch me. I want to touch you. When I'm with you, it's like they describe it in the books. Everything else fades away and all I see is you. All I think about is you. All I feel is you. The loneliness, anger, pain . . . all goes away when I'm with you.

Sometimes, I wish we could stay in this Blue Lake bubble forever and not have to face the world and all the stupid, senseless bullshit that comes with it. Sometimes, I wonder if I've built all of this up in my mind and it's not as earth-shattering as it seems. You make me feel seen for the first time in my life. You make me feel beautiful and sexy and like I could deserve a man as beautiful as you. I know fairy tales don't exist. My sister has always told me I set myself up for disappointment because I expect guys to act like the ones in my books. Maybe that's true. I don't know. I just know that I've never wanted to experience all the things I want to experience with you. No one has ever made me crave being kissed or touched the way I do with you.

Maybe the gods are rewarding me for enduring all the bullying and lies in my hometown, for being ostracized and forced to leave the only life I've ever known. Maybe I'm being given a gift for being the perfect daughter all these years that never made waves and always did what was expected of her. I don't know! Maybe it's that I never took any of those fumbling guys up on their offers and waited patiently for you. All I know is I'm yours, all of me. If you want me, and I think you do. I don't even care if it's not forever. Although I'm sure it would break me if it wasn't, because I'm convinced no one will ever make me feel the way you make me feel. No one will ever smell the way you smell. Kiss me the way you kiss me. Touch me the way you touch me. Make my body come alive the way it does for you.

It's physically painful that you're only a few steps away, across a cold tile floor, probably naked except for the soft cotton pajama bottoms I love that hang low on your hips. My mouth goes dry at the memory of how soft and smooth the skin of your chest is. The way it heats my fingertips when I touch you. The way your biceps ripple when I grip them tight, wanting more of whatever you're giving me. Is this what falling feels like? If it is, then here's the spoiler. It's better than the books, Julie. You're better than all my imaginings of what the guy I'd fall for would be. You're perfect and beautiful. And I don't mind saying it because you'll never read this anyway.

Good night, sweet Julian. I hope you dream of me as I'll surely dream of you.

Love, Ever

I close the journal. At some point, I'd sunk to the bed reading it—just that first page. I came to my senses after that. *I can't do this.* I shouldn't have done it. It wasn't for me to ever see. But I don't—can't—totally regret reading that one page. It's not dated, but it had to be after we'd been together—maybe before we slept together. It doesn't even matter. I'm euphoric with hope. And I'm more determined than ever to keep my girl. Whether I deserve her or not doesn't matter. She's mine and I'm hers. Whatever else happened or is going on, I know that much is true. She knows it too, even if she needs a reminder. I trace my finger over the last line. *Love, Ever.* I flip to the back and tear a blank sheet from the spiral binding, swipe a pencil off the floor and lay the blank page over her name.

After I trace it onto the paper slowly and precisely, I hurriedly scoop all the fallen items back into the drawer, including the journal, and replace the drawer back in the nightstand. Earbuds search forgotten,

I retrieve my phone from my pocket and pull up a contact I haven't used in three years.

Me: Hey Angel. It's Julian. I need a favor. Today. Available?

Angel: . . .

My knee bounces as I watch the three little dots. It's been a long time. Not sure I made a lasting impression. Random impulsive encounters don't always make the core memory bank.

Angel: Random, but yeah. Lucky you. How soon can you be here?

Me: 15?

A thumbs-up sets me in motion. I'm taking it as another sign from the universe.

***

An hour later, I'm in my Jeep ready to take the short drive back to Blue Lake, when my phone chimes with Ever's text tone. My heart leaps as I slide my device out of my pocket. I can feel my pulse in my fingertips.

Ever: Hey Julie, can we talk?

Butterflies and the pit in my stomach fight for dominance. I'm encouraged by her calling me Julie. *The universe is on my side, right?*

Me: Sure. When and where?

Ever: Here at sunset?

Me: Yep. Can I bring anything?

Ever: Just you ;)

Her cute reply and wink calm my racing heart. *The universe is on my side.* I let the crisp air of turning seasons rush through the windows all the way home. I don't play music and instead focus on the sights and smells of Cavern County. *Home.* I take in the oak tree-lined highways, the rolling foothills of yellow brush, the endless blue sky dotted with sporadic wispy clouds. Sunset will hit in a couple hours. Plenty of time to get home, shower, change and take a slow walk to Brew and my old apartment. My hand goes automatically to my chest. I don't rub though, and instead I tap it with my fingertips. The unhurried walk I hope will keep me calm and prepare me for whatever it is Everly has to say.

She loves me. I know she loves me.

***

Clouds make for spectacular sunsets. Tonight's looks epic. Another sign? At the top of the stairs to my apartment, I take one last look behind me at the lake view. Reaching for the door handle, I pause, ponder for a second, before I raise my knuckles to lightly rap on the door. She opens it within moments, a weird smile on her face. Because I knocked instead of walking in? Fuck, this is awkward. I forget the unease when her scent hits my nose. But it's mixed with . . . the aroma of her favorite meal? I want to reach for her, tuck the loose lock of hair behind her ear, kiss her on the soft spot below her earlobe, breathe in her sunshine scent.

I smile instead. "Hi." I stuff my itching fingers into the pocket of my joggers.

"Hi." Her weird smile is replaced by her sweet, shy smile I love so much. She reaches up and tucks the strand of hair behind her ear.

I swallow, watching her finger trail the shell and twirl the ends of the curling chestnut lock. Looking past me, she gasps at the sight of the sinking sun.

I turn my gaze to follow hers. "Incredible, right?" I knew the clouds would help paint a good one tonight.

"Yeah. Wanna go down to the beach for it? Or watch from the deck?"

"Whatever you want." I want to hug her. Should I ask if I can hug her? Is it weird to ask?

"Let's just watch it here. I made dinner. We can eat after if you're . . . Are you hungry?"

"Yeah. Smells delicious. Your favorite meal?"

Nodding, she smiles shyly and backs away from the door—both of us realizing we're still standing in the doorway of the apartment.

"Want something to drink?" The polite dance we're both doing is bordering on ridiculous, but we continue to play along.

"Sure, whatever you're having. I'll just head out to the deck." I don't wait for a reply, and she doesn't offer one. Maybe we're both over the absurdity of our pleasantries.

Ever brings two glasses of water outside and sits in the empty chaise, setting the glasses on the table between us. Tracking her movements in my periphery, I make myself calmly fold my hands over my lower abs and cross my ankles on the foot of the lounger. I take a breath from deep in my diaphragm and mentally clock the colors of tonight's sunset. Deep blue, purple, dark pink, burnt orange, golden yellow—almost every color. I want to hug her. Hold her hand. Pick her up and snuggle her into my lap. Feel her curl into me like she was made for it. And wasn't she? But I can't get ahead of myself. She asked me here to talk. I reel my shit in and wait. Another deep breath. Exhale. *She loves me.*

Chapter 33

Everly

That clean sandalwood scent—not too spicy, not too sweet. Equal parts clean skin, fresh air and just manly enough to make my mouth water. I want to touch him, hug him, kiss him. I tuck my hands under my legs, stretching them out on the chaise lounge. I could use a sip of the water I just brought out for us, but I don't trust my hands not to reach for him. I need to say what I asked him here to say.

"So beautiful tonight." The sky is brimming with so many colors and designs, it brings tears to my eyes. In some ways this makes me feel like the oldest eighteen-year-old on the planet. Like maybe only those who have come face-to-face with the fragility of life can stop and appreciate the simple gift of a setting sun. God willing, that usually means a bit more age and experience before you get to that place. Most of us race through life from one stress-inducing self-imposed deadline to another, never stopping to appreciate the last deadline met. Or have the luxury of stressing over minor things, like wrong coffee orders and stolen parking spots—something my dad was always quick to point out when he was home. I remember the sky the day we buried him. It was angry and gray, the air warm and muggy, but right after the service, the sun broke through the clouds and set the sky on fire.

I also remember the sky the day I read the words carelessly posted about me by malicious girls out of misplaced loyalty. That day I thought, just for a split second, maybe things would be easier without me here. The sun dipped behind a cloud in that exact moment, and the sky darkened before it began to pop back out. It sent beams shooting across the sky in camera-worthy vibes—no filter needed. It was so beautiful and bright it stung my eyes and allowed me to breathe.

His words pull me out of my introspection.

"It is."

I turn my head toward him, where my eyes fix on the deep penetrating blue of his. He's not looking at the sunset. He's looking at me. Tears sting behind my eyes. I blink as much to ward them off as to break the spell of his gaze. *Spit it out, Ev.*

"I . . . um . . ." Dr. Franklin, my high school counselor, once told me the trick to curbing nerves when speaking is to unload the thing in the forefront of your mind. Confess it to your audience and get them on your side. Of course, she meant for public speaking, and why it popped into my head now, I couldn't say. Except that the nerves feel the same.

He's watching me patiently, calmly.

I take a deep breath, blow it out through puffed cheeks and say the thing in the forefront of my mind. "I . . . love you." I exhale with the admission.

"I know." One dimple peeks out before he schools his expression into calm reserve again.

Looking down at my fidgeting hands, I continue before I lose myself in that glimpse of a dimple. "So much that I . . . I'm concerned I . . . I need to be okay with or without you." I pause to see if he'll say anything. He doesn't. "I know I have nothing to compare it to, but what we have"—I wag my finger between us, looking up into his face still composed and fixed on me—"is so good, I almost can't describe it with words. Maybe that's why we . . ." I look back down at my hands, purposely flatten them on my thighs and go on. "I'm trying to be sincere here, but . . . do it like rabbits."

His sharp bark of laughter kicks my eyes to his. The flame in my cheeks travels down my neck and settles on my chest. He stifles his laugh immediately at my blush, but the corners of his eyes reflect his amusement. Once his expression completely sobers, he still waits, quietly tapping his fingers on his chest.

"I don't like feeling insecure and . . . jealous. Or like I could lose you at any moment. I think the only way for me to battle that is to . . . feel more confident in who I am." I take a breath and add, "On my own." If I wasn't looking directly at him, I might have missed the panic. But I was looking, despite it flashing through his eyes like a streak of lightning and disappearing just as quickly. It gives me the boost of confidence I need to continue. "I don't want to lose you. Or us." I wag my finger between us again, prompting a slight nod from him. Encouraged, I forge on. "Can we . . . would you . . ." I trail off, unsure of myself again. "I've never done this before." I grimace on a shaky exhale.

He reaches his hand across the table between us and lays his palm lightly on the back of my hand but doesn't speak.

I turn my hand over automatically, lace my fingers with his and squeeze. "I want to date," I announce.

His eyebrows disappear under the longer strands of hair dusting his forehead.

Rushing on, I add, "I want to live here, and you live there." I gesture toward Allie's. "And we . . ."

"Date," he finishes for me when I pause too long, squeezing my hand. Then he lifts our joined hands and kisses the back of mine, relief etched in every detail of his body.

Every cell in my body exhales—his touch like oxygen.

"Yeah." I smile softly.

"Okay." He mirrors my smile, still holding the back of my hand and resting it on his cheek.

"Okay?" My eyebrows arch, my lips slightly agape.

His low chuckle tells me my answer as he sandwiches my hand in both of his. But he adds, "Yeah." He glances out at the now almost black sky. The night sounds of frogs and crickets grow louder, the stars brighter. "To be fair, I've never done this either."

"Never done what?" I'm genuinely confused.

"Dated." He says it with a laugh in his voice.

"Really?"

"Really."

"You and Taya . . ."

"Never went on one date," he finishes for me.

"Hmm. Is it okay if that makes me ridiculously happy?"

His baritone chuckle makes my whole face smile. "Yeah, sassy girl, it's okay. In fact, I kinda like it."

"Yeah?" I ask this boldly, feeling more like myself than I have in days.

"Oh yeah." There is no mistaking the desire behind his words, but he confirms it with his next words. "Can I kiss you? Or hug you?"

"Do I have to choose?" I smirk, even more confident now.

Without warning, he tugs my hand, pulling me onto his lap. I'm not sure I'll ever get used to how strong he is. But once the momentum of his pull lifts me off the chair, his other arm snakes around and under me and settles me quite impressively in his lap. Sitting sideways with my knees curled into him, I press my lips to his neck and inhale deeply. Like a drug, his scent soothes my senses.

I move my hand up his chest, across the soft fabric of his snug-fitting T-shirt and feel his slight wince. I pull back to look at him, but he just takes that hand and presses my palm to his lips. "Are you hurt?" My brows crease, making a line between my eyes.

Shaking his head, he murmurs, "Uh-uh." He releases my hands to frame my cheeks and bring my face to his. Velvet-soft lips brush mine, once, twice. The third time he touches them to mine, I tilt my head enough to fuse our lips completely. We open our mouths perfectly in sync, our tongues tasting, exploring, until I'm twisting and straddling him, deepening the kiss even more. Within moments we're both panting. His fingers are tangled in my hair; my hands clench the back of his neck.

He ends the kiss the way he started it—soft, velvet kisses—but his breathing is labored, like mine. Pressing his forehead to mine, he works to catch his breath. "Are we breaking the . . . is this okay?"

"I sure fucking hope so." I smile, still catching my breath.

"I love you, sassy girl."

"I can tell." I squirm a little on his lap, feeling every inch of just how much he loves me.

His hands grip my hips, halting my movements. "I'm going to need to know how this works. I want to . . . I want this—us—to be what you need it to be." He's saying this against my lips, his forehead pressed to mine. When I don't immediately respond, he adds, "Just tell me what you want, Ever. I love you. I always will. Nothing will ever change that. But I also want to love you how you need to be loved."

Because I'm sitting on him and he's wearing thin joggers and he's not a small guy, I feel every bit of his restraint. But his body can't lie. His bulge twitches against my center, sending a shock to the nerves there. And while I resist the urge to press into him, I find the courage to speak plainly.

On a long exhale, I say, "I want to live here alone, if you'll let me . . . rent it?" I don't wait for an answer and continue before I lose my nerve to be frank. "I want to roll it back a little from living together and act more like a new couple. I don't want to not have sex because . . . well, I like it and that seems like unnecessary torture. I just want a chance to become a whole person in my own right, separate from us. Know who I am beyond the couple. So if you're willing . . . can we date but still . . . have sleepovers sometimes?" I shrug afterwards and hold my breath, eyes down, forehead still on his.

Pulling his head back from mine, he engulfs my cheeks in his hands and waits until I bring my eyes back to his. The solar lights around the deck kick on in the growing darkness and illuminate his features. "Of course." He places a swift kiss on my lips. "I'm in awe of you, Everly Tate Davis. Are you sure you're not a reincarnated thirty-year-old?"

"What did I tell you about referencing women's ages?" I mock-scold him, hoping we're done with the serious portion of the program. If he heard that thought, he'd retract his compliance—which makes me giggle to myself again.

Holding up his hands in surrender, he answers, "My bad."

"Wanna go eat? I'm sure it's cold by now, but it reheats well." I nuzzle my lips into the space just below his ear. He smells so good and tastes even better.

Julian leans into my lips, and I feel the rumble of his reply in his chest. "M-hm." He stands fluidly with me in his arms. When gravity wants to pull my feet to the deck, I wrap my legs around his waist. His arms engulf me so completely our bodies fuse into one.

As he makes his way inside, I tuck my nose behind his ear, planting little kisses there. Once inside, I unwrap my legs and plant my feet on the floor.

Before he lets me go, he kisses me fully and unhurriedly. When he does end the kiss and step back, his eyes look almost black in the muted light of the living room.

I know that hungry look. Instinctively I lick my lips.

His eyes track the movement of my tongue. "You said it reheats well, right?"

"M-hm."

"Good." He sweeps me into his arms and carries me down the hall, purpose in every step, like he knows exactly how this night will end. "Ever?" He's nuzzling my ear when I hear my name on his lips like a question.

"Yeah?"

"I'm so proud of you." He sets me on my feet to look at me. With his hands resting on my neck and jaw, he continues. "I mean it. You're incredible. And you make me want to be better."

My smile makes my cheeks ache. I ignore the tiny tug of guilt over my college *experience.* "I feel the exact same way about you." He's already shaking his head, so I stop him with one finger on his lips. "I mean it. Julian, you are the most unexpected gift. And I want to be better for you too. For us."

"Okay, sweet girl. We'll be better together."

"That's the plan."

"There's a plan?" He winks, and I nod in response. "Oh, good." He rolls his eyes in mock relief. "I told you I've never dated before, so I might need a map."

"Me neither, so we can make our own map."

"I love you, Ever." He kisses me so sweetly.

"I love you, Julie. We've got this. You and me." I pet the scruff on his jaw.

"You and me." He draws lazy circles around my ears, piercing me with hypnotic blue eyes. I nod in agreement, but he shakes his head earnestly. "I mean it. Nothing can touch us. Not the past. Not the future. It'll always be you and me." He stops drawing circles and brings my face to his for a claiming kiss.

"You and me," I repeat, nodding.

"You and me." He echoes it like a mantra.

I stamp down the nagging thoughts fighting for space in my love haze, as well as the glimpse of unease I see in his eyes. I know what clouds my mind—my actions in Pismo. What's clouding his? A blonde-haired, green-eyed girl back from the dead? I stuff it all down.

Chapter 34

JULIAN

I have to tell her. She's going to find out anyway. Will she still trust me after? *Fuck.* I don't know if I'd trust me. It was dark enough during sex that she didn't notice, but the clock is ticking. I'm finishing the dishes and she's in the shower. She's going to see me without my shirt eventually and I'll have to explain.

As if I've summoned her, she slides her arms around me. Fresh from the shower, her scent fills my nostrils.

"Hi, boyfriend. Are we having a sleepover tonight?"

I dry my hands on the dish towel I'm holding and turn in her arms. "Do you want to have a sleepover?"

She nods as she presses a light kiss to my lips.

"Okay, sweet girl, whatever you want." I kiss her back. "But can I—can we talk first? I have something to tell you."

She takes a step back, sliding her arms from around me. She doesn't let go but lets them rest loosely on my hips as she tracks my face. Her eyes bounce between mine, trying to gauge what I'm about to say.

Neither of us likes surprises. And I hate that I'm putting that low-key panic in her eyes.

I take her cheeks in my hands and kiss her lips again, then her cheek, until I'm nuzzling her ear. Softly I speak into the shell. "I need to tell you something. Show you something."

She nods against my lips and backs up. "You said that already. So tell me. Show me." Her words are clipped, eyes like saucers searching mine for answers.

"Wanna go sit down in the living room first?"

"No." Her hands are resting lightly on her hips now, her eyes still bouncing between mine. "Just tell me what the fuck is going on, Julian. Spit it out."

"Okay." I hold my hands up in surrender and, standing barefooted in the kitchen, facing her, I tell her about my earbuds search and spilling her nightstand. As I talk, her hands fidget with the drawstrings on her sweats. "I didn't intend to read your journal."

Her hands drop.

"I swear I didn't, Ever. I just saw my name and I was so crazed . . . I'm not making excuses. There isn't one. I'm sorry, Ever." She looks up at me now, but I can't read her. I continue talking. "I only read the one page." Her eyebrows raise, and she nods slowly, like she understands, but her expression says she doesn't. When she drops her chin to her chest and starts rubbing her fingers across her forehead, I forge on. "I feel like a piece of shit. I really am sorry, Everly." I hold my hands out low at my sides, palms up. The movement draws her eyes up from the floor, back to mine. "Please say something," I plead.

"It's okay." She says it quietly, and I'm already shaking my head.

"It's not okay." I don't want her to let me off that easy.

"Look, Julie," she cuts me off. "Am I jumping at the chance to let someone read my journal? No. But you weren't trying to . . . intentionally invade my privacy. And to be honest, that letter doesn't say anything I wouldn't say to your face now. Maybe not back when I wrote it, but now . . . I probably already have."

"There's something else."

She purses her lips and waits.

I reach for the hem of my shirt, whip it over my head and watch her eyes roam my torso. I clock the moment she zeros in on it. She steps closer and reaches out her hand.

With her index finger she traces the fresh scabs of the tattoo. Her muted gray eyes fill and turn stormy. "You covered your tattoo?"

I shrug. "I filled it in and added your name." She's tracing the letters now. FOR EVER. Her name. My name for her. "It's your handwriting. From the letter." She looks up at me now with a couple long, slow blinks. Inquisitive, waiting, but . . . happy? *Please let her be happy.* I clear my throat and continue. "That's how I got your signature. I traced it from the page."

Now her eyes leave mine and drop to the tattoo again. Her cheeks puff out and she exhales, deflating them. She's nodding again, still not looking at me but the tattoo.

"I'm so sorry, Ever."

"You already said that." Like her words, her eyes are soft raising to mine. Her smile is crooked. Teasing? Her smile *is* crooked but claims her whole face as she reaches out with her index finger again and traces her name. "And you put me on your skin." Her eyes go a shade darker and brim with unshed tears.

"Don't cry."

As soon as I say it, one tear spills. She quickly swipes it, but another takes its place. She's breaking me. My sweet, sweet Ever. I reach out to cup the back of her neck and pull her to me. She wraps both arms around me so tightly and lays her cheek against my pec, shaking with sobs. The more she tries to control it, the harder she cries.

"Shh, Ever. I got you. I'm so sorry. I didn't mean to hurt you."

"I know. It's not that," she murmurs. "You're too good to me. I don't deserve you."

"Ever." I drag her name out. "Stop. That's not true." My voice is barely a whisper. I'm rocking her back and forth in my arms and saying anything that comes to mind to soothe her. She seems to completely forgive me, so why is she so upset? I say what I'm thinking. "What's got you so upset? If it's not the journal, then what? You're breaking my heart here."

With a watery laugh, she asks, "This one?" She traces the now-shaded heart lightly with the pad of her index finger.

"Hmpf," I half laugh. "Nope, that one's permanent. The one underneath it." I kiss the top of her head. "Don't cry, okay? Talk to me."

She sniffs and shakes her head. "I'm okay. I just . . . I'm happy, Julian. With you, with us, our life. I don't want anything to mess that up."

"Not possible," I say, my lips resting on her temple. "We are happy, right?" She nods against my chest and drags a fist down her cheek. "We deserve to be happy, Ever."

"We do. We are." She sniffs again and looks up at me, still holding on tightly. "The happiest."

I nod. "There she is. I love you, sweet girl."

"I love you so much, Julie." She tucks her head against my chest again, arms tightening.

"You and me, Ever." I sigh into her hair.

Her exhale is shaky, like her voice. "You and me," she murmurs.